I0831339

The Vastness of the Valley

THE VASTNESS OF THE VALLEY

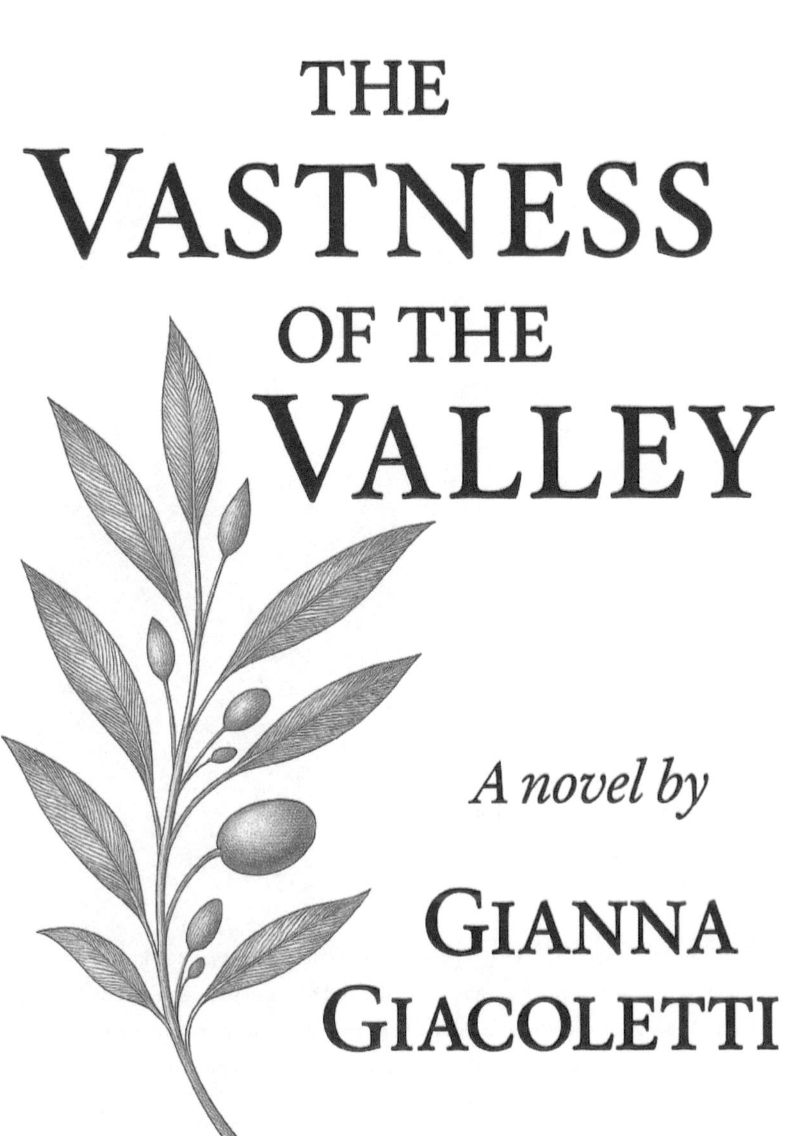

A novel by

GIANNA GIACOLETTI

The Vastness of the Valley

Contact: giannagiacoletti@gmail.com

ISBN: 979-8-9934140-1-0

First edition: November 2025

Disclaimer & Author Note

The plot of this book is not based on any one experience. All characters are fictional, and any resemblance to actual persons, living or dead, is purely coincidental. Certain businesses, restaurants and long-standing institutions are mentioned, but used fictitiously.

Growing up in Michigan, physician-assisted suicide (PAS) was a subject of conversation due to Dr. Jack Kevorkian's attempts to relieve terminal patients in the 1990s, famously stating, "Dying is not a crime." Much of the country called him Dr. Death, but his patients and their families considered him a hero and a friend.

While PAS is not yet legal in Michigan, as of 2025, there are over ten states where it is legal. The legality of the plot is not based on any one individual state law but is a generalization of all of them.

I will be the first to admit that I have not yet found a definitive stance on PAS. My opinion has fluctuated between pro- and anti-euthanasia based on personal life events and my faith. I still do not have a conclusive position.

As mentioned, the characters in this story are not based on real people, and the plot is fictitious. However, many real people are faced with this choice. My hope is that these characters provide insight into PAS, the decision-making process, and the aftermath. In no way is this meant to influence your opinion, but rather to open your mind to a very real and pertinent political topic in the United States, Canada, and Europe.

In loving memory of John Giacoletti

To Mom

For always believing I could do this and for demonstrating what a good wife looks like at her husband's bedside every day.

To Dad

For always trusting me with your story.

For being a brave patient until the end.

Rejoice with those who rejoice, mourn with those who mourn.

Romans 12:15 (NIV)

The Vastness of the Valley

FRIDAY

JULY 21, 2017 - PART A

WE DRIVE IN SILENCE to the hospital; neither of us has anything to say today. Michael keeps his hand on my thigh from the passenger seat, and every few minutes his worried grimace is accompanied by a tight squeeze. In response, I rub the top of his hand. Nonverbal comfort is all I have to offer.

A persistent and heavy undertone of fear has pervaded every day since Dr. Graham called last week. The minutes have passed like hours as Michael and I have dissected the few sentences she said on the phone, picking apart each word. Even through our denial, the insinuations in her request for a face-to-face appointment have been apparent.

As we drive to the hospital, I'm absorbed by the memory of our first drive down this road. The air in the car was charged with nervousness and buzzing with hope. Since then, Michael has lost a third of his weight. Bones protrude from his hips, his face is no longer bright and plump, his lips have thinned and paled, blending into the color of his skin, and his elbows jut out sharply. I can't remember the last time Michael ate something heavier than soup. Most days he struggles to keep down water. It's impossible to tell if his suppressed appetite is from the chemo or the invasive tumors infesting his organs and abdomen.

Michael's inherent positivity and instinct to fight haven't been strong enough to prevent his spirit from draining. His hope has dwindled exponentially with every round of poisonous infusions, each one wearing him down more than the last.

When Dr. Graham's team gave an appointment time, they asked us to be punctual. They explained that the doctor had double-booked a time slot to fit us into a full schedule. Michael and I understood what was said in the silence. Although our minds haven't strayed from today's outcome all week, neither of us has outwardly admitted what we're expecting. Over the last few months, we've indulged in the luxury of having the ability to avoid his prognosis, but that was stolen after Dr. Graham's one-minute call.

As we pull into the nauseatingly familiar hospital parking garage, Michael reaches into my purse for the orange medicine bottle filled with miscellaneous drugs. With shaking hands, he peels back the foil encapsulating one tablet and places it under his tongue to dissolve. This has become routine since the second cycle of chemo—just being close to the hospital conjures up queasiness.

I follow the garage ramp up, circling the levels mindlessly in search of a parking spot. An opening comes into sight as I turn the car onto the third floor. Once I've pulled in, I shift the gear into park, but neither of us moves; we don't unbuckle our seatbelts or rush to unlock the doors. We search the silence and blank cement wall in front of us for protection to shield us from the answers we're petrified to hear.

I squeeze Michael's hand, which is still resting on my thigh. He doesn't return the gesture, and I know his mind is somewhere else. His blank stare extends beyond the windshield and cement wall. There's no indication of emotion, only a fixed, empty gaze.

I lean my head back on the seat and let my tense shoulders fall as I join him in the transfixed stare before closing my eyes.

Over the last few days, I've prepared my mind for all possible outcomes regarding today's conversation. I've spent more time than I want to admit creating responses and plans for every prognosis. I've thought about what Dr. Graham will say, picturing her words floating as if they'll appear in a cartoon speech bubble.

What I haven't thought about is what happens *after* today's appointment. How do we leave the hospital? How do we tread through the halls carrying the heaviness of the news we both know is coming? How can we walk to the car with Dr. Graham's words ringing in our ears? How will I drive us home while paralyzed by our new reality?

With eyes still closed, I imagine Michael healthy and boisterous, laughing as he chases me past the bluffs and into the crashing waves off Block Island. Salty water sprays my legs as he sprints into the ocean behind me. The thin muscles lining his arms ripple beneath his tanned skin. He's reduced to a tall, shadowy silhouette as the sun shines from behind him. His eyes are gentle and twinkling, and joy lifts his lips into a toothy grin.

His image transforms into the shell of him that sits next to me now.

My thoughts spin. The only clarity I have is the sympathetic gut-wrenching horror that Michael must be feeling—looking into his future and running into a black wall of uncertainty, excluding himself from trips to the apple orchards when the seasons change or the Christmas parties that are too far away to plan for. The sinking feeling of not knowing if his days extend beyond the weekend, unable to plan beyond today.

My mind rests here, letting the truth of these thoughts seep into my brain. Michael must feel so alone, sitting in a reality that no one can fully join him in. Like we're living in different dimensions of the same world, layered over each other in an unreachable blur.

"I'm scared."

My eyelids flick open. I study him with wide eyes and allow my brain to painfully absorb his current state. His eyes are lifeless, nothing but emptiness beyond the brown irises. His skin is pale as it's pulled over the bones in his cheeks and the arch where his eyebrows used to sit. Like a child in his dad's clothes, Michael's long-sleeve shirt droops over his shrunken shoulders.

We both allow his words to linger as we take in their meaning without the interruption of attempted positivity.

Finally, Michael squeezes his hand wrapped around my leg and removes it. He sits up straight, turns toward me as much as the car and his weak muscles allow, and brings both of his cupped hands to my cheeks. With my face between his palms, we search each other's eyes for a comfort neither of us can provide, a comfort we know is not coming.

I'm not sure if there are words appropriate for this moment. No one tells you what to say when your husband holds death on his shoulders, crumbling under its weight while he's still alive. No one prepares you for the aching stillness between seconds when the final sliver of hope drags in anticipation of its release.

He kisses me, his lips dry and cracked, and rests his forehead on mine. We both cry, but not in the guttural way I was expecting. The tears fall in a quiet, steady stream, drawing out the pent-up hope that resisted the last few months. We cry for the expectancy of hopelessness, of darkness, like we're floating with tired legs waiting to drown. We stay this way, our heads leaning together and our hands intertwined, for as long as we can.

We can feel the minutes passing and know it's time to see Dr. Graham. I get out first and walk around to his side, meeting him with an outstretched hand.

"We can do this together." I squeeze his hand in mine, and he returns the gesture.

Once we reach the oncology department, things move quickly. The medical assistant leads us past the scale without stopping to take Michael's weight. We move down the hallway that has become too familiar, passing the patient rooms, and she opens the door when we've reached the end. There is no raised patient seat or metal sink. Commercial carpet replaces the tile that covers the hallway floors, and the walls are a light beige in place of the piercing white we've become accustomed to. A large desk centers the room, and we take a seat in its two blue chairs.

The medical assistant leaves once we've sat down. An earie silence hangs heavily in the air, enclosing us between the thick walls of this unfamiliar room. Michael takes my trembling hand in his. They shake in synchrony.

There's a framed picture of Dr. Graham with her family—two girls somewhere between six and ten and a husband who mirrors her long, thin figure. There are multiple diplomas and certificates hanging in brown wooden frames, all displaying her name. We wait only a few minutes, during which we anxiously reposition our crossed legs, before Dr. Graham knocks on her own office door.

"Michael, Anna, how are you both today?"

She knows the answer is not as casual as her question.

"How long do I have?" Michael blurts before she's even closed the door.

She doesn't answer. Instead, Dr. Graham is slow, quiet, and gentle in her movements, and it's evident this conversation is already becoming what we expected. She slides into her chair and opens the manila folder she brought in with her. She passes it across the smooth wooden desk so it's laying open in front of us, displaying copies of radiographs. I've become dauntingly familiar with these images, but my still hand flinches in Michael's. I can tell they look much worse than the last ones she showed us after his second cycle of chemo.

She remains silent, allowing us to absorb the images.

"What are our options?" Michael asks, recoiling and averting his eyes from the documents.

"Michael, that's your brain. The dark spots taking up a large portion of the space are tumors. A healthy brain wouldn't have any spots in the image. I consulted neurosurgery and the neuro-oncologist. This isn't something we can operate on."

Dr. Graham is leaning forward, pointing to the black mass on the page, but it's as if she isn't there, only her voice carries.

Michael and I nod to convey our effort to follow, both of us stunned by her words and already falling behind in the conversation.

"There's advanced radiation. The doctors I've spoken with believe this would cause irreparable damage. This tumor has put its roots in the deep parts of your brain."

"He was having migraines, but they kept getting worse," I say before I can stop myself. "Last week we were cooking, and he reached out for the counter. He said he couldn't see."

My hand becomes sweaty in Michael's, and my vision becomes blurry, which I realize is from the pooling tears.

"That's most likely an effect of the tumors," Dr. Graham explains slowly. "The team is willing to proceed with radiation if that's what you'd like. I do not believe it would extend the prognosis. It would decrease your quality of life. Your tumors are not responding to the treatments we've done, and they are spreading fast."

She flips through a couple of pages in the folder and reveals another radiograph with a large dumbbell-shaped black mass. She tells us it's a 14-centimeter tumor wrapping around Michael's stomach, which she believes has been a major contributor to his lack of appetite. She turns through the pages again, pointing to an image of his lungs, equally infected, then to the malignancies around his liver, one tumor 17 millimeters and another 18 millimeters.

Dr. Graham allows us to stare at the images briefly before closing the manila folder at her discretion.

"So, Doc." Michael's eyes are red, and his unsteady lip indicates he's holding back a hurricane of emotions. "Again, I will ask, what are our options?"

Dr. Graham proceeds to explain the different paths we can take. She opens with the option of transferring to a more specialized hospital because the surgeons here aren't willing to take the risk.

The next option is to continue his current treatment and add on more radiation. She doesn't believe the medicine will move faster than the tumors and prefaces that this choice may lead to an unbearable quality of life.

She brings up clinical trials, but Michael shakes his head immediately in response. She concludes with the option of palliative care, which consists of high doses of narcotics to treat the pain and possibly radiation to control the symptoms. If this is what we choose, we would meet with a doctor who specializes in these kinds of conversations tomorrow.

She stops there, allowing us to absorb the information she unloaded.

"Michael, I am not going to make you decide now. In fact, I prefer that the two of you go home and discuss what I've explained. Today, my goal is to give you options and discuss any reservations you may have."

"No." Michael's voice cut through the air.

I lean into him, clutching the loose material of his shirt as a lifeline. His arms wrap around me, pulling me in and covering me from the sting of her words. We pay no attention to Dr. Graham or the office. We don't consider that there might be another patient on the other side of the door awaiting their bad news. We hold each other and cry.

"How much time do I have?" I wipe Michael's cheek as he speaks.

"This part of the prognosis is not absolute," she warns, "it could be more or less."

"How much time?" Michael's words quiver as they leave him, fighting between self-control and frustration, fear and pain bleeding out of each one. He pauses, then whispers, "Please. How much time do we have left?"

"Pessimistically, one or two months. Optimistically, four to six months," Dr. Graham states, and for the first time I recognize a gleam of emotion in her eyes too. "We need to talk about the quality of life that you're going to have. The symptoms are not going to improve, they're going to get worse as time goes on. I want to prepare you for that."

We spend a significant amount of time discussing the problems that will arise. Michael will become delirious and possibly aggressive during his confusion. He may experience seizures or migraines like the one he had. He will most likely stop eating altogether, pained more by eating than by hunger. She or the palliative care doctor will increase his pain medications daily if necessary. She discusses the organs that already have tumors and those that are likely to become infected. His skin and eyes will become yellow, he'll have abdominal distention, and a lack of appetite caused by his liver failing. Changes in his mobility are almost guaranteed, excruciating pain while doing regular activities like walking, and possible fractures due to the cancer spreading to his bones. He'll experience consistent shortness of breath, frequently cough up blood, increase his use of the oxygen tank, and have chest pain from the overtaking of his lungs.

Her words immobilize me as I imagine the pain Michael will be in.

"So what will the actual cause of death be?" I ask with my teeth clenched. I know the answer, but I can't comprehend it; I can't believe it.

"Most likely starvation." Dr. Graham continues to be gentle in her mannerisms, but her words are no longer cushioned in their delivery. She is giving us facts.

Michael squeezes my hand reactively, and I watch the tears trail down his face. Fear bleeds into me through our touching skin.

"No," Michael repeats, "No, I'm not going to die like that."

His voice catches on *die* as the truth in Dr. Graham's words crash over us like a wave, and he realizes the inevitability of his future.

"It's been an honor to be your doctor through this fight." Her voice hiccups too as she reaches across the table and touches his hand briefly. Her eyes shine under the bright lights as they well with tears, and the tip of her pointed nose reddens.

She pulls her hand back and the space between us fills with silence. Michael's head continues to shake in denial.

I study both of them, my own emotions frozen as I wait for someone to feed the conversation with good news, depending on one of them to spew a string of words for us to hold onto hopefully when we leave. I wait for a single sentence that encourages Michael to keep fighting. But the room remains quiet.

"I'm going to give you resources on the options we've discussed, as well as additional information packets for options outside of our hospital system." She says, mirroring the grief Michael and I radiate. A single tear escapes down her cheek. She avoids eye contact as she sorts through another folder, pulling out different packets decorated with monochrome printing.

"Resources for what?" Michael asks with a hint of optimism that crushes me because Dr. Graham is not smiling. She's crying with us. This is not an option with a good outcome.

Dr. Graham places the information on top of the closed manila folder that has remained untouched in front of us.

"Physician-assisted suicide."

SUNDAY

FEBRUARY 1, 2015

THE AIR IS BONE-CHILLINGLY cold. It's one of the bitterest nights since I moved to Boston in the fall. Because the city is running in complete chaos, the police have created barricades of bright orange barrels to block off more than a handful of streets. There are more people flooding the pavement than on most Friday and Saturday nights combined.

I regret giving in to Harper's persuasion and leaving our cozy, warm North End apartment. We should be nestled beneath a blanket on the couch with an open bottle of wine. Instead of shuffling on icy streets, we could be watching the game between two exposed brick walls, smelling the grease from the pizza joint below as it wafts up through the floorboards. But we chose to spend our Sunday night fighting frostbite as we march to the strip of bars near TD Garden to cheer for a team we know nothing about.

The obsession around the Super Bowl is something I've never

understood. The whole game seems anticlimactic, and the ending is always a disappointment regardless of who wins.

I grew up "cheering" for the Bengals. My fandom entailed having the game play in the background while getting drinks with friends and wearing an old sweatshirt with the black and orange *B* painted on the front. Maybe if they had won a Super Bowl I'd be more interested.

But tonight, like a traitor, I'm wearing red and blue and storming the streets. Harper and I have joined the sea of people flocking to the already overcrowded bars.

Before we left, Harper conjured up a list of bars that she thinks will have a skippable line. She rattles them off now as we walk. I nod along in support, but I'm indifferent. I always have fun when she plans our nights out.

Despite leaving Boston for college, Harper found it easy to reconnect with her roots here. It doesn't surprise me that most bouncers recognize her. She's by far the most beautiful girl in any bar and captivates all eyes that find her. She easily ingrains herself in memory.

"So where are *you* leaning toward?" Harper asks, catching my attention.

"Somewhere I can feel my toes," I chatter.

"What about…" she starts.

"I trust you. Why don't you just tell me where we're going?" I grin. After years of friendship, we both know that's how the conversation would have ended regardless.

"Let's go to The Harp." She returns the smile. "It's not very far, and we can split a basket of fries. I'll even ask for a side of ranch for you."

"Is Adam working tonight?" I ask hopefully. The Harp is her favorite Friday night spot, based solely on the name. It's *my* favorite because her current boy toy bartends there. When he isn't drooling over her, he's proven himself to be useful; I can't remember the last time we paid for drinks. My job pays well, but not Boston prices well.

She nods and loops her arm in mine. The warmth of her body keeps me from shivering, and I cling to her for the entire frigid ten-minute walk.

As expected, the doors open for us as soon as Harper is within sight. I'm thankful we don't have to wait; I can't imagine joining the line outside. As we step through the door, the warmth hits my face, and my cheeks tingle from the abrupt temperature change. I shiver, forcing the chill off of me.

The music is loud but barely audible over the chatter of the fans. The usually dimmed lights have been replaced with Patriot-colored bulbs illuminating the tops of heads with a blue hue.

Harper spots Adam as we search the crowd for a familiar face. We walk past the various bars placed around the restaurant, heading straight to the one on the back wall. His thick dark eyebrows are pulled together in concentration while his hands mix drink after drink in a muscle-memory orderliness. In my mind, he's just one of the many men consumed by my best friend but when he comes into vision I'm reminded of his obvious charm; he's well-built with tattoos that emphasize his sharp masculine features.

When Harper catches his eye, he winks and forms a smile. His bright white teeth show between thick dark lips. He nods and raises the glass in his hand in acknowledgment before sliding it across the counter.

A few chairs sit haphazardly at a handful of tables, but most of them have been moved out to create more space. We maneuver through the crowd easily. When we reach the back bar, Adam formally greets us by handing us both a tall mystery beer.

Harper thanks him with a kiss; I thank him with a smile.

We find a vacant table and steal a chair from against the wall to hold our coats, responsibly stuffing our hats and scarves into the sleeves to avoid losing them on the sticky floor.

Two beers and one New England touchdown later, I'm more relaxed, warmed by the buzz of alcohol. As promised, Harper gets us a basket of fries to share. Between bites, we cheer or boo.

I understand the concept of football, but the yellow flags flying on the field almost every play hold absolutely no meaning to me. Harper has never indicated that she understands the game any more than I do, so we both find ourselves mirroring the responses of the aggressive, overreactive groups around us.

"Do you think they'll make it out alive?" I joke, nodding to the single group of men wearing Seattle jerseys. They're tucked away in the back corner, wisely keeping to themselves.

"Absolutely not." Harper bites into a fry and shakes her head, causing her golden-blonde waves to swing against her cheeks.

I imagine no amount of alcohol can protect them from the glares boring into their backs. My concern grows when the teams break for half-time. With the score tied, the crowd disperses like a sea of fish toward the closest bar for another drink, but the Seattle fans remain seated at their table. It isn't until a bartender kindly walks over to them that they order another round.

The game only becomes more disproportionate after the halftime stage clears. The New England attitude tangibly flares in a ripple across the bar.

"*What are you fuckin' nuts*?" someone shouts in a heavy Boston accent as the referee announces the reasoning behind his flag. Seattle is up, almost doubling the Patriots' score. There isn't much time left, although I know football minutes are not equal to sixty-second minutes. The energy in the bar starts to dissipate, and I worry about the inevitable angry street brawls that will break out if the Patriots lose.

"Need another round?" Adam asks, walking up to our table, a full beer in each hand. With all eyes glued to the TV, he's taken the opportunity to step away from the bar. He passes one beer to each of us, then wraps his hand around Harper's waist. I thank him as I try to figure out what number drink this is. I lose count without an answer as I float somewhere between buzzed and drunk.

I don't care much about the game's ending, but I'm captivated by the people surrounding me. The entire crowd is transfixed, their eyes religiously watching the TVs covering the walls. I've been living here for months, but tonight I've finally fed into the New England cult.

Mumbles around me turn to yelling, and I snap my eyes up to the TV. The game is within the last minute. Seattle has the ball. If there are any lingering doubts about the fans rioting in the streets, they instantly disappear. Tension fills the room, but the space lacks any dead air. Curse words covered in Boston accents prevent any creeping silence from flourishing. The seconds on the game clock count down. Harper and I finish our beers quickly, ready to jump out the door when the game ends to avoid the angry fans.

Seattle throws the ball, and an eruption of deafening cheers breaks out. I'm not sure if it's my beer-blurred vision or my non-existent knowledge of the sport, but I miss whatever happened. I don't waste time lingering on the semantics; instead, I join the sea of roaring fans. My body plays bumper cars with the large, unmoving men around me.

"Let's go!" Guys yell to me, charged by the frenzy around them. I scream it back to them, matching their excitement.

Harper's familiar voice carries over the crowd, and I look over my shoulder to see her mouth open in a cheer as Adam lifts her, arms thrown into the air. They're about ten feet away now, but I keep moving, driven by the buzzing atmosphere. People are chanting "*Butler*," and although I couldn't decipher Butler from Brady if asked, I mimic the cheering, giggling drunkenly as I shout and bounce between beer bellies.

I'm high-fiving extended hands, hugging strangers, and yelling as if I'm part of the team—until a freestanding foot stops me.

Without balance to catch myself, my tripping transitions into a fall, and my head dips down as it's submerged in a pit of shoes. While I'm trying to figure out what happened to all the faces, hands under my armpits lift me up like a child. Suddenly, my view is no longer ankles, and I'm standing back on my feet, staring at a navy-blue jersey wall. My brain rummages frantically, trying to organize the pieces from the last thirty seconds.

"I am *so* sorry!" A deep, shout interrupts my thoughts.

He's tall enough that the Brady jersey he's wearing doesn't look unreasonably large like it does on most people. My blurry gaze travels from his chest up to his face, where I meet a set of soft brown eyes. He's smiling down at me, revealing a row of tilted white teeth. Despite my drunk goggles, I can still decipher that he's handsome—a thinner version of the guy all the girls compete for with flirty eyes. I'm confused by his kind smile and the untraditional gentleness of his hands as they lifted me up and again now as they hold my shoulders to prevent me from swaying.

"It's no problem," I mutter.

"What?" he yells as he bends down to match my height. He turns his ear toward my mouth. His brown hair brushes my nose, and I'm very aware that if I move, my lips will be against his skin.

"I said it's fine. It wasn't your fault." I can hear the slur of my speech, and he jumps back in what I assume to be disgust. I open my mouth to make a petty comment, but before I can speak, I realize he's moved back because whatever was left of my beer has tipped and poured out sideways, victimizing his pants with a puddle.

I'm mortified. My attempted apology comes out in a series of stutters. All words, slurred or otherwise, are lost. In complete embarrassment, I dart through the maze of men back to Harper, who is still celebrating with Adam.

"I drank too much!" I shout. "I think we should go!"

Without asking questions, Harper nods, hands me my coat, and slips on her winter hat and gloves. Adam steals a kiss, and she whispers a sweet nothing in his ear, followed by an overtelling look before taking my hand and leading us toward the exit. I keep my head down in embarrassment as we weave between cheering faceless bodies. Harper gives out high fives with her free hand and thanks the host, who is too busy praising the TV to notice, before we slip out into the cold winter night. The chill fills my lungs with a gasp, and I'm left feeling short of breath but relieved to be inhaling fresh air.

We find the streets are no quieter. Applause leaks out of scattered bars and echoes between the cement road and brick buildings. Harper hooks her arm through mine and walks slowly, unable to multitask.

"Did you throw up?" she asks, digging through her clutch. "I think I have those little breath strips in here."

"No," I shake my head. "I just drank too much."

"Do you need water or something? Can you walk home?"

I roll my eyes but before I can answer, a distinct, audible voice layers over distant cheers. A quick glance over my shoulder confirms it's the guy from inside, still looking like he peed himself.

"Hey, you owe me a pair of pants."

"Excuse me?" Harper stops, and her head leads her body in a spin. I whip around with her, our arms still linked.

If my cheeks weren't already rosy from the cold, they're burning crimson with embarrassment now.

"What did you say?" Harper's eyebrows furrow disapprovingly at the stranger's demand.

"You owe me a pair of pants," he repeats. His bloodshot eyes don't waver from mine, and he ignores Harper completely. I look up at him like a guilty child caught in a crime, feeling the intensity of his focus on me. A curious churning in his eyes warm me, and although it takes me longer than it should, I see a gentleness behind them.

He isn't being serious. *Is he trying to be playful?*

"I, um, I'm really sorry." I mumble, confused.

"If you won't give me new pants, at least give me your number."

Is he flirting?

The seconds pass by slowly as I try to drunkenly decipher the situation. Harper catches on with much less trouble and raises her eyebrows visibly. A smile creeps onto her face, and her arm becomes unhooked from mine. She takes an obvious, deliberate step to the side to give us space but remains close enough to add to the awkwardness of the interaction.

He looks equally embarrassed and exudes palpable nervousness into the still bubble that's formed around us. I'm aware that the silence is hanging impatiently in the seconds it takes me to study him.

He rocks slightly, almost unnoticeably, from foot to foot while he waits. His eyes shift as he stuffs his hands into his pant pockets.

"I'm sorry, this whole thing played out much smoother in my head," he breaks the silence with a sigh. His head shakes and he releases a quiet, gentle laugh into the open air. He runs a hand through his messy, dark hair. His boyish nervousness is cute.

"Okay." I nod once. A smile plays on my lips shyly.

"Okay?" He takes a step backward, keeping his head down as he moves away slowly, feeling dismissed.

"I'll give you my number." My words release in a warm cloud that hovers in the space between us.

"Okay!" he repeats as he halts abruptly and extends his phone with excitement.

"I'm Anna. You can text me if you want to."

The words sound laughable as I say them.

"I think I will," he replies with his lips curled. He stands there glancing between me and my name in his phone. I wonder if he thinks it's a fake number or if he's too inexperienced to know how to close the conversation.

"Are you going to text me your name or tell me now?" I intend for this to be playful, but it comes out harsh, and I search for a way to soften it. "I'll need to know who to ship the pants to."

He continues to smile, "I'm Michael Leathem."

"It's nice to meet you, Michael Leathem. I'm sorry I spilled my beer all over you." My cheeks are still flushed.

More people pour out into the street as the bars begin to empty. Three guys standing outside The Harp call out to Michael, more drunk than me based on their almost indecipherable attempt to yell his name. He doesn't immediately turn around, and we hold eye contact, studying each other for another long minute before he breaks the moment.

"I'm not sorry at all." He shrugs with a quirky but confident smirk as he walks backward toward his friends, tripping at one point. He's still looking at me once he reaches the group, and he calls more loudly than he needs to, "I'll text you."

He doesn't text me.

Three days later, he calls.

SATURDAY
FEBRUARY 7, 2015

"DO YOU GO TO brunch a lot?" I ask in a nervous attempt at conversation. I tuck my overgrown bangs behind my ears, then pull them back to the sides of my face.

Michael sits across from me. We're tucked so close that our knees periodically bump beneath the small, wooden table. The surprise of his touch creates a layer of cold sweat on my palms.

We're centered between the conversation and clinking glasses of a dozen other matching tables that I assume have much less awkward pairings.

The menus given to us by the host look historic, decorated with ancient red and white checkers and laminated in thin plastic. The decor resembles an old diner but holds a pretentious, trendy atmosphere. The contrarian couples filling the space corroborate my assumption.

I look down at the bubbly font displaying *Avocado Toast* and the five other available dishes on the one-sided menu.

"Honestly?" Michael looks up from his menu. "Not really, I thought it would be a safe bet."

"What do you mean?"

"Well, it's pretty early, so you could eat breakfast, but if you're not a breakfast person, it's late enough for lunch. And mimosas are acceptable for breakfast, but if you don't want to drink, there's no pressure to."

His stare has floated back down to the menu lying flat on the table by the time he finishes. Although his face is still relaxed, his eyes dart across the menu, shifting uncomfortably from side to side. His hands rest on the table, fingertips barely touching.

Michael hadn't reached out to me since he called three days ago to formally ask me on a date. The conversation was brief; he had already chosen the day, the time, and the restaurant, so I had nothing to say other than yes.

I arrived at the restaurant a couple of minutes late. Michael was already seated when I walked in. He was looking around, studiously watching the waitresses as they flitted between tables, following their hands as they placed plates in front of other guests.

He stood up confidently when he saw me, but now he sits with his shoulders pulled close to his body, shrinking his size.

"Do you like mimosas?" Michael asks after taking a sip of water.

"I do," I reply.

"Want to play a game?"

When I nod, his layers begin to peel back; his shoulders blossom outward, and the quirky man I met last weekend starts to return. His hands wiggle with excitement as his posture straightens.

"There's a list of the different juices at the bottom of the menu. You choose mine based on your impression of me, and I'll do the same for you."

I grin and study him. The game seems universal, a good game to use on first dates, but there's an unfamiliar distance that exists in our conversation, a reservation that wouldn't be there if dates were regular.

The menu has as many juice options as food: orange, grapefruit, pomegranate, cranberry, peach, and pineapple. I don't need to look at the menu to know what I'm going to order for Michael.

The waitress wanders over, refills our waters, and asks if we would like anything else to drink.

I hesitate, the pressure growing, and wait for Michael to go first.

"She'll have the cranberry mimosa," he says confidently.

"And he'll have the orange juice one."

I sit back in my chair, attempting to mimic his confidence, challenging him with playful squinting eyes and a small smirk.

"So, I look like a cranberry girl?" I joke once the waitress has walked away.

Michael continues sitting with his regained posture, lighter after putting in our order.

He licks his lips as they curl, "I want to preface that the only interaction we've had is when you spilled beer all over me."

"Oh great," I laugh.

"At first, I was thinking pomegranate. But cranberry just feels like it fits. It's kind of an odd juice to have anytime outside the weird void between Thanksgiving and Christmas. You're small and have gorgeous green eyes but unexpected dark tattoos all over."

I tuck thin, mousy brown strands of hair behind my ears and absentmindedly rub one of the tattoos on my arm, "Go on."

"Pomegranate is good, but I like cranberry. It never tastes like you expect it to."

I nod, absorbing his observation.

"What about me?" He challenges with a tilt of his chin as his smile widens. Playful mischief spreads to his eyes exposing little wrinkles that expand from the corners.

"You've been picking lint off your shirt, but I don't think it's out of nervousness. I think it's because it bothers you." I pause, and he laughs in agreement, "I think when faced with a choice, you go with what you know. I chose the safe option because I think you do, too."

Our conversation flows after his icebreaker game. Michael's happy with his mimosa, and I'm pleasantly surprised by mine. The cranberry juice complements the champagne well, sweeter in the drink than it is on its own, and more refreshing than I expected. It tastes nothing like I thought it would.

When there's nothing but ice left in my glass, I order another.

We put in our food orders when the waitress comes back with our second round of drinks. I get a breakfast bowl, and Michael gets a turkey club—one breakfast, one lunch. I spend our conversation noting his mannerisms as he speaks, how he politely places his napkin in his lap, and how he makes an effort to cover his mouth if he starts laughing while chewing.

"Don't be obvious, but look at the couple to your left," Michael mumbles to his plate.

I whip around in my chair to see a pair of blondes laughing with each other.

"I said *don't* be obvious!" he chuckles.

"What about them?"

"How long have they been dating?"

I pause, feeling confused. I have no idea who these people are, therefore, I have no idea their dating history, but I slowly pick up on the game he's playing.

"They're not dating," I assert, "they're siblings."

He studies them briefly. "No shot. Look at the way they're laughing. Nothing brother and sister about that."

"They could be twins. No one is attracted to someone who looks like they could be related," I counter.

Neither of us speaks as we both do our best to nonchalantly stare at the pair trying to pick up subtle cues. She has long blonde hair, and after getting a better look, I notice her eyes are more green than they are blue. Her smile is big, her lips injected even bigger, and her long, white teeth are on full display as she laughs pretentiously. She has on black fashionable jeans and a tight, slimming cream turtleneck, which somehow makes her more desirable than any revealing top could.

"You're right, she does look too sexy."

"Objectively," he counters. His eyes deliberately meet mine. The intensity ignites a visceral reaction as his gaze permeates my skin, provoking a rush of adrenaline. My heart goes into overdrive, and my stomach is coated in a thick layer of trepidation. When the rush from his small, single word settles, there's a safe reassurance that follows.

"I'm judging so much. Look what you turned me into!" I say as an excuse to turn away and hide my blushing.

We collectively change our focus to the man, who is also blonde but a shade darker. I confirm his eyes are blue, naturally bright but illuminated now from the sun pouring in through the wall-sized windows. He sits returning her smile, but in a less composed way—jumpy and unstable like the excitement that comes while waiting in line for a rollercoaster. It makes him look younger than her. He's leaning into the conversation restlessly—hungrily—as she speaks.

"Early on in the relationship," Michael says without shifting his eyes from the couple.

"He's still pretty eager, maybe the third or fourth date?"

"Definitely. They haven't slept together yet."

I blush again at Michael's mention of sex, hoping he isn't paying attention.

"She was a client at the financial firm where his dad is the CEO. He asked her out, but she wasn't immediately interested."

"Nice touch," Michael turns to me and smiles, catching the tail end of my rosy cheeks.

We continue to make a story for the blondes, our laughter becoming louder with every additional detail. We project lives onto the oblivious couple. We'll never get an ounce of the truth, but I'm confident we've guessed a lot of the intricacies correctly.

Over two more mimosas, I learn Michael's a local, grew up *in* Boston, not outside in the suburbs—he emphasizes this seriously, as if it's his most important fact. He went to a Catholic high school in Boston, stayed local for undergrad and now for law school. He loves what he's learning and the work he did in his internship and has high hopes he'll continue with the same firm for another summer. I don't retain what type of law he's been practicing, but the brightness in his eyes and the fidgety eagerness of his excitement become imprinted. I ask about his family. He passionately explains the dynamic, unintentionally describing a very textbook, very traditional upbringing. He tells me about his older sister, who he picked on growing up and still antagonizes regularly, and his married parents, who punished him for doing so and still discourage their playful bickering. He elaborates superficially on his religious upbringing and briefly mentions the church he attends now. Outside of having a beer while watching football with friends, his hobbies seem limited to running and studying.

"I like to cook when I have time, but I think it's because I like to eat," he laughs softly. "I almost asked you over for dinner, but my sister told me it would be weird for a first date."

"You told your sister, huh?" I raise an eyebrow, catching the detail. We both blush. He continues his quiet laugh. I expect him to respond awkwardly and try to take back what he said. Instead, he finishes the bite he's chewing and looks up from the plate.

"I haven't asked her if it would be weird for a second date. What do you think?"

"Michael Leathem, are you asking me on a second date?" I tease with a smirk, feeling immensely more relaxed now than when our plates were full.

He blushes again and changes the subject with a shrug, "So, who was the friend you were with the other day? She didn't seem to appreciate my terrible flirting."

"Is that what that was?" I chuckle at his dry directness. "Her name's Harper. We were roommates in college and basically inseparable. She's from Boston, so when I got a job offer here, she was more than willing to move with me. Apparently, Boston has some kind of hold on people."

"If you haven't fallen in love with it yet, you will," he says with a smile. "Where did you go to school?"

"Ohio State. Made sense for me. I grew up a couple hours away in Toledo. But why Harper left Boston for Ohio, I will never understand."

"Oh, you mean *The* Ohio State University?"

I roll my eyes.

He asks me about my job and listens intently as I explain how I apply historic architectural design to the making of modern buildings. He nods at appropriate times and asks clarifying questions when he doesn't understand something.

Once I open up, my words fall freely. I tell him about my small apartment and the difficulties Harper and I had finding something reasonably priced. I bring up my little sister, Miller, who still lives in Toledo. She lived with me before I moved, and I admit to the emptiness that hangs in my apartment without her. We touch on almost every topic, but we steer clear of anything too serious.

When the waitress brings over the check, Michael stops her and hands her a card before I can even offer to cover my half. My pale cheeks give away my appreciation in a shade of red as I thank him. We occupy the table for another thirty minutes before the manager comes over. He explains, with Boston politeness, that they will be seating a reservation at our table, and the party will be arriving in fifteen minutes. I apologize, having learned this is common practice in busy New England restaurants. As I move my chair out to stand, Michael grabs my coat from its back and extends it to me in a disorganized chivalrous motion.

"I'd like to maybe see you again," Michael states as we walk out into a cold February gust.

"I'd like to maybe see you again too," I reply, standing in front of him on the sidewalk.

"I live close by. Do you want me to walk you to the T?"

I shake my head. "It was down on the way here, and I have some errands to run in the neighborhood."

"I had fun. I'd love to do this again, maybe cook for you next time." He's still smiling brightly.

I nod. I am both fully engrossed in this moment—the chilled air sharp against my nose, the blurry chatter of the Saturday morning crowd wrapping around us—and placed in the future in Michael's kitchen—sitting at a small round table in a crammed apartment watching him neatly spoon pasta onto the plastic plate in front of me, the walls bare, a roommate or two's voices carrying over as they talk on the phone or play video games through a headset.

The breeze carries the familiar minty smell of Marlboro from Michael to me. I breathe him in, holding the inhale and lingering anticipatorily. I bite my lip waiting for a kiss, but the moment holds no indication.

I take a step away from him, thinking he'll stop me, but he doesn't reach out. He allows me to leave. I look back after a few steps and catch him watching me, but when I repeat this halfway down the block, he's already gone.

My heart skips as I speed down the street, walking so fast that the pounding of my steps almost overlaps. I haven't been in a relationship since

I moved. I believe it's important to make friends and memories of my own before infecting the city with a relationship that might not last. I'd intentionally left all negativity across the country.

But Michael radiates positivity. He's nervous and open, grounded and easy—it's disarming. He makes the space feel safer.

As I walk, my stomach turns with excitement. The air bites the tips of my ears, but it makes the city feel sharp and alive. It nudges me to pay more attention to the cement beneath my feet than to lose myself in the memory of Michael's stare. Still, I hardly notice the increase in sidewalk and street traffic as the morning moves on.

Halfway home, I slip into one of my favorite bakeries. The tables are full, conversations softening the usual calming music playing overhead. But the buzz of the room feels like a continuation of my step rather than a contrast.

With a coffee in hand, I find a seat at the bar. I remove the lid and let the steam float up, wrapping my hands around the paper cup for warmth. I don't try to hide my grin as I call Miller. I'm eager to tell my sister about this nervous, attractive, oddly magnetic man that I think I'm going to fall in love with.

SATURDAY

MARCH 21, 2015

MICHAEL'S FINGERS TRACE OVER the black vines that run up my arm like veins. His head rests on our shared pillow. Passing car lights spill in through the basement bedroom window, leaving shadows dancing on his neck.

"What does this one mean?" His voice is heavy in the dark, and its hazy coarseness holds proof that the sun will be rising soon.

"It used to symbolize an olive branch, but now I just call it my warrior paint."

"What changed?"

"I guess I did. Either me or the church. I think the latter is less likely." My words hang in expectant silence, but I don't feel encouraged to elaborate, and he doesn't push me to.

"What about this one?" He touches the flower that sprawls across my ribcage.

"That's a lily of the valley. It symbolizes happiness," I pause, "They were my mom's favorite flower. She used to grow them."

"Like in a garden?"

"Kind of, we grew vegetables. The flowers look pretty, but they're toxic. Their scent keeps the animals away, they know how deadly they are. We would plant them around the garden to keep pests out." The shift in my mood at the mention of my mom is palpable, and I assume he noticed the past tense verbiage. I change the subject, "Tell me about a scar you have."

"This one is from stitches. I tried doing a flip into the pool when I was eleven or twelve and missed the water. The cement got the best of me." Michael rubs his finger over the mostly faded scar above his eyebrow. It's about an inch long and thin enough that it's barely recognizable as a scar; I hadn't noticed it before.

He tells me about a couple more small scars: a faint mark on his chin from slipping on the porch while spreading salt and shoveling snow, and an even older one on his elbow from a dirt bike accident. Although he was fine, the bike was not. He laughs lightly as he tells the stories that go with each minuscule mark. No tattoos, just faded scars and a dozen tiny moles scattered across his otherwise clean skin.

His hairy legs remain intertwined with my intentionally smooth ones as we spend the night whispering stories in the confinement of his twin bed. The passing car lights that leak in, painting our naked skin, become less frequent.

He tells me about his law school classes with enthusiasm. He admits he hasn't had a serious relationship since high school. He makes a purposeful mention that he never had a desire to take part in hookup culture. He says this with an awkwardness similar to the night we first met. I believe him.

Michael and I have spent a lot of time together over the last few weeks. For Valentine's Day, he cooked dinner for us and opened an expensive bottle of red wine. Yesterday, he insisted I celebrate my birthday with friends but surprised me at the end of the night with a pint of ice cream and a movie.

In between, we've gone on extravagant dates and spent mundane weekends pacing up and down the aisles of grocery stores. We've talked nonstop over breakfast and sat in silence at coffee shops while he studied and I read. He's officially met Harper and gone out with our group of girls. I've spent a lot of time with his roommate, Kyle, and watched Celtics games with a handful of his friends.

He's proved himself to be calm and hardworking. I've continued to grow more attracted to him but notice that he would blend into a crowd if it weren't for his height, which leaves more than half of his calves currently hanging off the end of his bed.

This is our first night together, and I've enjoyed the groggy late-night conversation that has flowed between us.

"What about you, what was your last relationship like?" His tired words melt across me, a calming wave that keeps my heart from beating as fast as it wants to.

"Not good," I attempt a nonchalant shrug as I pull the sheets closer to my chin, covering as much of my face as I can without it being noticeable. "We dated for most of college. He was the definition of a brooding artist."

"What happened?"

"He made everything in his life personal for the sake of art. He overreacted to everything. He'd call me his muse then pick fights that didn't make sense. We fought a lot, and eventually I shut down. We weren't happy—I wasn't happy. But his art was thriving. He didn't seem surprised when I told him I was moving away. I gave him the option to come. He didn't."

Michael's hand, draped over my bare ribs, runs up and down my back gently in support.

"I'm really glad he didn't." Michael kisses me deeply then leaves his forehead lingering against mine instead of pulling away completely.

"Yeah, imagine if I spilled beer on your pants and had no way of making it up to you." I nudge him, and he buries himself in my neck playfully.

He attacks me with a slew of clumsy kisses spread between my head and chest. I giggle and squirm, too ticklish to hold back.

I'm not sure if we agreed to fall asleep or if one of us dozed off mid-conversation, but I blink rapidly trying to block the sun shining in through the blinds. The light reflects off the recent dusting of snow, causing the room to be brightly illuminated.

We simultaneously wake up. Michael kisses me with dry lips and morning breath, but I don't mind.

"Coffee?" Michael asks, rubbing his eyes, "There's a coffee shop down the block."

"Please, for the love of every ground coffee bean, do not tell me it's Dunkin." I pull the blankets over my head and groan.

I *cannot* understand the obsession regardless of how long I've lived here. It's the cheapest coffee. Its popularity accurately depicts Boston as a city full of people who will pay thousands of dollars in rent for a studio apartment but refuse to pay more than a dollar for coffee.

"No, it isn't Dunkin, it's much better." He laughs and grabs sweatpants off the unevenly tiled floor.

He tosses me a thick cargo jacket and gray sweatshirt from the pile on his desk chair, then pulls a similar one out of the laundry basket for himself. "It's a Portuguese place with dark coffee and pastries I can't pronounce."

He proves himself honest; the toasted aroma of fresh brewed coffee and warmth of thick, authentic pastries crashes into us when we open the door. Out of the four tables, we chose the one closest to the window and allow the sun pouring in to keep us warm. Michael sips his coffee while I talk.

There's a noticeable progression in my comfortability as I jump between topics, mouth half full. I tell him how excited I've been to experience Boston in the spring, my anticipation to see the coastal beaches once summer arrives, the upcoming project at work in which I've been trusted with more responsibility, the city's neighborhoods that I love and hate.

Once I've eaten the last crumbs, we head back toward his apartment, slowly sipping what remains of our coffees as we walk.

Michael searches his pocket, pulling out a red cigarette box, and he holds one out to me as an offer. I shake my head and crinkle my nose in disgust.

"So it *was* cig smoke I smelled on you during our first date. How have you kept it hidden for so long?"

"I didn't purposely hide it." He interrupts himself to bring one to his lips and lights it smoothly. "It just never came up."

"I wouldn't have taken you for a smoker."

"Does it bother you?" Michael asks with raised eyebrows, although the cig is still hanging from his lips.

"I don't *love* it." I shrug. "You're not going to be able to go running if you poison your lungs. Won't be able to kiss me either, tasting like ash."

Michael leans in antagonistically, and I can't help but accept the smoke-filled kiss despite my threat.

"But seriously, what's the point? Why do it?"

"Because I'm a New Englander," he smiles, taking another drag and letting it go into the early spring air.

"And a dumb lawyer. What an oxymoron?" I tease.

"Fine," he declares. "I'll quit when I graduate."

"What?" I ask, surprised.

"I'll quit when I graduate," he repeats.

"Just like that?"

"Anna, I want you to like me. I can't have you thinking that I'm a *dumb lawyer.* Ten plus years of smoking is more than enough. Stick around until graduation and I'll quit."

"Okay." I smile up at him without doing the math.

"Okay," he repeats again. His brown eyes linger, their gaze holding me hostage.

His steps slow briefly as he looks around. He takes an extra stride toward a dark green garbage can, crushes the cigarette against the metal, and drops it inside.

"Starting early?" I ask.

"Oh no," he chuckles, pulling out a fresh one. He lights it and inhales dramatically. He takes my hand in his. "I better enjoy it while I can."

When we get back to his apartment, we both start packing up. Over breakfast, Michael prefaced that he had to go study this afternoon.

"You know, I don't usually like to do sleepovers," I say as I gather my remaining clothes, scattered around his room.

"Damn, I got a sleepover *and* breakfast? For the last couple of months, I thought you turned into Shrek after midnight." He smirks and shakes his head in contrived disbelief, "Figured I wouldn't ask until the wedding night."

My cheeks warm at his comment, feeling the earnestness behind it, and I nudge him playfully. "I hate the awkward mornings. You're always awkward, so I guess the mornings seem normal."

"I wasn't going to say anything, but watching you pick up crumbs piece by piece at breakfast was pretty awkward. Guess you're as weird as me." He chuckles, turns around to kiss me roughly, then continues to compile various things from his desk, shoving them into a backpack.

We leave together, me taking the T back to my apartment, eager to tell Harper about the night, and Michael walking to the law library. He describes studying how I imagine an asylum to be: two or three people sitting together, reviewing material separately in silence, no headphones, and no talking.

He kisses me before I go through the gates and texts me before I'm even home, warning me that he won't be looking at his phone. He promises to let me know when he's leaving the library.

Michael has created something I've never known before. He's always been clear and direct about his intentions with our relationship. I love that I never had to question where we stand.

When I get home, Harper is eating pancakes on the couch, watching a rerun of Gossip Girl. She immediately notices I'm wearing Michael's clothes and my disheveled hair. An excited grin takes over her cheeks as she clicks the remote to mute her show.

"Tell me everything!" she squeals and pats the open cushion next to her.

Harper gushes over the details, sentence by sentence. She asks a dozen questions and pries for more when I don't give a satisfactory answer. Her hazel eyes widen and her jaw drops as I go over our night. I tell her about dinner and the bar we went to with his friends. She asks when I started watching sports, let alone understanding them, and pries to see what I think of his friends. She digs for answers to what he's like in bed and what weighed into my decision to stay the night.

"You *love* him!" she giggles.

"I do not love him," I roll my eyes, finishing her list of queries, and steal a bite of her pancake.

"You're blushing! You totally love him."

"I don't love him. I do like him, though."

"Oh my gosh, you *like* him!" Harper's giddy with excitement. "If I hadn't talked you into going out for the Super Bowl, we wouldn't have gotten free drinks, and you never would have been drunk enough to spill your beer all over a stranger."

"You're ridiculous," I shake my head playfully, but Harper doesn't seem to notice.

She continues on her tangent dreamily, "Imagine the lawyer money. Promise I can come swim in your pool anytime I want. Do you think your hot tub will be open all year round? Your kids are going to be so tall."

We laugh, and I allow her to fantasize. Heavy butterflies flutter through my chest as she depicts my fabricated life.

By the time Michael texts me, I'm buried in my computer, struggling to produce a client's vision of a "historical" twenty-two-story all-glass building. We sporadically text back and forth for an hour or so before he goes to bed, and I follow soon after.

In the morning, I wake up to an invite to church.

Not only is this a first from Michael, but a first for this decade. The people in my life have given up on extending invites.

I don't reply right away. In the midst of contemplating the classic excuse of sleeping in, Michael calls. I hesitate before answering, but the early relationship excitement sways me to pick up.

I speak casually, pretending I didn't see his text, "Hey."

"Hey, I'm heading to church in the next hour or so. Want to come?"

I audibly groan.

"Please?" Michael asks softly.

"I can't make a decision on those details alone."

"Well, it's a medium-sized church, loud music, no sitting and standing and kneeling."

I consider the offer. I want to see Michael, and I want to get to know this side of him. He's made it clear religion is important to him, and, based on his character and approach to it, maybe his church would be intriguing. On the other hand, I'd have to go to church—sit between judgmental people listening to a preacher who probably spent the last week screwing up behind closed doors.

Michael takes my silence as an opportunity to continue his sales pitch.

"They have free coffee." I can hear the smile laced into his words, and I'm unnerved by the whirlpool it creates in my stomach. "I'll be there in thirty minutes. We can hop on the T together, assuming it's running."

"Fine," I drag the word out dramatically.

I hang up without explaining that I left the church a long time ago, and the volume of the music today could never make up for God's silence throughout my life. I don't tell him that my personal philosophy remains shallow; either God doesn't exist, or, if He does, He's a cruel, sadistic God. Either way, I have no desire to give Him praise.

Thirty minutes later, on the dot, I hear a knock at the door. While waiting for Michael, I've brushed my teeth, put on mascara and lip gloss, and changed into jeans and a sweater. I add his borrowed cargo jacket despite it draping over my shoulders.

"Ready?" Michael asks immediately as I open the door. When I come into full view, he smiles, "I like my jacket on you. It looks good."

Michael hands me a coffee, the same order I placed at the coffee shop yesterday morning. His attention to detail makes me smile.

We leave quietly, careful not to wake Harper, who remains sleeping behind her closed door.

"So, are we going to ignore last night's sin, or will we burn up when we walk in?" I attempt a joke on the walk to the T.

"I promise we won't burn. Well, I won't, maybe you will." Michael's chuckle following his bad joke doesn't make me feel better. He senses this and extends his hand for me to hold. I accept the offer, allowing my hand to be swallowed by his, juxtaposed in size.

After a quick ride, we step off the T in Somerville. Church is only a few blocks away, but I get more nervous the longer we walk.

"So, what should I expect?" I fidget with my purse.

"Absolutely nothing. A couple hundred people, good music about Jesus, and a hot coffee refill with unlimited access to cream and sugar." He squeezes my hand and looks down, towering over me even in my heeled boots.

We finish the remaining two blocks in silence, which feels uncomfortable to me, but Michael shows no signs of uneasiness.

The building is composed of old brick that's painted black to give it a more modern look. The upgrade draws attention in comparison to the historic homes that make up the rest of the neighborhood.

There's a large cross near the entrance and scattered bold "*Welcome Home*" signs along the sidewalks wrapping around the block. People smile and greet us as we walk in, and, to my surprise, I don't spontaneously combust.

"See, you didn't even spark. Not a single flame." Michael's whisper and caring smile bring reassurance but fail to erase the compunction that's hammering in my chest.

I take the promised coffee refill from a stylish wooden table. Michael gets a donut from the adjacent table, and we walk past more smiling greeters. No one calls Michael by name, but they all say it's nice to see him again. I wonder if they mean this literally, as in they recognize him, or if it's one of the scripted greetings given to them by a communist-like church dictator.

The auditorium hums with chatter and happy laughter. It's set up like a movie theater with cushioned stadium seating and carpet reminds me of elementary school story time. The dim lighting adds to the projected atmosphere.

"Where do you want to sit? Where do you think you'll be most comfortable?" he asks. My eyes jump across the long rows of cushioned self-folding seats.

"At home in my bed," I reply sarcastically.

"Seriously, Anna. I want to sit where you're comfortable." Michael's looks down at me, his brow bending gently.

He's trying to help feel more relaxed in a place he knows I naturally don't, and I'm ignoring his effort.

"Well," I contemplate, looking around. I'm overwhelmed by the vast options. "Let's just sit where you normally do."

Michael leads me down the aisle then extends his hand to usher me into a row. I choose a seat past the middle to avoid being the center of the crowd.

I fiddle with the buttons on my jacket and swirl my coffee while Michael sits motionless.

There's a screen on each side of the stage and a third one in the middle. On them is a countdown to what I assume is the start of the service. Three minutes pass with nothing but silence between Michael and me. Periodically, he squeezes my hand, but he says nothing.

There's a steady trickle of people into the auditorium until the screen gives a two-minute warning, which induces a flood of families through the doors.

The once intimidating auditorium feels smaller now that most seats are filled, and the faint buzz of conversation becomes a roar.

With a few seconds left on the clock, band members walk out on stage. Before they begin playing, a hush washes over the room, row by row. A catchy drumbeat counts in the rest of the instruments, and the singer yells a loud, cheerful welcome. The lights dim into oblivion, only the blue stage light remains. The hue highlights the standing bodies that almost completely fill each row.

It feels like a concert; the band leads the song while the audience sings along, guided by the lyrics flashing across the screens. Michael sways to the beat, occasionally rubbing my back. He doesn't sing, but I can see his Adam's apple bob gently as he hums.

I appreciate the unfamiliar music regardless of its meaning and nod along following Michael's example. Mindlessly, I read the lyrics as the crowd sings them out. Each word is inserted with the purpose of inspiring, and if I wasn't as aware of how absent God can be, I may fall victim to the whimsical beliefs of the church.

The first two songs are loud and upbeat, but before they start the third, the drummer puts down his sticks, and a calm hush washes over the crowd. The piano player's fingers are gentle as they tap the keys. The vocalist's words come out soft but pronounced. The church joins together to sing the familiar hymn.

When I close my eyes, I'm taken back to when my hair was longer, woven into a thick braid with a ribbon tied in it. My right hand is tucked safely into my mom's and my left one is wrapped around Miller's. Miller and I sing the words clumsily, still too young to know all the lyrics, but my mom's smooth voice covers our mistakes as she sings along. Her song is strong, and the lyrics pour out as a proclamation. She holds her free hand open, palm up, in front of her in praise.

Eyes still closed, standing in a large auditorium free of wooden pews, my lips silently form the words, recalling them from memory:

Prone to wander, Lord, I feel it,
Prone to leave the God I love;
Here's my heart, O take and seal it,
Seal it for Thy courts above

After the service, Michael offers to take me to lunch before he goes to the library. We decide on lobster rolls at a restaurant near my apartment that we frequent.

On our way there, we make casual conversation, and, although it lurks in the shared air, both of us avoid the topic of church.

We get to the restaurant before the afternoon crowd fills its tables. An aroma concocted of warm bread and strong coffee welcomes us as we're seated. From the view of our two-person table, it looks like we're hovering over the water.

The small building is suspended over the river on stilts that remind me of a Carolina beach town. While most of the walls are made up of thick wooden panels, the back wall is covered in a large window spanning its length. Early afternoon light brightens the room and illuminates our wooden table.

Our waitress greets us as she sets down two waters. Michael places our usual order before she gives us menus: two lobster rolls, warm with butter, and one basket of crispy sprouts. The waitress jots our order down on a notepad then turns back to the kitchen. When she's a few paces from the table, Michael leans in toward me attentively.

"Ready to have the conversation?" Michael asks, "What did you think of this morning?"

"Well," I begin. I pause to ponder before continuing, "The music was good, the coffee was free, and people had constant smiles."

"That sounds like positive feedback," he's hesitant.

"It reminded me of *The Stepford Wives*."

"Not so positive anymore." Michael's expression is still kind, but there's an earnest undertone as he continues, "I'm serious, Anna. What did you think?"

"I appreciate you including me in this part of your life," I pause, searching for a gentle way to continue, "but I don't think church is for me."

"Jesus is for everyone," he counters, more relaxed. His shoulders fall slightly, and a faint smile pulls on his lips.

"Maybe, but I don't think I want it to be for me."

"That's fair," Michael nods, "why not?"

I debate the level of detail to include in my answer. I know I need to be honest, but how much truth can I omit before it's a lie?

"My mom would take Miller and me to church most Sundays. We would walk there after school once a week for Catechism. She prayed over us before bed and sang us hymns if we couldn't fall asleep. But she made the mistake of going to the church in a time of need."

"Did they help?"

"If they did, I probably wouldn't hate religion so much," I scoff, but refine my tone before continuing. "They pushed her out, pushed all of us out. I had a complicated family. They didn't want our problems there."

He leans back in his chair, places his fingers on the edge of the table, and nods in contemplation. I assume he's pondering whether he wants to push for more information or leave the conversation where it is. In the pause, the waitress drops off the food and refills our waters. We both use the convenience of the interruption as an excuse to change the topic.

For the rest of lunch, we discuss trivial things. He talks about applications for internships and the various topics of his upcoming exams. He patiently explains pertinent laws, even though I'm sure he has taught them to me before.

Once we're finished eating, Michael lays down enough cash to cover lunch and a tip. Conversation flows normally but holds a slight trace of reservation. He walks me the remaining few blocks to my apartment and kisses me goodbye at the building's entrance.

Harper's home when I walk in, and we bounce ideas on things to do outside. Although still chilly, the sun is shining. We toss on light jackets and walk toward Quincy Market.

The discomfort of the lunch discussion still lingers despite the temporary distraction, so Harper carries most of the conversation, but I'm happy to be her listening ear. Lately it feels like we haven't had much quality time together. Harper started working at the funeral home her dad owns as what she calls, despite my discouragement, an "event planner." She's also taken up bartending in Seaport on the weekends for extra cash. Between her schedule and mine, we don't have much overlapping free time.

We spend the afternoon walking around Boston, snaking the blocks and slipping in and out of bookstores and boutiques. We end our adventure back at our apartment, cheese pizza in hand.

We're cognizant of the passing time as the light that pours through the bedroom doorways into the windowless living room begins to fade.

We open a second bottle of wine and each break off another slice of pizza. I won the coin toss for DJ, so Mac Miller sings through our small portable speaker as Harper gives me Adam updates. She's thinking of ending things, but the timing is complicated by his upcoming birthday.

"I didn't think I'd get bored with this one," she shrugs casually, but I can see the disappointment hidden in her expression.

"It just means there's still another man to meet."

"Speaking of men and meat," her face brightens, and she refills both of our glasses before wiggling further into the blanket draped over her lap. "What's going on with you and your hotshot lawyer?"

I roll my eyes and exaggerate a groan.

"Come on! I gave you full Adam details. You haven't talked about Michael all day!"

I shake my head, "He took me to church."

"You say it so negatively. He *took you to church*, and you *went.*"

"I guess."

The air freezes between us. Harper knows me well enough to feel my churning mind. She stays silent, waiting patiently as I work through the fleeting thoughts.

"I think it's a core part of him, Harper. I think he's prolonging asking me more because he knows he'll either have to compromise his morals, or he'll have to leave."

"Is there an option where *you* compromise?"

It's a good question. Is there a situation where he doesn't compromise, and I do? Am I willing to lose Michael for a grudge I hold against a God I don't know even exists?

"I bet if you talk to him, he'll listen." Harper says.

Maybe he would listen, but I don't think my reasoning for hating God would make a difference. It comes down to whether or not I want church in my life; the rationale feels less important.

"He won't understand my perspective," I decide and let out a heavy wine-filled sigh. "He has happily married parents who did so well they retired early and have paid for everything. He grew up living the American Dream, his sister is a successful engineer, and his parents still do weekly dinners with him. He easily got into law school and is at the top of his class. He's never struggled."

"I don't think you have to struggle to be compassionate. You should give him more credit," Harper shrugs and again refills our glasses, giving me the option to end the conversation.

"I just don't see my opinion on religion changing." The heaviness of the truth weighs on every word.

"Never say never." Harper breaks the tension by extending her glass playfully and I clink it in a cheers.

We stay up for hours, laughing and bouncing between topics. We jump from serious conversations to playful ones without skipping a beat. Eventually, we call it quits with most of the second bottle drained and decide to go to bed. Harper dips into her room after kissing the top of my head. I throw away the finished bottle, cork the almost empty one, and shove the box of pizza in the fridge.

I'm in the middle of brushing my teeth when Michael texts me. I smile as his name lights up the screen.

Michael: done studying, want to come over?

Me: Harper and I had a few glasses of wine. I'm going to stay in.

No more than three seconds pass before he texts back.

Michael: Looking for company?

Me: I'd like that

Michael: Be there in 15

Michael arrives with characteristic punctuality. When I open the door, he greets me with a warm kiss and a bottle of sweet red wine. I grab two clean glasses while he uncorks the bottle and unpacks his day.

I'm ahead at work, and my first meeting isn't until the afternoon. I use this as an excuse to have another glass despite what's already running through my veins.

After a couple glasses, we take our party of two to my bedroom to avoid waking up Harper, who's presumably sleeping in her room. The few walls and hollow wooden door between us don't muffle any sound.

There's a brief moment of sloppy kissing and clumsy undressing, but we laugh at our lack of coordination and surrender to the wine's intoxication.

We lay together comfortably, exchanging slurred compliments and whispering nothing of substance to each other in the dark. The warmth of our naked bodies accumulates under the sheets. Michael's hand intertwines with mine. We drunkenly watch as our fingers do flips over each other, the tips brushing against the other's.

"I want to talk to you," Michael says abruptly. The boldness feels out of place in our light, incoherent, sleepy conversation.

"Okay…" I reply cautiously.

"I have a non-negotiable." Michael's voice is heavy as it falls into suddenly still air. The noise outside seems to die down in response. Even the heat vents fall silent.

The creeping awareness of my nakedness makes me insecure, and I peel myself away from Michael so none of my skin touches his. His shifting posture signifies that he feels my growing reservations.

I remain silent while I attempt to read the lines on his face.

"I want a wife who will go to church with me on Sundays." Michael's tone is stern but unwavering. There's no indication of discomfort in his statement. His words land in bold confidence like he's throwing a winning set of cards onto the poker table.

"We have a lot of time to talk about this stuff," I stall.

Harper and I's conversation flashes through my mind. I haven't had time to think about what I want. I haven't weighed out the importance of remaining mad at God versus the devastation of losing Michael.

Michael's brow furrows. His eyes study both me and the space around us like he's doing calculations in his head, analytically balancing the risk and reward of the words he's let go.

He hesitates a second more before speaking, "I know, but can you agree to that one thing?"

"This feels like a bigger conversation, Michael," I say, my words quivering with the fear of losing him.

He kisses me gently, holding my cheek in his hand. I'm warmed at our skin's reconnection and watch his expression change again to something more tranquil, "I want to have the bigger conversation, too."

I nod, my body relaxing as his does.

"But Anna, I'm going to make you my wife one day. I need to know you can make this promise."

I'm overwhelmed with a flutter that zips down my body and absorbs any breath held in my lungs. I can feel my neck flushing, and I return his examining stare, but pair it with a smile. We both allow silence, me in deliberation and him in anticipation.

I think of every excuse. I could tell him I don't even remember his birthday. I could argue these promises are leaps and bounds ahead of where we are right now. Or that it's more common for relationships to fail than to succeed. I could explain my body's usual response to a request this big: that commitment is always paired with the urge to escape like a running deer startled from the crack of a breaking stick in the woods.

But with Michael, I don't feel any of that.

"Okay," I breathe into the silence and let the weight of my head fall into his palm, "I promise."

"Okay," he copies, squeezing my hand.

SATURDAY

APRIL 11, 2015

MY CLOSET IS EMPTIED onto my bedroom floor in a tornado-like pattern. Not a single article of clothing fits over my skin the way I want it to. My shoulders look too bony, my chest looks too prominent, my stomach shows too much, my face is too pale. I stare at my reflection, angered by what I see, frustrated by the shape my body takes in the dress currently encapsulating it. I'm normally not an insecure person, and I hate that today is turning me into one.

Harper lies on my bed with her long, tan legs stretching up against the wall, forming a ninety-degree angle with her body. She's remained silent as I've vented about each shirt, dress, or ill-fitting pair of jeans that I've tried on just to tear right back off. With every outfit change, my confidence has dwindled, replaced by an unfamiliar and growing sense of self-doubt.

"I am out of clothes. I have nothing left," I groan in defeat. "I have less than an hour until they get here. How am I supposed to get ready in an hour? What if they're early?"

Harper doesn't respond, absorbed in the blue light of her phone. Her bottom lip pouts as her nails taps away at the screen.

I clear my throat, then shout, "Harper!"

"Sorry!" She jumps and rolls over so her wavy blonde hair sprawls evenly across her back. "I didn't know you were talking to me."

"Who knew meeting someone's parents would be this stressful? I thought I was easy, breezy." I fall back onto the bed and cover my face with a pillow.

I didn't plan ahead like most people would have. I hadn't even thought about what to wear until this morning. I had days to try on clothes, go shopping if needed, make up an excuse for why I couldn't make it if I ended up completely defeated. But instead, I waited until this morning to even open my closet. Now I'm feeling the repercussions of my procrastination.

"Boutique Harper is now open," she says in a cheesy French accent, and I throw the pillow off my face with a rush of encouragement.

With Harper's help and closet, I settle on light jeans—not a single hole in the denim—and a black silky blouse that falls perfectly at my waist and covers all the tattoos on my arms. I pair it with black leather boots from my closet and a clutch from Harper's, and I feel my confidence slowly rise back to baseline.

Michael hasn't reached out to me since this morning. The bitter, nervous lie in my head spews that it's because he's forgotten about me. Thankfully, it's combated with the confident truth that he simply doesn't realize how nervous I am because he doesn't think I should be; I can hear him in my mind telling me exactly that.

When he'd asked me a few days ago to get lunch with his family this weekend, I'd agreed without much thought, excited to meet the people who raised him. This morning, while sipping my coffee, I realized I hadn't even interacted with my own parents in years. That was the single thought that sent me into a spiral.

A knock at the door interrupts my vain outfit inspection. Both of our eyes react by widening larger than the moon, and we freeze for no more than a millisecond before Harper springs out of bed toward the door. I hear Michael conversing with Harper, but it doesn't sound like anyone else is with them.

I inch out of Harper's room into the hallway, peeking around the wall that boxes in the kitchen. When I confirm Michal is alone, I take my first step out of hiding.

"Hello, beautiful," Michael smiles when he sees me. He holds my gaze; his eyes are like flowing brown lava stirring with excitement. "You look great."

Michael is wearing a black cotton t-shirt and beige pants that fall straight down his skinny legs, stopping at a pair of black Nike running shoes. His outfit, composed of one of the many identical Hanes shirts he owns, is not surprising, and I'm comforted by his lack of effort.

I have the preconception that he comes from a very affluent family. He's never said anything that confirms this, but he hasn't said anything to convince me otherwise, either, and I've been receptive to clues. His dad recently retired in his early sixties. His mom is considered retired, but she works at the office where she spent her career from time to time, primarily for the social aspect.

His possibly wealthy family reminds me of my less-than-well-off upbringing and feeds insecurities I didn't know I had.

I do a little anxious shake before burying my head in his chest, allowing him to wrap me up and absorb my nerves in a way only his all-consuming arms can.

"Where is everyone?" Harper asks my unspoken question as I continue to hide in Michael's embrace.

"They're meeting us at the restaurant," Michael states. He wraps his fingers around my shoulders and inches me away from him so he can see my face. "I didn't tell you that, did I?"

"No, you missed that detail." I bury my face back into his chest and shake my head.

"I'm sorry," he whispers into my hair. His fingers spread across my back, each one pressing into me with comfort.

I can breathe again, like the mere contact of his fingertips pulls the anxiety out of me, exchanging it for a full breath.

"Ready?" Michael's body shifts, and he nods goodbye to Harper. She waves and mouths, "*good luck*" —as though Michael is immune to seeing her silent lips. He chuckles in response.

On the walk to the restaurant, I'm too nervous to ask any questions. Michael's sister, Amber, and her husband, Logan, are visiting from Michigan, which is why he wanted me to come to lunch this weekend. I thought it might be too soon, but he made no indication that he shared this belief. His parents, who live in Boston, have been eager to meet me. They offered lunch with the whole family, thinking there would be less pressure with Amber and Logan, although it feels like the opposite.

I remind myself that these considerations mean that Michael talks to his family about me.

We finish the walk in silence, but before we cross the final block, Michael stops and uses his hold on my hand to pull me close to him.

"Hi," he whispers. As he speaks, I look up at his smile, the sun partially blinding me.

"Hi." I squint.

"Big breath," he coaches. We breathe together, and he squeezes my body into his on his exhale. "You're okay. You look beautiful. They're going to see you, get to know you, and love you. It's going to be fun."

"Okay," I agree with a nod feeling his confidence seep into me. The mini-speech is so characteristic of him that the stability calms me.

"Are you ready?" Michael asks.

When I nod, he closes the pep talk with a gentle kiss, letting his eyes linger closed. He plants another kiss on the top of my head then removes his hand from my waist to lace our fingers together. Joined at the hands, we cross the alley and walk through the restaurant doors.

Halfway through lunch I admit to myself that Michael was right: I am okay, his parents do love me, and so far I'm having fun.

His dad opened the meal with a prayer that I willingly bowed my head for. Since then, it's been an easy lunch. Logan and Michael have continuously talked sports with his dad, who asked me to call him Scott, throughout the duration of the meal.

Michael keeps his hand either placed lightly on my leg or entangled with mine when we're not talking together.

His mom, Elaine, also insisted on being on a first-name basis. She spends most of lunch teamed up with Amber peppering me with questions.

I quietly observe the dynamics of the table. Logan is playful with Scott in a familiar way, as though he has been part of the family for decades, and I wonder if that is normal for in-laws. The conversations are cohesive and free flowing, lacking the formality I expected.

Scott is an older version of Michael but with a less sharp face. The tip of his nose has rounded with age and his hair, although still full in volume, has turned silver. His thin-lipped smile is crooked, and he speaks with a thick Boston accent. He's dressed as simply as Michael, and when he gets up to use the bathroom, I catch a quick glimpse of simple all white running shoes.

Elaine, on the other hand, is a Boston Proper; her accent is heavy, but she speaks more pronounced, each letter being heard even when they're supposed to be silent. She's short with a black bob that has grays sprinkled into the roots. Her face shows no sign of aging other than the crow's feet that are only evident when she smiles, much like Michael. She smiles a lot, a close-mouthed grin that beams warmth.

Amber, despite being open and kind, is more intimidating than I imagined her to be. She's hyper and loud. Her eyes are judgment-free, but I can see the thoughts darting behind them. She focuses for no more than a few seconds before something else catches her attention. But her active role in the conversation shows she is noting everything, both said and unsaid.

I can see how Logan and Amber balance each other. He's masculine, a couple of inches shorter than Michael but much thicker in stature. He has big arms and though he's lumberjack-like, his husk is more muscle than fat. He speaks grumbly and deep. His features make a good juxtaposition to Amber's round, petite figure and her animated way of speaking.

Michael squeezes my thigh beneath the table periodically in reassurance, and I can feel his eyes shift to me sporadically. The invisible string that connects us is sturdy. Even when he's talking to Logan and Scott, I can still feel the stability of his presence. Michael has cultivated a strength and assurance in our short relationship that gives me the confidence to join conversations without him.

I notice Elaine catching Michael's protective check-ins too.

At the end of the meal, both Logan and Michael insist on paying the bill. While they playfully bicker, Scott sneaks out from the table, walks up to the front counter, and gives the young waitress his card. By the time they notice, the server has already brought the bill back, and it has been signed by Scott.

"Amber wants to get a cannoli while we're in town. Do you guys want to come?" Logan asks the group.

"Please! It'll be fun!" Amber says as she grabs her large purse from the booth and slides out behind her mom. She squeezes my shoulder, confirming her invitation before looping her arm around Elaine's.

Michael eyes me from his towering position. His smile grows as he takes my hand, following behind the group. I jump at the opportunity of what feels like a brief moment alone with him.

"Thanks for inviting me," I whisper, leaning into his arm as we walk.

"I knew you'd have fun." His lips curl in childlike excitement, giddy and anticipatory.

The bakery is a short walk from the restaurant. I listen to the overlapping conversation topics as Michael and I walk silently. Scott and Logan are in deep discussion about the NBA, ragging on the Celtics for their losing record. Elaine and Amber's voices layer with updates on job changes.

We pour through the door, spilling into the cozy warmth of the bakery. The sweetness of dessert invites us in, and we fall silent as the rich aroma of chocolate and vanilla washes over us.

Scott gets a box of cannolis while the rest of us pull chairs around two small tables. By the time he sits down with us, Logan and Amber have broken away, making the second table their own. The back of Amber's espresso-colored hair faces us as they share romantic whispers, fully engrossed in each other.

"How have things been since you moved to Boston?" Elaine smiles at me warmly as she pulls a cannoli from the box. The late afternoon sun glows behind her, illuminating her silhouette.

All Leathem eyes shift to me hearing the question. The nervousness reignites.

"It's been good. My best friend from college is from Boston, and she moved with me. And Michael's been a great tour guide." I feel myself blushing and I shift in my seat.

"Has he taken you to Newport yet?" Amber asks excitedly.

"Amber, it's only April," Michael says and rolls his eyes.

"Yeah, but it can be nice in the spring, too."

"I'd love to go to Newport," I chime in shyly.

The wholeness of Michael's family makes me feel young. Two parents, fully functioning and close-knit, exude a safety that is unfamiliar to me. It projects an umbrella of protection and allows space for me to experience the same childlike excitement as Michael.

"I'll take you." Michael pulls me closer me with the arm he has draped around my waist, hidden beneath the table.

He looks down at me. My eyes are locked on his, mesmerized by his stare, lost in its intensity. My lips tingle with a smile, and I bite the inside of my cheek to contain it. The warmth of his breath brushes my nose as he exhales.

We hold our gaze until the silence of the paused conversation settles over the table. His family leans in toward us expectantly.

"I'll take her." Michael breaks our eye contact as he nods and glances around at his family. For the first time since the night of the Super Bowl, Michael seems flustered.

We leave our afternoon dessert with protruding bellies and big smiles. The anxiousness has settled, allowing me to laugh genuinely. We come to a point where we need to separate, our houses being in opposite directions. Michael casually says goodbye to his family. He promises Amber and Logan that he'll visit once law school allows, which they joke is never, pairing their sarcasm with dramatic eye rolls.

"It was so good to finally meet you," Elaine says, hugging me goodbye, a sweet summer smell escaping from her hair, the fresh floral scent so familiar.

"Thank you for inviting me." I hug back, breathing in the scent one more time: lily of the valley.

She pulls away but keeps her hands on the backs of my arms. She examines my expression, which I'm sure reads confusion or unease because I'm not sure why she paused nor why she's studying me. My gaze falls uncomfortably.

"My son loves you," Elaine says definitively. A gentle smile pulls her cheeks up. Mine respond with a crimson flush. "Be good to him, you fit in well."

I swallow the dryness in my mouth, feeling nothing bob down my throat. I don't know what to say or which of the many parts of her two sentences to respond to. Elaine steps back, and Amber interrupts the interaction by hugging me. I'm thankful for her bouncy attitude that scares away the tense air between Elaine and me.

The rest of the goodbyes go quickly, and soon Michael and I are walking away, waving one last time over our shoulders.

I only live a couple of blocks from the bakery, so we get to my house before we have a chance to unpack the afternoon. Michael lingers speechlessly before kissing me goodbye at my door. I want him to stay, to laugh with me about my silly insecurities going into the day, but the uneasy stirring in my stomach prevents me from verbalizing it. He doesn't say anything either. He warned me prior to lunch that he would have to study afterward, but I still feel deserted when he leaves.

I call for Harper once I'm inside, but the silence tells me she isn't home. I'm more drained than I've been in months, so I take the chance to breathe in some alone time. Whispers of insecurity surround me on all sides.

Is he leaving because I'm not normal enough for his family? How could I ever fit in with such a traditional family when I've never had one? They only liked me because I was pretending to be someone else. He must have seen an outward callousness toward the normalcy of his family dynamics. He isn't coming back. He doesn't want someone who is broken.

Besides the occasional honking or the revving of an engine from the street below, a soothing silence soaks the air in the apartment. The faint buzz of electricity acts as steady white noise.

I exchange Harper's clothes for sweatpants and set the borrowed outfit on her dresser before closing my bedroom door and falling into bed. I collapse in the soft comforter and tuck my sweatshirt's arm around my fingers to hide my hands as I curl into a fetal position.

I'm exhausted from something I can't find words for. The day weighs on me heavily, and the stale apartment air makes breathing uncomfortable.

If Harper comes home at any point, I don't hear her through my closed door and loud headphones.

The lack of light coming in through the window exposes the passing time, but I still feel paralyzed, stuck in a melancholy quicksand. I've been spending all day sorting through fleeting thoughts, trying to pin down what has created the funk.

My mind keeps pulling up memories of my mom: her small bulbous nose and long straight hair falling onto her shoulders as she laughs, the veins in her hands popping as she pulls weeds out of the garden then pats the dirt back down. My memories of Ohio with her in them are bright, lively, and warm. Memories stored after her death come up bleak and pale, like Midwest winters where everything blends into a sea of soft gray.

The comparison between my childhood and Michael's family experience leaves me feeling inadequate. I've never known a family like his; never seen a marriage last into their children's adulthood, never seen money troubles not end in divorce and drug addictions in death. Sickness, in one way or another, has always followed the marriages that I've known and looked up to.

The more I play back my parents' mistakes, the more my emotions collide in overwhelming waves.

I call Miller, and I'm thankful she picks up despite being in the middle of studying. She's the only person who can understand what I went through because she went through it, too.

"I'm guessing this means it didn't go well?" she asks when she hears my sad hello.

"No, it went great," I reply.

"Why don't you sound happier then?"

"They're a white picket fence family," I sigh. "I don't fit in."

"Did they say that?"

"No," I hesitate, knowing the words sound silly, "his mom actually told me the opposite."

Miller listens to my failing confidence, saying little in return and acting mostly as a sounding board.

"You can't let Mom and Dad's dysfunction haunt you forever," Miller says into the phone once I've finished venting. "We've envied kids with two parents our whole lives. You have an opportunity to get that through Michael. It's a healthy relationship, don't push it away."

"But what if he leaves too?" My words catch unexpectedly, not realizing how many emotions were brewing.

"You'll find another family to be a part of. In the meantime, you'll have me."

Miller doesn't lie or make promises that he won't leave, but her words bring comfort. *I'll always have her.*

Before hanging up, I wish her luck on her upcoming final exams, then check the notifications I've ignored.

Harper: Be home in the morning. Walk of shame incoming

Michael
Two missed calls

No follow-up texts. I call back reluctantly.

"Hey," Michael's voice is breathy when he answers, "I was wondering when you would call back."

"What are you doing?"

"Running," he responds heavily.

"It's almost midnight," I state.

"I couldn't sleep."

He pauses, and I stay silent, still feeling anxious.

"You hate them, don't you?"

"What?" I ask, surprised.

"You didn't invite me in, didn't call me back, didn't text me." Insecurity pours through the phone. Regret washes over me.

"Michael, your family is great. I had a really fun day."

"Oh." He says, slightly lighter.

"Want to come over?" I ask in a plea, hints of desperation decorating each syllable.

"Yes. I'll run home and shower, then come by."

I hang up the phone and allow the imprisoned air in my lungs to escape in a rushed exhale.

I practice a speech of explanation until I hear a familiar knock at the door.

Michael and I spend the next couple hours entangled together, half-dressed under my bedsheets. I offer my perspective on the day—only the positive feedback.

Michael seems to hold a defensive posture, as if waiting for an insult to be hurled, but as I speak, he becomes softer, and his thumb brushes my shoulder. His eyes are as gentle as his touch.

"My family was different than yours," I say looking up, searching the ceiling for a place to start. "My dad wasn't a great dad. He was in and out of jail for DV, possession and distribution, assault and battery."

As I say this, Michael flinches, but he kisses me tenderly in the space between my words.

"And my mom's love always came with hate," I sigh, continuing to ease into my family's skeletons. "Not for me or Miller, or even my dad. Mostly for the orange bottles that controlled her. She had a more consistent relationship with Xanax and Vicodin than she did with any of us."

I think back on my parents' marriage, their volatility and violence. Their lack of understanding for the other's problems and disrespect toward any progress. Neither of them had an example of a stable marriage. Really, they didn't display signs of observing any type of successful relationship.

"But my mom," I restrain the welling tears and continue, needing to empty myself. "She painted the colors of the day. When she was happy, the days were vibrant and full of life. But the days grew dark and gloomy as she became more addicted to pills."

Michael rests his lips on my shoulder, quietly listening. A calmness spreads through the space between us in the midst of his patient understanding.

"The garden started dying when she stopped tending to it. My dad became more reckless the more she used. Eventually they both went off the rails. He ended up in jail, my mom ended up dead, and Miller finished high school near my college campus. She became another roommate to Harper and me. We were all better off separate."

"I'm sorry." Michael says, tired and tender. He leans his head against mine. I breathe him in, exhaling pent-up pain. Michael's brow remains furrowed, as it was throughout the conversation. His eyes are deep tonight, making it impossible to read the thoughts collecting at the bottom.

We sit in silence; I fidget with my bangs, flatten the sheets over my chest, and readjust my pillow.

"Thank you." Michael's cracked voice echoes after an eternity of stillness. He clears his throat before he continues, "for telling me about everything."

The end of his sentence is followed by a pause in which he stares. His eyes dart side to side as he looks between mine, and he kisses me. His lips press into mine, his hand slips through my hair, and he pulls me close to him.

"I'm sorry I wasn't always there to protect you," he breathes, eyes closed, forehead pressed to mine. "I'm here now. I'm not going anywhere. I won't leave you."

SUNDAY
AUGUST 23, 2015

THE SOUND OF THE train beyond the four walls leaks in so loudly we can feel the track's vibrations. We lie in the dark, the yellow hue from the streetlights outside paints stripes across our bodies as it sneaks in behind broken blinds. The train's rumble fades as it moves further away, and we lie in bed quiet and still, soaking up the silent moments between our heavy breaths. I rest my hand gently on Michael's chest. I'm curled at his side, my breath in rhythm with the rise and fall of his body. He traces the vines tattooed up my arm out of habit.

Today was loud. I've been joining Michael and his parents for church on Sundays. His family picked us up this morning. On our short drive, his dad spat a dozen theological questions at me. He asked where I stood with my beliefs, pressed on how we'd raise kids if I'm not a Christian, brought up baptism. His concerns were legitimate. His intentions were kind, but his delivery was not.

After Michael and I hit the six-month mark in our relationship, his parents started openly asking more questions about our future. But today it felt more like an interrogation than a discussion.

I answered as politely as possible, but I remained truthful, so I know my answers weren't sufficient.

I'm still warming up to the idea of being with someone who is as dedicated to their faith as Michael is. The two of us have frequent in depth conversations about where I stand. I don't feel as strongly as I did at the beginning of our relationship. Michael's display of love and kindness has been very different than what I've experienced from the church. But contemplating the idea of being open to following Michael in his faith doesn't equate to me jumping into being baptized as his dad suggested. Unfortunately, there didn't seem to be a middle ground for Scott.

Michael picked up on my discomfort and intervened when appropriate. He kept my hand squeezed in his throughout the conversation.

He loves his dad in a way I don't understand, and I could tell he was struggling to balance respecting him and standing up for me.

My body warms feeling his hand against mine now, as it was in every church service we've been to. He keeps me close to him, protects me, keeps us connected.

I stare at his jaw, feeling small tucked between his chest and arm. I often study his mannerisms, his posture, the way he looks while engrossed in a new court case. I'm determined to etch the small moments into memory in case he breaks his promise and leaves.

Tonight, he lies silent and still. He closes his eyes but periodically flutters them open once he notices he has succumbed to the tugging exhaustion.

The vents above us rumble and blow cold air down at us. It ruffles his hair, which has dried distraughtly after the shower, extending in every direction, overlapping without tangling.

His breathing is slow and melodic, his chest rising to fill before emptying under my hand. I rub the small dip below his sternum with one finger, then trace his collarbone sticking out strongly before moving on to the thin muscles running visibly down his arm. I love his tall, lengthy body, his brown eyes, gentle movements, peaceful and calming voice, his laugh when he finds something genuinely funny, and his deep chuckle when he's unsure.

I love him.

"I think you're my soulmate." I say quiet and fragile, breakable in the dark room.

"I'd better be," he laughs quietly.

His response is matched with my silence. He leans over and kisses my head, his warm breath lingering after.

Michael pulls away from me so we're eye to eye. His nostrils flare against mine as he breathes. He looks serious, his gaze bouncing between my two eyes with a heavy, thoughtful stare.

"You're my soulmate, too." He responds smoothly.

His sentence doesn't end there. It dangles on an invisible string, hanging in his caught breath waiting for the final words to fall. The air remains unmoving in my lungs as my heart rate speeds up. I feel the words before he says them, covering us like a sheet in the dark room, a small space that's warm and safe and just for us.

"I love you, Anna Dawson."

The words tumble heavily. My lips part without hesitation, and the same words boomerang back to him.

"I love you, Michael Leathem."

His smile grows, and I feel the energy welling before I see it in his eyes. He's looking at me with a hope I've never seen in anyone before. There's a joy exuding from him so prominently it's tangible, and I reach for his face, begging to absorb all that he's feeling.

His lips meet mine gently. His hand brings my face to his.

"You're my family now," Michael pours his words into the darkness between us, and I've never felt so warm.

SATURDAY
OCTOBER 17, 2015

"WE ARE NOW BOARDING all zones." The staticky flight attendant's voice carries over the adjacent section of seating, and the remaining passengers rise in synchrony. Michael squeezes my hand as we stand up together, swinging our backpacks over our shoulders.

Michael wears his excitement proudly as we stand in line waiting for our plane tickets to be scanned. He takes each small step forward with a tall, open posture and a wide grin.

He called me immediately after Amber announced her pregnancy to the family in late April. Kids hadn't come up in conversation before his sister's call; I hadn't realized how much he was looking forward to being an uncle. Since the baby was born last weekend, Michael has gotten dozens of pictures. He's openly gushed at his nephew's tiny fingers wrapping around Amber's, his dark eyes as they widely look into oblivion, and the smallness of his body compared to Logan's.

I'd happily agreed to go visit Amber and Logan in Michigan when Michael asked me to join him. His parents were already there—they'd gotten on the first flight out and arrived before Amber was even home from the hospital.

I'm excited for a crowded house and to see a cohesive family covered in joy. I'm excited for normalcy.

"Here, I'll take your bag," Michael says, reaching to me. We agreed he could have the window seat since I'd end up leaning on him anyway.

I pass him my bag and after he's shoved it below the seat in front of mine, I slide in next to him. Before I have a chance to touch the seatbelt, Michael passes me a small package of sanitizing wipes. He gestures to the straps lying limply next to my waist then pulls out another for himself, opens it, and wipes down his tray, window, armrests, and seatbelt. The heavy scent of Clorox coats our row as the cloth streaks the plastic around him.

"You never know who sat here before you," he says while shrugging, seeing my questioning side glare.

"You excited?" I change the subject while completing the obligatory cleaning.

"I can't believe there's a baby in my family. My sister has a *baby.*" Michael squirms, eagerness wiggling out of him.

"I can't wait to find out what his name is." I've been waiting less than patiently for the telling of their secret.

"I know! Even my dad didn't let it slip."

"He's going to look so small in your arms." I smile at the thought: Michael's oversized hands cradling the small bundle of blankets as two little arms stretch out, tiny fingers wiggling in the air.

"You think I'm going to hold him?" Michael turns to me, shocked, the used wipe dangling from his fingers.

I take the wipe from him and stuff it in the pocket of the seat in front of me, then take his hand in mine. "He's your nephew, you're his *uncle.* Of course you're going to hold him."

Michael thinks in silence before the familiar, giddy smile takes over his face. "I don't know how to hold a baby."

My lips curl into a smile, joining his, and we laugh as our lack of baby experience becomes apparent. Neither of us has friends who are parents, and besides Miller and a couple of stray cousins, I don't talk to my family, so I've missed out on seeing any babies that may have come along.

The flight goes by quickly. Michael sleeps most of the way, and I sit back with closed eyes listening to music.

As we descend, the bright colors of fall overtake our windows. Vibrant orange, faded yellow, and deep reds cover the flat land below. I wasn't expecting the state to remind me so much of Ohio, but from the sky, it looks like a more colorful version of where I grew up.

Scott and Logan pick us up from the airport, which is much bigger than I expected. When they pull up, Michael and I rush to jump into the back of the big silver truck, trying to avoid adding to the congestion of the passenger pickup loop.

"How's Amber?" I ask reaching for my seatbelt.

"Exhausted," Scott laughs and shakes his head.

"How's the baby?" Michael follows up immediately.

"Won't let anyone else hold him without screaming until he turns red."

"So maybe I won't be holding him," Michael whispers to me with his eyebrows raised.

When we pull into Amber and Logan's subdivision, we're greeted by a line of neatly trimmed pine trees. We pass a few dozen houses, all beautiful brick with two or three-car garages. They have sprawling grass yards and porches and pools—very different from the Boston scenery I've gotten used to. Most houses have pumpkins on the front steps or Halloween decorations in the windows to prepare for trick-or-treaters.

I can picture the little feet peeking out from ghost costumes bouncing from house to house, filling a tiny pumpkin-shaped bucket. It's a good neighborhood, and I imagine some houses even do the full-size candy bars. Maybe we'll visit next year while the baby is still too young to indulge in his treats.

Michael jumps out of the car as we pull into the driveway, grabbing both his backpack and mine and leaping steps ahead of the rest of us. He leaves the front door wide open for the three of us trailing behind. Elaine greets us at the door and directs us to take off our shoes, wash our hands, and change clothes before holding the baby. She shows me to the bathroom since Michael is already eagerly bounding down the hallway to change.

After I've washed up and slipped out of my airplane clothes, I join Michael in the living room. Logan and Scott are leaning over the back of the couch. Michael sits next to Amber, hunched over her shoulder.

"This is Mason," Amber says when I get closer. Although her eyes have dark shadows beneath them and she lacks any hint of makeup, she glows brighter than I've ever seen her. Her smile holds a new, lively joy.

"Mason," I repeat in a whisper. When I see him in his tiny entirety, he steals my breath. His dark eyes are large and glossy, disproportionate to the size of his face in the sweetest way. The rest of his features are preciously small—his faint eyebrows, doll-like nose, miniature fingernails, and little curled ears. His skin looks like porcelain: pale, smooth, and unscathed.

"Isn't he perfect?" Michael asks, looking up at me with tearful eyes. I nod, too enamored to speak. I'm completely transfixed by the mini-miracle in Amber's arms.

"Do you want to hold him?" Amber asks Michael, and he nods ferociously. He glances up at me in search of reassurance. I give a slight nod for encouragement, feeling the stinging behind my eyes. She gently extends Mason to Michael. His eyes light up as she transfers the weight into his hands.

Mason looks so much smaller juxtaposed to Michael's figure than he did in Amber's arms. Michael's adoration is so prominent it radiates into the space around him. My heart aches at the love emanating from the pair. I can't help but picture a slightly older version of Michael sitting next to me, holding our baby.

"He hasn't even fussed," Logan remarks with annoyance.

"He knows his uncle is the coolest." Michael shoots him a toothy grin.

The peaceful jubilance lasts only a couple of minutes before Mason makes it known that he wants to go back to Amber with a loud stretching cry. She glances at the clock, does some quick math in her head, then opens her arms for him.

"I'm going to put him down. Will you guys order food?" Amber asks, bouncing Mason as he screams the smallest cry I've ever heard.

"Anything you're in the mood for?" Logan asks with caution.

"Nothing spicy. No broccoli or cabbage."

"I didn't know such a small body could have such a big explosion without ever actually eating a piece of broccoli," Logan shakes his head once Amber's down the hall. "We're still working on figuring out what's okay for her to eat and what's not."

We settle on Mediterranean food, adding an additional grilled chicken dish with no garlic and minimal spices for Amber.

Logan and Scott go to pick it up while Michael and I spend time visiting with Amber and Elaine. They talk about Mason while we listen, intrigued by the new life in the family. We hear about his perfect little coo, the features that look like Logan and the ones that look like Amber, the feeling of his fingers in their hands, and how Amber recently learned that there's a point past deliriously tired. Elaine jumps in with funny stories of Michael and Amber as babies and compares Mason to both of them. She lights up as she speaks, proud of her new status as grandma.

"He can already recognize my voice and pretty soon he'll be able to *really* see, and his eyes will follow things, and he'll snuggle us back." Amber beams as she spews her baby knowledge. We're interested, but none of us give the reaction she hoped for. She changes her posture and shakes her head as she continues, "Okay, enough baby talk. I need adult conversations about anything else."

"Patriots are up three-two for the season. I think they finally got their game figured out," Michael ventures.

He receives an eyeroll from all three of us in return.

"Okay, maybe not *literally* anything else."

"How's school?" Elaine asks.

"It's fine," he shrugs.

"He's still ranked number one in his class. It's a lot more than *fine*." I nudge him, and he smiles with a boyish blush.

While Amber rests, Elaine shows us Mason's bedroom. Even though he'll be sleeping in the bassinet next to his parents for a few more weeks, they decorated it perfectly. There are silhouettes of jungle animals painted in white along the bottom of the gray walls. The crib has matching gray sheets, and there's a short bookshelf already half full. The dresser, which is small because it only holds newborn clothes, I suppose, has a foam changing pad on top and a tray fully stocked with diapers. They look no bigger than the ones I put on my dolls growing up. Michael walks around the tiny space. He comments on the smallness of the clothes and the thickness of the book pages, outwardly enamored by this new, unexplored world.

When Logan and Scott get back, we devour the food. Besides Amber, who has plain chicken and rice, all of us have multiple heaping plates of chicken, rice, grape leaves, Fattoush, and bread with hummus and garlic. By the end of dinner, we're all leaning back in our chairs with distended stomachs.

Amber brews a new pot of decaf, and we all help to clear the mess. Scott and Elaine sip their coffees while we chat casually over the cleared table until Amber expresses her exhaustion. Dinner was only interrupted once, but since Amber's breastfeeding, she has to be the one who responds to Mason's cries. We respect her fatigue and disperse quietly. Scott and Elaine go to the guest room, where they're sleeping, and Logan helps get the pull-out couch in the living room ready for Michael and me.

"I'm shocked Elaine is letting you sleep together," Logan says. He carries pillows from the hallway closet over to the couch while I help Michael pull sheets over the bed corners.

"You don't have any other rooms," Michael laughs, "and it's not like we're getting any privacy in the living room."

"Yeah, but still, you know how your parents get. They didn't let Amber and I sleep near each other even when we were engaged!"

"Perks of being the younger child," Michael grins and wiggles his eyebrows at me from across the bed.

"And *this* is why your mom doesn't let us stay together," I laugh and throw a pillow at him.

"Don't do anything that could get me in trouble," Logan says, "I'm going to bed. Hope you guys are heavy sleepers, that baby's got lungs on him."

Michael and I finish making the bed, not only tired from the morning's travel but preemptively exhausted from tomorrow night's flight as well. Unfortunately, Michael has class on Monday, so our stay is short.

Scott and Elaine poke their heads around the corner to say goodnight. Michael and I take turns changing into pajamas in the bathroom.

After we've both brushed our teeth, we click off the lights and slip beneath the covers. Within seconds, both of us have our eyes closed, and a wave of quiet peace washes over the room.

"He's the cutest baby alive," Michael says with a yawn.

"He is," I reply, smiling.

"He's so small and helpless."

"Mhmm."

"Do you think our baby will be that cute?" Michael's words cause my eyes to shoot open, powered by a rush of adrenaline. I turn my head only to see Michael already looking at me, watching my reaction. He wears a subtle smile—as though he didn't bring up babies—but he shows no signs of a joke as he stares back with sincerity, patiently waiting.

He wraps his arm around my waist and pulls me closer to him. He fiddles with the material of my sweatshirt, his fingers meeting the skin of my lower back. His calmness soothes my pounding heart.

"I think they'll be even cuter," I reply, my smile escaping.

"I think you're right."

Michael says before sneaking a quick kiss in the dark. But he comes back, slower and more tender. My eyes linger closed, but I can feel his gaze as his breath warms my nose.

"I love you, Anna Dawson."

I open my eyes, and he kisses me once more on the lips, then one last time on the forehead before closing his eyes again.

"I love you, Michael Leathem." I whisper back.

I snuggle with the blanket as I normally would with Michael, making sure to leave a respectful amount of space between us.

I'm only woken up once during the night, and it's by Michael who wants me to hear how cute Mason's cry is after it woke him up. I sleepily nod, then fall back asleep until I hear movement in the kitchen. I can tell whoever is awake is trying to avoid being loud since the kitchen is open to the living room, but the sound of brewing coffee jolts me awake, my body eager for caffeine.

"Good morning," I whisper as I slide on a sweatshirt and tiptoe to the kitchen.

"Coffee? It's regular," Amber asks, gesturing to the full pot.

"Please," I nod. She gets me a mug, and we sit down together at the table. I breathe in the steam and sigh gratefully after taking my first sip.

"I'm not a bad mom, I promise. My doctor said I could have a half cup," Amber raises her mug, filled to the top but closer to the color of milk than coffee.

I smile somberly, feeling a surge of sympathy for Amber. She's under so much physical stress—losing sleep, constantly breastfeeding, living on the clock of a newborn—but she's also been putting so much pressure on herself to be a good mom.

"I wouldn't have the self-control to stop after a half cup," I say. She continues to stare down at her beige-colored coffee, so I add, "You look great."

"You don't have to lie," Amber scoffs politely.

"I'm being honest. You're glowing, and you look so happy with Mason."

"That's very nice of you," she replies, then leans over and whispers, "I feel like total shit. I haven't gotten any sleep, my boobs hurt all the time, and I'm on week one out of eighteen years."

Amber confides in me while the others are still asleep. She tells me how she feels disconnected from her friends, but she's too tired to care. The only thing she ever thinks about is Mason. She checks his breathing multiple times when he's sleeping, and, if he isn't in her arms, there's a panic that's constant throughout her body. She's having trouble trusting Logan to do the simple things like change Mason's diaper. She's never felt so far apart from her husband in the entirety of their marriage.

She stops when Elaine walks out into the kitchen, and I watch as she transforms herself, putting on a smile. Elaine is happy to sit with us, but when she does, the conversation shifts away from Amber's venting.

One by one, the family gathers in the kitchen. They creep in to pour themselves a coffee, then join the rest of us at the table.

Soon, we're all sitting around the dining room table, and our whispers turn into a cluster of normal-volume conversations, forcing Michael to wake up.

We spend the morning helping Amber with chores around the house. We urge her to get rest since her body is still healing and tell her to take advantage of having family here. I try to be gentle in my encouragement after the morning's conversation. She looks at me for reassurance before agreeing, as though we're in on a secret no one else knows—which is probably true.

Michael and I take over baby duty in the afternoon while Logan runs to the grocery store to restock diapers. When Mason's awake, we can't stop looking at him, touching his tiny feet, and giggling at his yawns.

I'm hit with instant sadness when Scott gives us a thirty-minute warning for the airport. I'm not ready to leave Mason or the rest of the family. Although I know I'll see Michael's parents in a couple of weeks when they get back to Boston, having the whole family crammed under one roof has been a cheerful change.

"I'm sorry we can't stay longer," Michael says while hugging his sister.

"I'm happy you got to come, even if the trip was short." Amber waves her hand, shooing away his apology.

"Thanks for having us," I say when it's my turn. The group is distracted by their goodbyes, but I still lower my voice, "Call me if you ever want to talk."

She squeezes me mid-hug. "I can't wait for you to officially be part of the family."

On the flight back, Michael sleeps, but I'm still wired, drunk on the smell of newborn. I spend the entire time wondering what our baby would look like. Would he grow into a body as big as his dad's or inherit my petite stature? Would he get my green eyes, or would he come out of the womb with brown eyes that hold all his emotions like Michael's? Would it be a sweet girl who has my fair skin and does ballet? Would we have one kid or two kids? Or more?

Michael brings a steady security to our relationship that allows me to look at the next steps. He cultivates a space for me to picture a life and a family—*our* life and *our* family.

I look over at him. His mouth has fallen open, and his head rests on the closed window shade, one hand against his head and the other in my lap. His legs are bunched up, and his knees are pushed together from the closeness of the seat in front of him. He looks so peaceful, like a quiet boy rather than a man.

"I love you," I whisper in his ear, and he smiles in his sleep.

SATURDAY DECEMBER 12, 2015

THE ENDING OF THE winter semester for all of Boston's colleges, paired with the sudden chill, leaves the streets bare as the sun begins to sink. We walk hand in hand to a steakhouse in celebration of Michael's law school graduation and long-anticipated job offer.

Michael has been in school for his entire adulthood, and the ending of his education signals a new season of life for him. This is the most important transition he's gone through, but we've been avoiding any conversations about the inevitable changes that come with his graduation. Michael is quick to breeze over any topic relating to our future, which creates a space for my insecurities.

I remind myself that he sought my opinion and included me as he processed each job offer: the pay, location, probable hours, and clients. He was elated after each interview, his quirky goofiness and stubborn ambitious side coming together on full display.

But a nagging negativity haunts my mind. Just because he has included me in the decision-making process doesn't mean he plans to include me in the next steps.

He took an offer in Cambridge. Multiple law firms, both in and out of state, recruited him, but he didn't want to leave the city. His life is here, all the friends he's made from elementary to law school, and his parents live close by.

But tonight, I'm pushing all insecurities aside, temporarily breaking the haze of uncertainty covering the future. Michael's mom planned a family brunch next weekend, but I wanted to do something special for him tonight. I made dinner reservations at his favorite steakhouse and sent an invite to all our friends for drinks after. I know he's probably tired from the ceremony this afternoon, but it's too monumental of an accomplishment not to celebrate today.

When we get to the restaurant, we're escorted past the quiet murmurs of other tables and are seated near the grand piano. Its keys are gently played by a man in a striped button-up shirt sending hushed romanticized versions of modern music around us.

A thin, blonde man in an all-black suit introduces himself as he sets waters in front of us and asks if we've looked over the drink menu. Wanting to make tonight special and knowing Michael will take an egregious amount of time to look over such a long list, I jump in without missing a beat.

"We'll take whichever bottle of sweet red you recommend."

I hand the wine list back to the waiter, wondering if he's even old enough to legally drink.

Michael's oddly quiet as he skims the menu. The nervousness in my brain is fueled. Knowing Michael will pick out a seasonal menu item I'll love, I spend the passing time by glancing up at him, trying to read his expression.

I remind myself that tonight is about celebrating Michael's accomplishments and nothing else.

I imagine he's overwhelmed by the change in his schedule and the unfamiliarity of the weight of law school being lifted. He might be nervous about the daunting bar exam, known for failing everyone on the first attempt, or the gathering of so many people tonight. I'm sure the pressure of today's cigarette being his last at least amplifies his anxiousness of the other stressors.

Our bottle arrives, and the waiter pours me a sip to taste. I perform the pretentious but expected swirl of the glass and drink the splash of wine, then nod in approval. He pours us each a "full glass," which equates to about a quarter of what Harper and I pour ourselves at home.

"Do you two know what you want?" the waiter asks, looking first at me then at Michael.

"Can we start with the calamari? For dinner, the Wagyu medium rare for me, and she will have the duck, also medium rare. We'll also get the fennel salad to split?" Michael orders with a simplicity that exhibits his gentle chivalry. He looks at me briefly, making sure I have no objections. I smile back in approval; everything he ordered sounds delicious.

"Any allergies or dietary restrictions?" the waiter asks.

Michael shakes his head.

"Great, I'll be back shortly with bread and oil."

As I watch Michael's brief interaction, I'm reminded of the reasons I love him, his kindness and consideration, the masculinity in his gentleness and leadership. I rest my chin on my hand, smiling dreamily.

"What?" he chuckles and blushes.

"Nothing, you're just so handsome."

"I love you too," he says knowingly. He's gotten extremely good at hearing the *I love you* in my everyday verbiage.

The food surpasses the memory of our last meal here. We savor the richness and perfect cook of the meat, enjoy the fresh crunch of the fennel salad, and relish the bold aroma of the wine as we refill our glasses until the bottle empties.

"Do you remember our first date?" Michael asks, piling the scraps of his plate onto his fork.

"It wasn't that long ago," I say. It was less than a year ago, but the progression of our relationship feels drastic in comparison.

While I wait for him to continue, I swirl the stem of my glass between my fingers, wondering where he's going with this.

"Remember that game we played?"

I nod, thinking back. Not only did we play on our first date, but a lot of dates thereafter. We found couples while walking in the park or dining at restaurants and would guess how long they'd been dating, what kind of families they came from, their jobs and pets. When we started dating, it was something we did often, but it slowly fizzled out. I can't remember the last time we played.

"What do you think people would guess for us?" Michael asks, more relaxed.

"In the morning before coffee, they'd guess we're a cranky old married couple," I laugh, "but I guess we probably look like a married couple right now, too."

"I like that guess." His smile widens.

We take time looking over the dessert menu but decide to stop at a local bakery before heading to the bar. I pay, fighting Michael's persistence to lay down his card.

We go back out into the cold night, hugging our light jackets as we walk. Our finished bottle of wine warms any exposed skin.

"I think Douceur is still open," Michael suggests.

Douceur, one of our favorite bakeries, is in the direction of the bar we're holding the celebration at, so I agree. I loop my arm through his as we make our way down the quiet street.

We rush into the small shop and rub our hands together for a hurried warmth. It feels more evident now that the sun has set that neither of us dressed warmly enough for the freezing winter night.

There isn't much set out behind the glass, and we're told that anything they have left for the night is on display. We shiver as we skim over the remaining inventory. One of the employees stirs together a chocolate cream in the mixer, sending a sweet scent into the air around us. Another kneads the dough in front of him into the shape of a croissant. I thought I was full from dinner, but I salivate as I watch them.

After some deliberation, Michael and I settle on two chocolate pastry twists.

"Want to eat here?" Michael asks, gesturing to one of the few tables in the shop.

"Yes, please," I say, my fingers still regaining feeling.

Michael hangs his coat on the back of the chair, but I opt to keep mine on. We sit down and take our first bites.

"I forgot how good these are." I close my eyes and allow my small, drunk taste buds to savor the sweetness. "You know, the first time I came here was with you and your parents just a few months ago."

"Thank you for celebrating me tonight." Michael slides his half-eaten pastry aside. He takes my hand in his. My frozen fingertips buzz in the warmth of his palm. "I want to celebrate with you when I pass the bar exam, too."

"Of course!" I say with a mouthful of pastry. I blush and bring my free hand up to cover my mouth until I've swallowed the bite. He gives my hand a familiar squeeze, and I copy the act in return.

"I want to celebrate everything with you. When we buy our first house, every promotion we get. A dog then a baby," Michael's squeeze intensifies as he continues to speak, but his face remains unstrained.

He leans in closer to me and uses his free hand to reach into his coat.

"Michael!" His name comes out in a squeal, my breath escaping in a gust. I struggle to fill my lungs, but my eyes fill easily with tears.

"Anna, I loved you from the second I saw you. I fell in love with your clumsiness and beauty first, but you impressed me with your playfulness, resilience, love, support, and intelligence. I know it hasn't been long, but there isn't a doubt in my mind that you're the person I'm supposed to spend the rest of my life with, and I don't want to wait anymore."

I'm hearing the words he's saying, nodding along fervently, but my eyes remain on the open box in his hand.

"Marry me." It isn't a question, but his words hang in the air, waiting to be answered.

"Yes, yes, of course!" I cry into the hand that still covers my open mouth. His smile is serene as he reaches for my hand, pulling it from my lips, and slides the ring on. I hold my hand out and move it side to side, watching the diamond sparkle. It's a large, edgy gem sitting on a simple band. It would look out of place on anyone's hand except mine, where it fits perfectly, as if it were made just for me.

"Michael!" I gasp again. He gets out of his chair and pulls me up, then presses his lips to mine. The claps of the two employees fill the bakery as they cheer for us.

"Let's go celebrate. I hear all our friends are waiting for us." He kisses me again.

The nerves and tears blur the walk to the bar. When we walk in, we're greeted by Amber, Miller, and Michael's parents. Miller hands us each a glass of champagne and hugs me tightly as the room yells *congratulations*, shouts coming from every direction.

Our friends fill every corner of the bar, but Harper's tear-filled hazel eyes catch my attention first. I swing my arms around her, both of us shaking as we cry.

"I can't believe you kept a secret!" I laugh. She reaches out and snatches my hand to inspect the enormous diamond for herself.

"I swear he picked it out on his own!" she squeals, "I told him there was no way I could see it and not tell you."

"It's perfect. I couldn't imagine anything better."

"Or bigger," Harper smirks at me. "I'm so happy for you, but I can't believe I'm going to lose my favorite roommate!"

"And I'm losing my favorite half of the closet!" I whine bittersweetly. We giggle as I show off the ring's sparkle under the dimmed lights.

Michael finds me somewhere between laughing and crying with Harper and drapes his arm around me. With hands joined and giddy tears, the two of us circle the room thanking people for coming. I'm amazed that so many people kept quiet. While I thought I was planning a party for Michael, he was cleverly using it to celebrate our engagement.

I take time to thank Amber for traveling. She returns the gratitude and thanks me for giving her a break from baby duty.

"I'm so happy you came. I'm proud of you for leaving Mason and trusting Logan!" I hug her, knowing how hard it's been.

"The house will be a disaster, but his mom and sister are on standby. I needed a trip away."

Miller interrupts our conversation by swinging her arms around me in an embrace.

"Need a refill?"

"Please," I hug Amber one more time before Miller and I go to the bar for another glass of champagne.

"Can you believe you're engaged?" Miller says after we've requested the drinks from the bartender.

"I had no idea he was going to propose. We hadn't even talked about rings."

"He did a great job," she says, taking my hand in hers and shining it under the faint light of the hanging bar lamps. "How are you feeling?"

I can hear the understanding in her words, the question behind her question. It's like she has been reading my thoughts.

"I wish Mom and Dad could be here tonight," I sigh, twirling the ring around my finger. The room behind us is full with family and friends, but the heaviness of the missing conversations is obvious.

"I don't think either of us actually wants Dad here," she laughs lightheartedly, "but Mom knows."

"You think so?"

"Yeah, and I think she's proud. You found someone with a humor as lively as hers. Someone who's endlessly positive like she was." Miller smiles sadly and her eyes twinkle. Her words waver as she speaks, "She'd be so happy for you tonight."

I want to ask her if she believes in heaven and if she thinks our mom is there, but I leave the conversation for a different day.

"I love you," I bump her with my hip as the bartender puts two drinks down in front of us. She nudges me back, and we cheers our full glasses.

"Hello, beautiful," Michael draws out the syllables, smiling as he returns to my side. My face brightens, and my smile widens at the sound of his voice, still in shock. He lifts my chin up for a drawn-out kiss.

"Ew," Miller comments. Michael laughs as he waves down the bartender to get a glass of champagne for himself.

"To the Dawson girls, who are *both* joining the Leathem family," Michael raises his glass, nodding to Miller. She blushes, grateful to be included.

"To my sister finding someone who I can trust when they vow to love and care for her forever," Miller adds, weaving together honesty and intimidation. The three of us clink flutes.

As we turn around, Michael's roommate Kyle begins drunkenly tapping on the karaoke mic, trying to get the group's attention.

"I'd love to share stories of these two," Kyle says between microphone screeches, "As the roommate, I have many."

He wiggles his eyebrows, and the crowd lets out an expected laugh. Michael looks over to his mom, then down to me and covers his reddening face. Kyle is so unpredictable, and he's right; he has more than a handful of embarrassing stories.

"But I won't because Mrs. Leathem is here, and she'd kick my ass like she did in middle school when she caught us smoking cigs. So, I'll just say that I've never seen Michael so happy. I never thought he'd meet someone, let alone someone so beautiful and patient. To Anna, who voluntarily cheers for the Patriots!"

Michael draws me in by the waist, pressing a tender kiss to my head, whispering softly into my hair that he loves me.

Kyle passes the mic to Harper, who shares her version of his speech. With the mic now fair game and alcohol being served generously, sweet speeches turn into funny stories that bleed over into karaoke. Friends and family get up and sing terrible off-key versions of Taylor Swift and Billy Joel while the rest of the crowd sings along.

Michael and I make our way around the tables, trying to thank everyone individually before people start to trickle out.

Eventually, the party begins to die down, and we seize an opportunity to sneak out.

We break out into the cold, laughing hysterically, drunk on champagne and high on happiness. As we stumble home, we reenact the speeches, giggling at my surprised jaw drop and at Michael's nerves during dinner. I replay the conversations Michael avoided about the future. It makes sense now, knowing that he was trying to keep this a secret.

We make it back to my apartment in record time.

The door isn't fully closed by the time his mouth is on mine. He leans into me, pushing me against the living room wall, and reaches to the side to lock the door, then lifts me, spinning around the living room. My legs instinctively wrap around his waist as his lips slide from my jaw to my collarbone.

His breath is warm on my neck. I shiver and lean my head back, closing my eyes. Our lips continue to press heavily against each other, breaking only in short intervals to take clothes off layer by layer.

We stumble in the dark, taking turns pushing the other backward toward the bedroom. We don't stop for the light or to close the door as we move collectively to the bed. My hair is tightly wound around his fingers, and my nails are on his back as we fall to the mattress. I breathe unevenly into his chest as he lets out a stifled moan.

He freezes and looks down at me. His hand's grip turns into a soft palm, and as his body relaxes, mine does too.

"I love you."

His demeanor changes as he releases the words, becoming softer but deeper. His eyes look into mine, closing only when our breaths meet between overlaying gasps and moans.

Between the alcohol and the late hours, the night becomes a blur of Michael pressing into me, our bodies deflating, a few minutes of sleep, then restarting the hour. Each time his tongue touches my skin, I notice the slight increase of light slipping in around the curtains.

We wake up with our bodies intertwined. We soak up the morning light and memories from the night. My heart skips, and I pull my hand close to my eyes, worried I hallucinated. Michael's laughing by the time I process last night's events.

"It's beautiful." I smile and bury myself against him while both kissing him and staining him with tears.

We spend the day between the bed and the couch. Harper gives us full rein of the apartment to celebrate, promising to give us at least a two-hour warning before she comes back. Around noon, Michael makes us scrambled eggs and pancakes from scratch to feed our overworked appetites.

We spend hours reminiscing about our first date and all subsequent ones while a *Harry Potter* marathon acts as background noise. We fill conversations with details about his job, types of weddings we find elegant or cheesy, the best months to get married, and how many people are too many. He tells me the story of how he chose the ring. We compromise on which neighborhoods to start our apartment search and form an agreed-upon timeline to move in together.

As we giggle over forgotten memories, I float into a fantasy world where we spend our youth laughing over drinks and our Sunday mornings making breakfast before church. A series of fictitious decades that are too close to only be imagined, where we enjoy routine chores and nightly dinners. Together, we become wrinkled from time and retire to a lake house in Vermont buried somewhere in multi-colored trees where no one can find us. We spend a long life together celebrating anniversaries and promotions. We enjoy the silent company of each other on the mundane days. In this life, we have friends and babies, and we replay our wedding videos on our anniversary and cry every time. We vow to love each other through the kids' teenage years, when time has shriveled our lips and decades have outdated our kitchen. Michael promises to still kiss me regardless of our finances and the disgusted faces our kids make at us.

We kiss and talk and enjoy the closeness that only comes from the synchronization of becoming one until the sun has set and a layer of darkness rests over our naked bodies sprawled across the couch.

"I don't want to live without you," I whisper with sleepy eyes long after midnight.

"You don't have to. We're going to spend the rest of our lives together."

"I get to die first," I say this with a sudden but tangible fear that there's a possibility I'll have days without him next to me.

"I'll take one for the team," he replies with closed eyes, "I'll die one minute after you, so you never have to be alone."

"You promise?"

"I promise."

He nods and leans over to kiss the top of my head. His eyelids lift, heavy with drowsiness, and his brown eyes meet my green ones for a long, serious stare.

"You really promise?"

"I really promise. You won't ever have to live without me."

SATURDAY

APRIL 9, 2016

TWIRLING THE BOUQUET OF flowers between my fingers, I stare blankly at my reflection in the full-length mirror. I tug on the cream-colored lace dress that now feels too tight. The new sparkling ring feels uncomfortable against my pinky knuckle; my toes are pinched between the unforgiving fabric of my shoes; the brightly colored bouquet in my hands looks gaudy instead of lively the way it did earlier.

"*Wife*," I whisper out loud, feeling the syllables nip my lips as they're pushed out. I smile pretentiously as though I'm introducing myself to a stranger, "I'm Michael's *wife*."

I look like I've aged in the hour since I last saw myself. This version of me looks unrecognizable. A cheap bride with a diamond ring that belongs in a gallery, not on my hand. I'm a knockoff trying to play the part of the girl Michael imagined himself marrying. I wonder when he'll figure out I don't know how to be the wife he wants. I have no reference for a successful marriage, or proper communication, or gentle love. His family worked so hard to build a generous man, and he's pouring all of it into me—an empty cup who spills the kindness given. I don't know how, but I know I'll break the beauty he's offered me.

The version of me trapped in the mirror doesn't offer any answers.

Our closest friends and family joined us for a small ceremony at Fan Pier Park. At Michael's request, Kyle officiated our short exchange of vows overlooking the city and the ocean. Elaine was upset that I didn't want a big wedding. She was even more disappointed that Michael agreed with me—he said he wanted an intimate ceremony since our vows were only between us and God. During the wedding planning, Elaine made her feelings clear with subtle, pointed comments. To mitigate her disappointment, I tasked her with planning the reception dinner, which got her excited. I think she just wanted a way to feel included since she wouldn't get the chance to have a mother-son dance.

After the ceremony, we all made the trip back to our apartment to overindulge in alcohol before dinner. Elaine and Miller, my two personal wedding planners, went ahead of the group to ensure everything was set with the reservations.

"You okay in there?" Harper's calls from outside the bathroom. Laughter from the small group gathered in the living room echoes down the hallway and slips under the door. When I don't answer, Harper lets herself in.

"Hey," I say and give her a sad head tilt with tear-filled eyes.

"Hey," she repeats gently. She moves toward me, stopping when our shoulders touch, and turns to face the mirror. Her eyes meet mine in the reflection. "What's going on in that head of yours?"

I shake my head and look to the ceiling in an attempt to hold in tears. "I feel like a different person now."

"You look like the same old Anna to me. Your hair's still mousy brown, but Miller put it up in a cute little bun instead of it being straight. You have on more makeup than usual, but it's not too much. And your dress is gorgeous, but I'd venture to guess you bought special white sweatpants for after dinner."

"I did," I grin through drying tears.

"Now give me a real smile, Mrs. Leathem." Harper draws out my new name and nudges me with her hip. She pivots in front of me, blocking my reflection. Her fingers carefully wipe any dampness on my cheeks. "You're going to mess up your makeup, and I worked too hard for it to be ruined before dinner."

I roll my eyes jokingly, but I'm thankful for her cheerful positivity. She pulls me by the hand out of the bathroom to rejoin the group. When I stumble out from the hallway, I'm greeted with a big cheers.

I don't know if anyone else sees it, but Michael looks different too. He looks bubbly. His brown eyes are big and hopeful like a cartoon drawing. He's energized, like he's been rested and renewed, as he pops around making conversation with everyone, being more social than I've ever seen him. When our eyes meet, he beams brightly and jumps over to me, leading with his outstretched arm that immediately wraps around my waist to dip me for a kiss. He tastes like vodka and happiness.

"Shots!" Kyle yells, interrupting the heavy, drunken gaze between Michael and me.

"Shots!" Michael repeats after kissing me again.

We take the shots Kyle poured. Michael passes us all another one. After we lose track of how many we've had, Harper begins corralling the group through the door. Drunken happiness has taken over, and we're all stumbling, laughter roaring between us.

"Okay, everyone out!" Harper demands, herding the room with authority, waving her arm as though she's directing traffic.

"Come here," Michael says gently as his long arm reaches to grab my hand. He spins me and pulls me into him before I can walk out the door.

I stagger, feeling the height of my heels beneath the heaviness of the alcohol. Harper winks at me as she closes the door behind her. It's only the two of us left in the apartment.

"Well, hello, beautiful." Michael draws me closer to his chest.

With a single kiss and the warmth of his embrace, my body relaxes. I find comfort in him, and immediately I know that although I may feel different, Michael is still the same.

"We didn't get a first dance." Michael takes a step back, "So, Mrs.

Leathem, may I?"

I take his outstretched hand, and we sway to the silence. I bury my face in his shoulder, smelling the alcohol on my breath as it's reflected back to me. I glance at my hand in his, looking at the wedding band that now accompanies my engagement ring.

"Our first kitchen dance as a married couple," I smile and lean my whole body's weight into his, "I'm a *wife.*"

"You're *my* wife," Michael looks down at me, beaming proudly. He searches my face, and I see his eyes water for the first time today. "I just love you so much. You're my number one priority. It goes you, and everything else comes second."

I'm overwhelmed by his love. I see it in the depths of his brown eyes. I feel it in the grip his hand has on my waist. I hear it in the tearful grumble of his voice.

"I love you," I say back.

Dinner is a warped, blurry haze. When we arrive, the table is full of food. I nibble, but I'm too distracted to eat. People give toasts throughout the dinner. We all drink too much and start to get sloppy. Kyle trips in the middle of the restaurant while going to the bathroom. I knock over my water, and it soaks two of the dishes on the table. Harper breaks her wine glass, leaving glass shards in her seat.

Elaine and Scott pay the bill and leave as the waitress drops off one of each dessert. Multiple spoons fight for the sorbet, I break off a piece of baklava, and Michael pulls the plate of cheesecake toward him to stake his claim.

As we take our final bites, Kyle raises his glass with a toast to the newlyweds and taps his chocolate-covered knife against it. The rest of our table follows his lead, using the custom to prompt us to kiss. A soft *ting, ting, ting* echoes through the restaurant, drawing the attention of the diners around us.

"This has to be the last toast of the night," Michael says quietly under his breath as he leans over in his seat. Our noses are touching, his skin heating mine, but he pauses before leaning in to kiss me.

I sit still in our moment, a split second that feels like we're alone. The clinking around us continues but fades into a muffle, and all I can hear is the exhale of his breath. It's warm as it meets mine, alcohol seeping out. I can decipher each of his fingers as they grip my thigh under the table.

"I love you," I breathe. He presses his lips to mine before I've gotten out the last syllable. I can feel his smile in our kiss as it thins his lips. The cheer of our table gets loud, but we stay with our foreheads slightly touching, breath colliding, fixed in the stillness of the space between us. I never want to move.

Once the table's clean, we're expecting it to be far into the hours of the night, but it isn't even midnight yet. Kyle urges us to keep going, but my nerves prevented me from eating dinner, and my alcohol intake surpassed the food eaten hours ago. The effects are kicking in, and the nausea is spiking.

I'm not coherent enough to understand if they go to the bars, but Michael gets us a ride home.

We've barely made it through the doorway before I'm sprinting down the hallway to the bathroom.

I groan as dinner expels into the toilet bowl, a muddy mixture of Mediterranean that looked much better going down than it does coming up.

"Michael," I call weakly between coughs. He doesn't answer right away. My stomach quivers. "Babe?"

"I'm coming!" Michael calls back, and I hear his footsteps moving quickly against the hardwood floor. His head pops around the corner, and he sets a water glass down next to me. I shake my head, refusing to pull my face out of the toilet bowl in fear of the food regurgitating.

"I'm so sorry." My voice sounds deep as I hold back the bile fighting to come back up, "This isn't how we're supposed to spend our wedding night."

Michael rubs my shoulders as he laughs. He sits down next to me, leaning his back against the open door. I don't look up, but I can feel the softness of his gaze on me. "We have every night after this."

"You're too nice to me," I cry before another course of our meal comes up.

"This isn't the first time you drank too much, and it definitely won't be the last." Michael's lightheartedness makes me chuckle too. The groggy sound echoes in the toilet.

Michael leaves to change out of his suit and brings pajamas for me with him when he comes back. Between bouts of sickness, I slip out of my already unzipped lace dress. Michael holds my arm to steady me as I work to pull up the flannel shorts he brought over. I raise my arms, and he slides a sweatshirt over my head. As I lay back down, I realize these aren't pajamas at all, they're Michael's boxers and hoodie. My *husband's* clothes. This makes me smile.

Michael sets up a pillow and blanket for himself on the hardwood right outside the bathroom and gets comfortable on the floor next to me.

Mascara has built up under my eyes in a black, crusty layer. My once-cute bun now feels like a hairsprayed rat's nest as I weave my fingers between knots, hoping to swap it for something less constricting. The tile is cold under my knees, and as soon as I get a break from bouts of nausea, I wrap myself in the towels spread out around the bathroom.

Michael lies with his eyes closed a foot away from me. He offered a hand for comfort earlier, and his arm remains outstretched on the tile. I lean over and tuck it into his chest, then adjust his blanket so it covers him entirely. Once he looks comfortable, I move back to the toilet bowl.

I think back to the child in a twin bed that felt so expansive, listening to my mom tell stories of garden fairies and talking gnomes, staring through the dark at the glowing stars stuck to the ceiling. I don't know how the little girl who was scared a monster might reach up from under her bed grew into a brave woman. I don't know how I did it without my mom's guidance, without her light to scare away the monsters hiding in the dark.

I think Miller was right; she would have liked Michael. They would spend summers laughing in the backyard. She would make a salad out of vegetables grown in her garden, and he would say how much better they tasted than store-bought ones. Maybe in another life I'd bring him home to her, and she'd love him too.

My life's timeline has always been separated by her death—while she was here and after she was gone. The days without her were monochromatic, soaked in black and white. But Michael brought the light back, washed me in colors, and created a new point in the timeline—before him and with him.

"Thank you," I whisper as I rest my head on the towel-covered pillow Michael set up for me. I lie sideways and sip water through the straw, watching Michael's steady breathing as he sleeps.

MONDAY
MAY 16, 2016

"I THINK I'M OFFICIALLY on the Kane Garrick murder case," Michael says from the table, his face glued to the text on his phone screen. He pours us each a glass of wine, not breaking his stare, as I move the empty dinner dishes to the sink.

"That's exciting!" I slide back into my chair across from him.

"This is the biggest case I've gotten. I can't believe they're trusting me to be part of this."

"They know you'll win, that's why they chose you." I smile supportively. He passed the bar exam a few months ago and has already proven his worth at the firm.

One of the firm's partners has a friend who has a friend who requested a recommendation for a lawyer—something like that. Regardless how his firm got the case, it's a huge accomplishment.

"What's your role going to be?"

"I'll be doing a lot of research, reading through past documents, making questions for Garrick, things like that. I'm somewhat limited since the case is in New Hampshire."

"Is that where they're holding him?"

"Yeah, that's where he's from. Really unfortunate, in most other states the death penalty wouldn't even be on the table." Michael shakes his head and takes a drink. The red of the wine stains his lips turning them a deep maroon.

I'm stunned by his words. A heavy chill reverberates through me causing the hair on my arms to prickle. My body begs to react, but my muscles are frozen. My shock must be evident because Michael tilts his head as he stares perplexedly at me.

"Didn't I tell you?"

"That you were fighting to take someone's life? No, you left that part out." The bitterness of my words singe the air between us.

"Anna, I'm not fighting to take his life. I'm fighting for justice for the family," Michael replies unbothered and takes another sip of his wine.

"But if you win, his life will end."

"Not necessarily–"

"But probably."

"*Possibly*, not *probably*. The jury will unanimously agree he's guilty. But I don't think the judge will sentence him the death penalty. The circumstances aren't black and white."

"The fact it's an option is infuriating."

"Anna, there's substantial evidence that he killed his wife. I'm not saying he deserves to die, but he deserves to be proven guilty. I'm on the team representing the *family*." Michael's face is painted with confusion as he speaks, as though he doesn't see the ethical dilemma.

I knew if they put Michael on the case, he would be representing the state of New Hampshire. He'd told me the defendant was being accused of two counts of murder—one for his wife and the other for the unborn baby she was carrying. National news stations have been all over the story.

Garrick doesn't deny that he did it, but he hasn't admitted guilt either. At just thirty-three, he'd already served in the military overseas for a decade and had been taking a cocktail of prescriptions for PTSD and other mental health diagnoses since returning: Ambien, Xanax, muscle relaxers, pain medications, antidepressants.

Apparently, there were multiple accounts of him blacking out. He had been sleepwalking periodically over the last few months, proven through texts from his late wife. Sleepwalking turned into sleep cooking: a hospital report stated he had severe burns that were attributed to their gas stove. He even jumped into the pool once, where he woke up completely disoriented. So, while he doesn't deny killing his family, he also doesn't admit to it because he doesn't remember.

"This isn't worth fighting about, it's my job."

Michael's posture has shifted. He leans toward me, shoulders fallen, resting his weight on his elbows. His hands move up and down against his cheeks as he buries his face into them, expelling a clear sign of disappointment.

I want to be excited by his accomplishment, but I can't see past the possible outcome.

"Yeah, your job and all of your morals compromised," I mutter. I down what's left in my glass, push the chair away from the table, and carry it to the sink to wash the dishes. Any tranquility has been sucked out of the room.

Michael breathes in heavily, watching me from the table. "What the judge decides is out of our control. I don't even think he'll get the death penalty, but if he does, it's a legal option."

"Does that make it right?" I fume. "Because it's legal? At what point do we stop thinking about the crime and start thinking about the human behind the crime? Is your moral compass no higher than the law?"

"You act like I chose this case because I wanted to see someone die." Michael's lips droop with discouragement. "How are you not on my side with this?"

"You're trying to play God! You're letting the judge decide whether or not to take this man's life!" I continue as I scrub dinner's dishes. I reach for the wine glass, noticing the deep burgundy that stains the rim—sticky and black like the color of blood.

"It's either the death penalty or he rots in jail. Which is the better option?"

My anger flares, fueled by my inability to answer. Is death more humane than sentencing him to life in prison? Taking away his autonomy? Is this what mercy looks like?

"Taking this case sets the precedent for your moral standing at work."

"We're going in circles. This is my job, Anna!"

"Tell that to your God! Or don't, considering He can't even hold you accountable to be a decent fucking person."

"Damn it!" Michael slams his hand against the wooden tabletop in a burst of frustration that causes me to jump. "I have bills to pay–*our* bills. I'm doing my *job*. I'm standing up for those who can't stand up for themselves, and you're accusing me of playing God?"

"I don't want any of this shit if it means you have blood on your hands!" I throw the half-washed plate down into the sink, which causes the remaining dishes to rattle, then storm down the skinny hall of our apartment and into the spare room.

Michael is quick to follow. There's a heaviness in his footsteps as they march behind me.

"I'm not taking his life. There is no blood on my hands! I'm proving that he did something he *obviously* did! I value his life, but I also value justice for the family!"

"You're a religious contradiction. You care about charging the crime, not caring for the criminal." My hands find Michael's chest, and I attempt to push him to the other side of the doorframe so I can close the door. "Get out!"

Michael doesn't budge. He glares down, towering over me. "You're not listening."

"I'm listening to every word," I spit. "A life for a life, right? God no longer has a plan for him because he messed up. Why not just end it here for him? Get out!"

His stare burns into me as the rage in my eyes competes with his. My teeth grind. His jaw clenches. I see a slight flicker across his face, and I can't tell if he's holding his breath or holding back words. The flash of darkness passes as he sighs, and the anger disappears from the depths of his eyes.

"Fine."

He steps back, and I close the door, louder than normal but not a slam. There's only silence on the other side, but I can feel him there. My adrenaline drops and I let out an audible sigh as I slide down the wall behind the door.

After a few minutes of stillness, I wonder if I was wrong about him being there. Eventually, I hear a body shuffling, then each of his footsteps distinctly as they pad against the hardwood floor down the hall. There's a quiet pause as they disappear briefly before moving back in my direction.

"I got water." His voice slips smoothly through the space under the door.

I don't respond.

"Want some?"

I crack the door stubbornly. A full glass glides across the hardwood, but when his hand disappears, I close the door.

"Thanks," I say after a few more minutes. The exhaustion of the day has started to wear on me.

"I'm going to change out of my suit," Michael says, reading my mind. I can hear his strain as he gets up, "in case you want to get out of your work clothes, too."

I look down at my untucked blouse and unbuttoned pants and sigh dramatically before slowly opening the door in defeat. The floor releases a familiar creak as I step out of the office. Michael's silhouette greets me in the doorway as the hallway light spills into the darkness of the office from behind him.

We're quiet as we change, both taking up more space in the silence.

I want to apologize for picking a fight, for the disrespectful words I said, for the judgment I passed. I want to explain that I understand this case doesn't reflect his morals or character. But instead, I slip into bed around midnight without having said a word.

Michael is present in the groaning shower as the old pipes work hard, then in the sound of rushing water. I fall asleep, exhausted, after setting my alarm for work tomorrow.

I wake up partially when my body shifts on the mattress. There's nothing beyond the darkness of my closed eyelids. Most of my senses are dulled in the sleepy haze, but I feel Michael's hands pulling me into the safe warmth of his body, his arms wrapping around me. A sleepy kiss is planted on the back of my head, then we both drift into our dreams.

In the morning, I wake up to an empty apartment. The space is too small for my overflowing guilt that fills it.

I'm not an expert, not even a self-proclaimed one, but I have done a lot of research on the death penalty. Being married to a lawyer has forced me to study subjects in unthinkable depth so I have an argument prepared if we disagree. I've come to the conclusion that the judicial system fails more times than not. Evidence thrown out because it was inappropriately acquired, alibis dismissed because the one witness was "unreliable," and facts given to the jury that induce assumptions about the defendant that may not actually hold any truth.

I know Michael holds a similar view. He values life from a religious perspective and believes it isn't for us to take, regardless of what that person has done. He always does his best to stand on the right side of the moral spectrum, and I need to trust that he'll do that for his cases, too.

While at work, the increasing guilt causes a steady decline in my productivity. I need to apologize. I shouldn't have added more stress to an already tedious and time-consuming case.

Once the day is over, I go to the grocery store and pace obsessively through the aisles. Cooking was never one of my selling points in the pursuit of becoming Michael's wife, but the idea of having a homemade dinner ready on the table makes for a good apology. In my basket, I have penne pasta, parmesan cheese, and a zucchini. I'm not sure what I'm planning to do with these ingredients, but I add cherry tomatoes and burrata to my basket. I settle on the Anna Special—a slump consisting of anything that looks fresh and whatever is going to go bad in the fridge.

Once I get home and unbag the groceries, there's about an hour left until Michael should be getting home. I wonder if he'll stay late today to avoid me based on his early morning disappearance.

I change into shorts and one of Michael's sweatshirts, put music on, and begin my failed attempt to balance singing, dancing, and cooking. I let my playlist shuffle, singing at full volume as I mix the random items from the grocery store with chicken sausage I found in the fridge set to expire next week.

"Either you're getting better at singing, or I'm falling more in love with you."

I'm startled as familiar arms wrap around my waist. Michael kisses the side of my head, then rests his chin on top. I turn around to face him, and my mouth opens to pour out an apology, but my words are blocked by his warm lips pressing against mine.

"I know," he breathes in the seconds our lips are apart.

I kiss him back, standing on my toes and looping my arms around his neck. I hear the stove heating the boiling water click off and the sound of the cutting board sliding across the counter before he lifts me onto the laminate.

"I'm sorry I got so mad," he says.

Michael holds my chin with his fingers and lifts it so my eyes meet his. He reads the unspoken apology in my irises and accepts it with a slow kiss.

He whispers that he loves me, his breath heavy as his forehead falls into the space between my neck and shoulder. He kisses me again, this time harder.

"I'm sorry," he exhales into my shoulder. He says it over and over, his jaw clenching between words. His shoulders pull together under the growing pressure of my hands. His body tightens more with every repeated syllable as his gentleness and forced restraint evoke a hunger in his eyes.

Michael pulls my blouse over my head and tosses it on the ground behind us. His fingers snake around the button of my pants. The heat of his palm sends ripples of desire through my body as he pulls me closer. He shakes off his clothes and his muscles tense when his skin meets mine. Last night's argument dissolves, and our sharp words are blunted as we touch. His name falls from my lips and bounces off the walls in a faded echo as he melts into me.

An hour later, our bodies lie sprawled across the floor slick with sweat, and the kitchen is a muddle of displaced clothes. While we wait for the pizza on the way, we contemplate the root of the question that caused the disagreement: *Who gets to decide when it's our time*?

SATURDAY

JULY 2, 2016

"CAN'T WE PICK OUT a name *after* we pick out the dog?" I sound whiny, but I have been offering names for the entirety of our three-hour—and counting—drive. And while I've been trying to throw out names that we *both* agree on, Michael shows no interest in compromising.

We provided our contact information to a dozen local shelters and specified a handful of breeds we're interested in. After a few weeks of waiting, we finally received a call informing us that someone was rescuing a litter of Dalmatian puppies from a puppy mill. We'd waited almost two weeks while their vaccines were confirmed and their health was checked. Last night, we were told the puppies were ready to be adopted. We also found out that it was a long, windy drive around arching hills to Vermont. Neither of us protested, both too eager to meet the puppies to care about the distance.

For the first portion of the drive, we excitedly discussed the personalities we'd see in the tiny animals. We solidified that we both prefer a boy. We vocalized what spot patterns are cute, whether we like a pink nose or a black one, and agreed that we would only bring one home if we both fell in love.

All that's left is to agree on a name.

"Sure, we can pick the name after." Michael nods, and if I weren't sitting within range to see his smirk, I would have believed his tone. But the passenger seat is too close to ignore his toothy smile.

I give him an exaggerated eye roll.

"I still don't know why you don't like Butler. Butler won the game for the Pats on the night we met. It's symbolic."

"It's ridiculous. I'll end up calling him *Butt*, what kind of nickname is that?"

"You don't have to call him that. You can call him Malcolm, Butler, Malc. Unlimited options!"

A childlike smile spreads across his lips as soon as we pull off the highway onto an endless road. Up until this point, the drive has been relaxing, winding widely around a hilly landscape covered with distant towering trees. Now, the bright green leaves fold into each other, creating a cave around the straight road ahead of us.

I roll down the window to let in the smell of summer as I stretch my hand outside. The soothing smell of warm grass and damp earth threads through the passing air as the peeking sun spills onto my cheeks and illuminates the vines up my arm. It's nice to see the opposite proportion of trees and skyscrapers.

The GPS tells us we've arrived, and our location is on the left. Michael puts on his signal hesitantly as we pull onto the empty road. The forest is dense around us, and only the thin dirt path beneath our tires parts the branches. An engulfing tree canopy matches the long driveway. It breaks as a small brick house comes into view.

There is a makeshift gravel driveway at the end of the trail with an old, but well-kept, red pickup truck parked to the side. A house sits in a large clearing that spans acres. It's big enough to be mistaken for a farm if it were carpeted with dirt and seed. Instead, it's covered in grass that's semi-tamed. Beyond the backyard sheds, it becomes overgrown, overtaking the rest of the property. There are puppy pens sporadically spread throughout the backyard. In each, small bunches of hair wiggle around in what looks like a single mass.

A thin, older woman with pale, leathery skin and thick crow's feet begins walking toward the car. She has on a long flowing skirt and a tank top that displays her equally weathered shoulders. Her aged lips form a welcoming smile. As she gives a single wave, Michael slows down the car and rolls down my window.

"You can park anywhere on the gravel." The woman guides us with a shaking finger before taking a step back to give us space. We oblige and park at the top of the driveway.

The sun is hot on my skin as we step out of the car, but it's counteracted by an unexpected crisp breeze. I pull my sweatshirt over my head, happy I came prepared. Michael doesn't notice the chill as he shifts his weight between his feet, giddy with excitement. He introduces himself to the woman who tells us her name is River, confirming she is indeed the woman we spoke to on the phone.

"I fostered for a while, years actually. They transitioned into asking me to hold puppy litters since I have the space." She extends her arm, referencing the flat open land behind us. "And now I'm a mini adoption center. I have a few litters here now."

"We're interested in the Dalmatians," I say.

"Dalmatian puppies are in the shed under the heater lamp. They rescued Mama, too, but I put her away. She's been protective of her babies." River shakes her head in disappointment as she speaks, "Terrible situation. Some of them are still a little malnourished. But feel free to take a look around at the others too. You never know which one you'll fall in love with."

Michael wastes no time and hustles across the grass straight to the shed. River keeps me for a few more minutes, talking about the puppy mill, her own dogs, and her late husband. I feel sad for this lonely woman surrounded by only trees and dogs. I can't imagine continuing through life without Michael.

River ends the conversation on her own, telling me she'll be in one of the many puppy pens if we have any questions. I thank her before following Michael, far behind.

When I get to the shed, he's staring into the small pen, looking more nervous than a first-time dad. I stand at his side, clasping his hand in mine, and we both take a moment to absorb the sweetness of the puppies in front of us. Small spots covered in hay, baby teeth biting at ears and tails. Some of them are playfully pummeling each other, forming a ball of chaos. Others are sleeping or lapping water with tiny pink tongues. One little oddball is chewing on the hay.

"Are you going to pick one up?" I lean my head against his arm. My eyes float up to watch him gaze lovingly at the tiny animals.

"I don't know how to pick up a puppy."

"You didn't know how to hold a baby until the first time either."

"Pick one up for me?" Nervousness exudes as he speaks, "A puppy, not a baby, please."

When I nod, his excitement returns contagiously. I reach into the pen feeling little licks and floppy ears and pick up the one that has been eating the hay. Michael's eyes light up as I pass the puppy to him. It wiggles around in his hands, and Michael's smile grows bigger.

We end up sitting on the ground next to the pen, swapping between puppies, letting them chew on our fingers and nip at our clothes.

One by one we decide that our hearts aren't undoubtedly stolen by any of them, regardless of how adorable they are.

While I go to talk to River, Michael hops between puppy pens, inspecting each litter at arm's length. Even from across the small field, Michael's energy is radiating as he steps over the pen and squats in the grass, petting each one.

"Babe!" Michael shouts after a minute, interrupting River and me. He's holding up a little brown puppy Lion King style. I turn to excuse myself from the conversation, but River's lips are already pulled into a smile.

"I've seen that face before," she says as we both look out at Michael from across the yard.

"Who's this?" I ask, walking up to the pair. Michael's speechless, laughter taking away any chance of words.

"This is Butler," he says finally and hands me the floppy-skinned puppy.

"The mom is a boxer who lives here in town," River says once she's joined us. "She got loose and was gone for a couple of weeks. Came back right when the family was about to give up. Didn't take long to realize she had a half dozen babies growing inside her. They're about ten weeks old now."

"What do you think he's mixed with?" I ask, giggling as the biscuit-sized puppy licks my cheek.

"We have a lot of dogs in the area, so it could be anything. Pit bulls, a couple of labs, some shepherds. If your apartment has restrictions, I'm happy to sign the papers as a lab mix."

We walk away with a puppy certificate, clean vet records, and the promise that we'll get him neutered. Michael insists on driving home but takes his eyes off the road to glance over at the puppy in my lap a dangerous amount.

After four hours and three potty breaks, we finally make it back to the apartment. Butler heads straight for the shoe collection near the front door, and I mentally prepare for a year of training.

Overcome by excitement, neither of us thought our puppy plan through, and we both regret it. Getting a puppy on July 4th weekend has to be in the running for the worst decision ever made. Butler cries and howls and shivers fearfully at the sound of the first firework. Both Michael and I decided to stay in after realizing our mistake, but nothing we do calms him. We try to distract him by playing and giving him treats. At one point, Michael sends him to his crate sternly, but after a few minutes of continuous crying, he takes Butler back out and we all snuggle. Despite our best efforts, nothing soothes his little panicking body.

"Well, we got one full day with him in the honeymoon phase," Michael says with closed eyes, exhausted.

We're sitting on the floor near Butler's food bowl. Michael cycles through picking up Butler, who squirms in his arms, putting the puppy down, then picking him back up when he starts to whine.

"Could be worse. I can't think of how right now, but I'm sure it could be," I moan, equally distraught.

"What do we do?"

"Pray that tomorrow comes faster."

After cleaning up multiple puppy accidents and listening to Butler howl for hours, the fireworks finally stop, and we put him in his crate for the night. He falls asleep immediately.

Michael and I tiptoe to the bedroom, careful not to wake the sleeping menace, and get ready for bed, tired from a night full of puppy tantrums. Both of us change and brush our teeth with super-human speed, then flick off the lights and jump into bed. We settle in quickly, not knowing how much sleep we'll actually get—small, sad whimpers woke us up before sunrise yesterday.

"I can't believe we made it." I keep my eyes closed as my sentence falls into the dark. We lie only inches apart, our noses so close that I can feel the warm exhales as he breathes.

"The quiet is so nice," Michael responds groggily.

"The worst is over. That has to be the worst, right?"

"Only until we have a baby."

I pause, thinking how we've coparented Butler for the last forty-eight hours. I wonder what it would be like to have a crying baby in the other room instead of a whining puppy.

"Do you think we'll be good parents?" I ask, smiling at the thought of a mini Michael in my arms.

"I think you're going to be a phenomenal mom."

I'm not sure if Michael's eyes are open or closed, but I know he can feel me blushing.

"Come on." I tug gently on the leash attached to Butler's collar, doing my best not to pull his twenty-pound body too hard as he resists the stairs. "Come on, Mac, let's go."

"Babe, you have to stop calling him that. You're confusing him."

"You told me the nickname possibilities were endless." I raise a single eyebrow in Michael's direction.

"His name is Butler. Mac doesn't even make sense."

"Butler–as in Malcolm Butler." Hearing his name, Butler's floppy ears perk up, and he cocks his head to the side, joining the conversation, "Malcolm–as in Malcolm Miller. Better known as Mac Miller. Therefore, Mac is a perfectly reasonable nickname."

Michael roughly pulls me into his chest with a quick outstretched arm and kisses the top of my head as he buries it in his shirt.

"Ew, you're all sweaty!" I playfully push him away. Butler barks at us, ready to join in the fun.

"Come on, Butler," Michael says with authority. Butler immediately responds by hopping down the steps. I roll my eyes at his selective obedience.

Over the last couple of weeks, Michael has been using the first half of his lunch to go for a run, then join Butler and me for our afternoon walk. *Walk* is a generous term; we usually take one lap around the block, then go back home. He still has a couple of weeks until he gets his final vaccinations and can go to the dog park.

Michael said it was important to leash train him as early as possible. He's been taking time to work with Butler for a couple of hours every day. He'll sit with his long legs extended while Butler rolls between them like a tiny ball of hair. So far, Butler has learned most basic commands, although he only listens to Michael.

By the time we've made it around the block, Michael and I are sweating, and Butler's tongue flops loosely as he pants. The three of us take a moment to drink water and cool down in the air conditioning. Once my body has returned to a normal temperature, I go back to work, but Michael stays in the living room with Butler. I can hear him praising the puppy. Joy fills his laugh as it travels down the hall to the office. I listen to the two of them, smiling as I type on my computer. Michael's happiness and Butler's small barks make it easy to relax. I smile to myself as I absorb the mundane peace of our life.

SATURDAY
AUGUST 6, 2016

THE CONVERSATION OF MOVING had come up consistently for months before Michael was able to persuade me. It crept into all our free time—into TV commercial breaks, during our walks with Butler, and dinner table conversations.

I fought back a lot at first. I love Boston. I love our friends and the life we've established. I know Michael does too. He loves that his parents live close and appreciates having his childhood friends integrated into his everyday life.

But Baby Mason is in Michigan. When we booked the flights last October and Michael held his nephew in his arms, it was game over. He made the decision to move to Michigan that day, even if it was never said out loud.

Michael was persistent and used every persuasive skill possible. But it was Amber who tactfully sold me on Detroit with the promise of more babies to come. I finally agreed to move.

Michael easily found a law firm he liked in metro Detroit. I used distant connections to get a contract job. I would be working with builders to design entire neighborhoods of new homes. I preferred commercial buildings, but I took the job, grateful to have an income established before the move.

After a dozen extensive calls with our realtor, we accepted Amber's offer to stay in her guest room and spent the week looking at houses. The more we explored, the narrower our search became. We ended up focusing on Birmingham, a small suburb about thirty minutes from Detroit, with a popular downtown area. Although it's a more expensive city, it's still much cheaper than Boston. We quickly found a three-story home and fell in love. When our offer was accepted, we headed back for a second trip to close and get our first car using Amber's GMC discount. All that was left to do was pack up our things.

To avoid driving a huge moving truck across state lines and to prevent the embarrassment of getting stuck under the Boston bridges, which were built too low for a U-Haul, we ended up purging anything replaceable. We shoved what we had left into some boxes and rented a van for the trip.

The drive, which passed faster than expected, ended up being over fourteen hours after gas stops and periodic potty breaks for Butler. Michael volunteered to drive the entirety of the trip. The radio was broken, but we renewed our excitement through conversations about the anticipated fresh start. We would be there for Mason's first birthday and now had the luxury of Miller being only a short drive away. We pulled into the driveway as darkness settled in—*our* driveway.

Drained and stiff, we shuffled inside. I emptied the overnight bag filled with snacks, an air mattress, bedding, and toothbrushes. In a single motion, we moved Butler and his crate inside, blew up the air mattress, flipped on the gas fireplace, and stripped off our stinky clothes. We fell asleep without hesitation.

I wake up now in the middle of a very empty living room. Michael lays next to me peacefully sleeping, mouth ajar. The sun pours in brightly through the big windows lining the back of the house, revealing a full view of the small fenced-in backyard.

The house feels even bigger than it did in the dark. Last night, we made our bed on the living room floor, too tired to haul the air mattress up to our bedroom on the third floor. From where we lay now, I can see up to the second floor. Just beyond the railing is a carpeted loft with a bedroom on either side. I wonder if we'll fill them with kids one day—if this will be the house we raise a family in. Will Michael spend an afternoon installing baby gates on these stairs? Will we decorate the walls with family portraits? Will we spend our nights leaning over the kitchen island exhausted as we load a bottle steamer?

These walls are a blank canvas begging to be painted with memories we haven't made yet. In time, this house will become a collection of the best moments life could offer.

I smile to myself feeling rejuvenated by the imagined future and sit up. Michael bounces from the disproportionate weight distribution. He grumbles and pulls me back down, then shifts me flush against him.

"Five more minutes." Michael's raspy groan echoes in the emptiness as he pulls the blanket over his exposed shoulder.

Butler, having heard the sound of Michael's voice, begins barking from his crate. His tail thumps powerfully against the ground in excitement. The possibility of falling back asleep becomes further out of reach with every thud.

I shake Michael, "Okay, five minutes are up. Come on, it's move-in day!"

"Mmmm," he grumbles, rubbing the sleep from his eyes.

"Coffee run?"

"Okay, okay," Michael yawns and stretches his arms far over his head.

I do a quick search and find the closest coffee shop. Access to coffee is much more limited than in Boston. Usually, I would be happy to get fresh air and take Butler for a walk, but the anticipation of the day chases away any desire to explore.

"It's further than I expected. I'll get it delivered."

Michael nods. His butt sinks into the deflating mattress as he sits up, still rubbing his eyes.

I put in an order for coffee and pastries, typing in our new address with heightened enthusiasm.

"I bet Butler wants to check out the new yard," I encourage. Michael crinkles his forehead and gives me a look from the corner of his eye.

"I'm moving." He rubs his face one more time, awakening his goofy side. He grabs me playfully and pulls me into him, kissing my head a dozen times.

"Okay, okay, you're awake!" I laugh and pull away from the headlock. Butler cries from his crate, wanting to be part of the fun.

Butler gets the zoomies the second we open the crate door. We watch as he runs around his new space excitedly.

Our order arrives once we're both dressed, have our teeth brushed, and our water bottles refilled. We take a sip simultaneously. It tastes like coffee, but it lacks the zing of Boston coffee.

"You miss it too?" Michael asks, reading my expression.

"Yeah," I reply with disappointment, "I didn't realize how much I'd grown accustomed to Boston caffeine."

The afternoon comes and goes and soon, the sun is pouring in from the west-facing windows.

As we sort through the bedroom boxes, the doorbell rings. It's echo reverberates up the floors, startling us both. Although we had become immune to the fuzzy, violent sound of the apartment buzzer, the chime of a doorbell is new. Butler's barks follow the sound immediately.

"We have a doorbell!" I squeal in a whisper. Michael's laugh follows behind me as I hurry down two flights of stairs.

"You made it!" Amber shouts before the door is fully open. She springs into my arms, wrapping me in a tight squeeze.

"We brought over the boxes you had delivered to our house." Logan rubs his hands together and nods back to his thick, American-made truck parked behind our Budget rental van.

"Why don't you two *strong* men bring the boxes inside for us to open?" Amber bats her eyes at Michael and Logan, who both respond by rolling theirs but kindly oblige.

"I have to meet Butler!" Amber says, looking over to the crate. Butler jumps wildly at the sound of his name and digs down into the plastic beneath his bed.

"He's in timeout after he spent the first half of the morning chewing the corners of the stairs," I say with a head shake. His whine grows louder as we walk toward him. Once I've unlatched the door, he zooms out, leaping into Amber's arms. She giggles and lets him lick her chin as he jumps up.

"He's still in training," Michael grunts as he walks through the door, a box in hand.

Worried he'll escape out the front door while we carry in boxes, I put Butler back in his crate then cover it with a few towels. Hopefully if he can't see us, he won't feel so left out.

The first box takes Amber and me thirty minutes as we pull out shiny new dishware, pausing each time to *ooooh* and *ahhhh* in admiration.

By the time the men have emptied the van, we've only made it through three boxes. Michael looks unimpressed from the front door as he and Logan take off their shoes.

"Those are shelves for the office," I gesture toward two heavy boxes leaning against one another on the steps, "Will you carry them up?"

The men do as asked, and Amber and I snicker, egged on by their annoyance.

We unbox cookware and dishes, doing our best to fill the kitchen cabinets and drawers. The difference in space compared to the Boston apartment is so drastic that we end up leaving a lot of the cabinets empty. Amber nonchalantly suggests we use them for baby bottles.

"Are you looking forward to the job change?" Amber asks as we open the first of three matching boxes and follow the paper directions to put together the kitchen island stools.

"I hope I measured these correctly," I sigh to myself before answering. "Yeah, honestly, at first, I was a little disappointed. I loved my job in Boston. It was my first 'adult' job outside of summer internships and my apprenticeship. But I think change will be good; I'll have new problems to solve."

"Moving is hard, but moving to a new state and starting a new job is really hard. Trust me, I know."

I think back on my move to Boston. It was only two years ago that I started a new job and moved to a new state with Harper. Now I'm doing it all over again, but without her.

"Knowing my brother, he'll be more reassuring than Logan was," Amber offers when I don't reply. She gestures to the screwdriver in my hand, and I pass it to her as the boys come downstairs.

"Well," Michael says loudly, "we may not have a table, but at least we have one stool for the island."

"Get out of here!" I toss a stray piece of styrofoam at him, but it deflects in the air and lands next to me.

"Nice throw," Michael winks.

"There's no way you guys finished moving everything."

"Far from it. We're putting the bookshelves together, but we can't make any more progress without the tool set."

"Fine! But we're keeping the screwdriver." Amber extends the old, out-of-place tool.

"I guess we'll have to use the power drill," Michael sighs sarcastically and reaches over me, stopping before and after grabbing the tools to plant a kiss on the top of my head. He ruffles my hair as he walks away.

Amber and I finish assembling the remaining two stools while chatting about Baby Mason and how she's been feeling as a new mom. She tells me he's been sleeping much better since we last saw him; thus, so has she.

"Do you think you'll have another?"

"I want to say maybe, but I know we will. Not for a few more years, though. For now, one baby has proven to be more than enough."

"I can't wait!"

"You need to contribute to the pot before I make another addition." Amber raises her eyebrows, filling her sentence with the unspoken question.

"No way." I shake my head.

"You bought a three-bedroom house. What are you going to do with all the space if you don't plan on filling it with babies?"

"We have new jobs, and we need to make new friends. Besides, Michael provides enough childlike energy."

We move our conversation upstairs to hang clothes, but I remain stuck on Amber's words.

After confirming that we'll have the rest of the furniture delivered on Monday, Michael and Logan call in pizza to be picked up. They drive separately, so Michael can drop off the emptied rental.

While they're gone, Amber and I walk through the house, admiring the few additions we've made. The kitchen is beautiful. Sunlight pours in through the large windows in the adjacent dining room. The three stools we assembled are neatly tucked into the island. I run my hands along the soapstone countertops, admiring the smoothness.

Upstairs, Amber and I inspect the bookshelf the men built. It sits, waiting to be filled, in the loft, which Michael plans to use as his office. The far corner bedroom will be my office. It's empty except for three floating shelves. The guest bedroom and bathroom on the other side of the loft are also bare; we haven't even started looking at furniture yet. Amber and I skip the third floor entirely in our tour. The master, which takes up the whole level, is filled with nothing more than boxes.

After the four of us fill up on pizza, exhaustion sets in. There's a mutual understanding that the day has come to an end for the four of us.

"Let me know if you need our help on Monday! I have a few babysitters on deck," Amber offers, hugging me goodbye as the bright sunset shines through the open door behind her.

Michael and I continue unpacking. We agree the day was long enough and settle on emptying what **OFFICE** boxes we can without desks.

Butler bounces between Michael and me while we unpack. He rolls around on the carpet and zooms up and down the stairs, slipping on the hardwood floor when he gets to the bottom.

After filling the shelves with books and rearranging them twice, I walk out of my office and into the loft to see if I can help Michael with anything. I'm instantly greeted by his two paintings—one of a lion and the other of an elephant, both black and white—placed on both sides of his two degrees. The four frames sit side by side, resting against the wall adjacent to my office, ready to be hung. Michael had insisted on keeping them when we moved into our first joint apartment in Boston, although I never "got around" to hanging them. He was strangely sentimental about keeping them even if they remained boxed up in a closet—which is what I *thought* the plan was in our new house as well.

"No way," I stop in front of the pictures.

"Just listen," Michael says, following my glance and reading my thoughts.

"I'm not going to *just listen*. You're a lawyer. I stand no chance in this argument if I *just listen*."

"But–"

"No *buts*, we agreed that these would not be hung."

"Actually, you *told* me they weren't going to be hung, and I nodded. We technically never even had a verbal agreement."

In real time, I watch our first moving argument begin to unfold. He stands firm that it's his office space, and he should get to hang whatever he wants. I respond with the very obvious argument that the wall he chose to hang them on is the only wall upstairs that is visible from the front door. I don't want these pictures to be the first things guests see.

"You got an actual office, I have this open space."

"Then take the office, Michael," I retort, annoyed.

"But I want *you* to have the office," he says calmly, giving me big puppy eyes. "All I want is to hang two pictures. You have decoration freedoms over the rest of the house."

I look up to the gentle face that towers over me, seeing the softness in his dark brown eyes. His lips are curled into a slight smile, their resting position. He waits for my reply in patient silence.

"Rock, paper, scissors?" Michael reaches his hands out in a ready position.

"Best two out of three?"

He nods, and we begin the countdown.

I lose twice.

"Rules are rules," he shrugs and grabs a hammer off his desk, then twirls it tauntingly in his hand.

"Fine," I say, "but I'm not happy about it."

"I love you," he says as he kisses the top of my head.

"You better," I fake pout. "I'm going to let Butler out, then make some tea. Do you want any?"

"I'd love some," Michael smiles, continuing to swing the hammer.

I'm still searching the boxes for the tin of tea bags twenty minutes later when the hammering stops. The sound of Michael's footsteps shifts from the carpeted loft to the hardwood stairs.

"I found a measuring cup to boil water in the microwave, but I have no tea," I frown from my spot on the floor and hold up the glass.

"First project to tackle tomorrow: empty the kitchen food boxes." Michael says while digging through boxes on the island counter, Butler at his feet.

I sigh and push away the box in front of me in defeat.

"I guess tonight is not a tea night," Michael says as he sits down next to me, clearly giving up as well. He pulls me closer, and I lean back so my head is in his lap, looking up at him.

"Can you believe how much space we have?"

"We went from a Boston apartment to a three-level house. We have a kitchen island and never have to share an office again."

I laugh, "Okay, it wasn't that bad."

"Yeah, not that bad," he says sarcastically.

When we find the energy, we rummage through the remaining food boxes like raccoons looking for a late night snack. They mostly consist of random condiments, baking materials, spices, and protein bars. Finally, we stumble on a few bags of popcorn.

"Shall we?" I hold one up, shaking it excitedly.

When the microwave beeps, we get settled under the blankets on the air mattress. Our squirming causes each other to clumsily shift up and down.

With popcorn bits between blankets and greasy fingers, we christen the new house. We whisper in the dark, romanticizing our Boston apartment. Michael says the absent street sounds leave this "city" house feeling silent. We get excited over our jobs; Michael starts a week from Monday, and I start the week after that.

The fireplace warms the living room as we snuggle into the blankets sleepily. We drift off to sleep, our phones left uncharged and the air mattress half-deflated.

TUESDAY
JANUARY 17, 2017

"I HOPE THEY GIVE me the antibiotics, then let me leave. I hate being late," Michael says with uncharacteristic annoyance. We're almost to the urgent care halfway between our house and the restaurant where we have a reservation with Amber and Logan.

About a month ago, Michael caught a pretty bad cough. He ran a fever that lasted for a few days. After trying Tylenol, ibuprofen, and a variety of over-the-counter cough suppressants, Michael finally caved and agreed to go to urgent care. Once it affected his daily running, he was more motivated to surrender to his body's need for antibiotics. With so many infections being passed around in the winter months, I'm convinced he got something from Mason, who now goes to daycare full-time.

We stayed busy over the holidays, checking off all the Christmas activities that Michigan has to offer. We went ice skating in downtown

Detroit, drove up to Frankenmuth for chicken dinner and fudge, watched the Lions lose at Ford Field, and took Mason to the zoo to see the lights. He's not even two, so I don't think he comprehended anything he saw, but Michael and I had fun.

Then came New Year's Eve, where we soaked ourselves in icy Michigan air, heavy and damp from the recent snowfall, for over six hours. At midnight, we shared a numb-lipped kiss. If it wasn't Mason who spread this infection, it was picked up at one of the many public places we've been to.

"I'm sure it will be quick!" My voice is coated in attempted positivity as we pull into the busy parking lot. We struggle to find a parking spot, and Michael's dread rises as we get out of the car.

When we check in, the receptionist blandly delivers the bad news that it will be at least a thirty-minute wait. With our reservations in an hour, Michael contemplates leaving. If we leave now, we'll be on time for dinner, but I know Michael won't come back. I text Amber that we'll be a little late, then find two open seats.

Michael's name pops up on the TV, taking its place at the bottom of the waitlist.

The waiting room is overcrowded and full of wet coughs, sniffles, and a concoction of videos playing out loud despite the signs advising against it. Occasionally, a mom will call to her kid to come and blow his nose.

Whatever Michael contracted seems to have infected everyone.

I try to concentrate on the book I brought in preparation for the wait, but it's impossible as the sound of germs contaminates the small space. Michael keeps one hand on my leg out of habit and uses the free one to scroll through work emails. From my peripheral, I catch his eyes shifting up to the TV every couple of minutes in hopes that he somehow drifted to the top of the list.

After much longer than thirty minutes, a short, blonde in navy blue scrubs calls Michael's name. He leads us behind the doors and around a workstation placed in the middle of a rectangular room surrounded by about twenty patient doors. He gestures us in through an already open door. We enter the small room decorated with sterile metal and white walls. I squeeze myself in behind Michael and sit uncomfortably on the single chair stuffed into the corner of an already crowded room.

"What brings you in?" the technician asks as he wraps a blood pressure cuff around Michael's arm and sticks a thermometer under his tongue, then jots down the vitals.

Once the thermometer is pulled out of his mouth, Michael describes the wet cough he's been having. The technician nods his head, his eyes darting between Michael and the keyboard where his fingers type hastily. It takes about five minutes to go down a list of mostly yes-or-no questions presented on the computer screen.

"The doctor will be in shortly," he says. He finishes typing, then smiles and exits the room swiftly, closing the door loudly behind him.

I pull my book out and read for about twenty minutes before a light knock interrupts the silence, and a woman's head peeks around the door.

Her cheeks are plump and covered in freckles. She carries extra weight, which feels ironic since she advises people to lower their salt intake and get in their daily steps. Her white coat stretches to the roundness of her torso.

I'm too distracted to hear her introduction, but when I look up, she's extending her hand to Michael. Her short red hair bobs in sync with their handshake.

"So, what's been going on?" She sounds out of breath as she takes a seat on the backless chair, then turns to face the computer to skim over his chart, seemingly for the first time.

"I got sick after the holidays and haven't been able to fight off the infection," Michael replies to the back of her head.

"What symptoms have you been having?"

"Lots of coughing, a lot of fatigue. I had a fever when I first got sick."

"Anything else you can think of?" She scoots herself off the chair. In one swift motion, she strips the stethoscope from her neck and puts one side in her ears and the other against Michael's chest.

"Not off the top of my head."

"Are you coughing anything up?" She moves the stethoscope from his chest to his back.

"Not at first, but for the last couple of weeks I have been."

"Is it green or yellow?"

"Not really either."

"It sounds like you have what's going around. I'm going to call in an antibiotic. Take it twice a day for ten days. You should be feeling better toward the five-day mark, but make sure you finish it anyway. By the time the antibiotics are gone, you'll be feeling back to normal."

"Thank you," Michael responds shortly. He shifts in his seat and checks his watch, eager to leave.

"You are free to go. Stop by the front to make sure we have the right pharmacy. It should be ready tonight, so you can take your first dose in the morning. Take Tylenol if your fever spikes again."

She turns and smiles one more time before leaving, her face drooping with exhaustion when she thinks we're out of sight. Michael waits for me to put my book in my purse, then grabs my hand, and we hurry out.

There's a new batch of coughing kids in the waiting room. I make an effort to hold my breath until we get outside into safe air.

"Pleasant lady," I say sarcastically as we cross the parking lot.

"Too long of a wait for a five-minute interaction. Will you text Amber and let her know we're on the way?" Michael asks as he simultaneously puts on his seat belt and backs out of the parking spot. I hurry to buckle mine before he pulls onto the road, then text Amber.

Amber doesn't reply, but when we get there, she's already seated at the table. She's twirling an empty wine glass between her fingers and is accompanied by Logan and the half-empty beer he holds in one hand. She waves dramatically when she sees us, causing Logan to turn his attention away from whatever basketball game is on the TV. Michael and I cross through the sea of chatter, swerving between full chairs and laughter.

"Sorry we're late. You know how urgent care is." I roll my eyes. I hang my coat on the back of my seat as I climb into the high-top chair.

"Never urgent," Amber shrugs.

"Don't worry about it, Amber has kept herself busy downing two glasses of wine," Logan jokes.

"Hey, you volunteered to be the DD!" Amber laughs and scrunches her nose playfully at him.

We order appetizers for the table, and I put in two drinks in an attempt to catch up to Amber.

Amber gives us updates on Mason: the small friends he's made at daycare, the words he's started communicating in sign language, and the YouTube videos that he's obsessed with. She adds how exhausting it is to make sure he doesn't hit his head on corners she didn't even know existed, how messy he gets trying to feed himself with a spoon, and his deep disdain for the bathtub. She claims to miss the infant stage, but I clearly remember the complaints of not sleeping and breastfeeding, which made her feel like a cow.

Amber and I talk about work while Logan and Michael chime in enough to pretend that they're listening. Their eyes are glued to the basketball game playing on nearly every screen in the bar. They interrupt themselves mid-sentence to react to big plays and nudge each other like kids when someone scores.

After we've finished dinner and paid our bills, we walk out together and say our goodbyes in the crowded parking lot. Our words escape in the form of steam as we talk, breathy syllables floating through the air. Amber shivers and pulls her coat closer to herself as I hug her and Logan goodbye.

Michael clears his throat a few times on the short walk to the car, but once it starts, he breaks out into one of his familiar coughing fits. As he hacks, his hand clutches the collar of his shirt. I rub his knee in support, pained as I watch him gasp for breath.

"I hope those antibiotics work," Michael strains to speak. He shakes his head and rubs a hand over his watering eyes.

"Me too," I nod.

TUESDAY

JANUARY 24, 2017

A WEEK INTO THE antibiotics, Michael is still having frequent coughing fits. Each one feels more intense, and there are seconds between coughs where he gasps for air. His lack of sleep has been impacting his work and, understandably, his mood.

"Do you think I should go back to urgent care?" Michael asks as I pass him a sudsy plate to load into the dishwasher. Red specks of the spaghetti sauce Michael made by hand stick to my fingers. My hands scrub the dishes roughly as I try to conjure a solution.

"Why don't you call Kyle? Isn't he dating a doctor now?"

"That's a good idea!" Michael's eyes light up with hope as he looks up at me, bent over and half-buried in the dishwasher.

"Go text Kyle. I'll finish the dishes." I nod at his phone on the dining room table.

"I love you, but I am absolutely not letting you load this dishwasher."

Michael is obsessive when it comes to the dishwasher. He loads the racks with precision in a Tetris-like pattern. I'm sure he could wash every dish we own in one cycle if I challenged him to it.

When the last cup is loaded, Michael wipes his hands then tosses me the towel. He leans over to press his lips into my temple as he walks past me to his phone. I dry my hands then shuffle my socks across the wood toward him. Using my head, I wiggle between his extended arms. He finishes the text, then pulls me into him tightly.

His breath is steady, but with my head resting against his chest, I can hear the force of every inhale. His shoulders fall as he releases the heavy air.

Our embrace is interrupted by a reply from Kyle. Anita, his girlfriend, is an emergency room doctor—or a resident. Kyle uses the words interchangeably, which confuses Michael and me, who have no medical background.

"Kyle said she'll call me now." Michael squeezes me tightly and walks to the living room.

I follow him, taking a seat on the adjacent side of the large L-shaped couch. I pull out my phone to look busy while I eavesdrop.

Michael says hello politely before he gets straight to the purpose of the call, asking her if he should go back to urgent care or get antibiotics somewhere else. After an unreasonably long series of questions, Michael thanks her and hangs up. I glance up from my phone in anticipation.

"Anita suggested I go to the doctor again but to my primary doctor this time. She said I should try to get in as soon as possible."

I nod in agreement as Michael calls the office I've been going to, which stays open late on Mondays and Tuesdays. He explains the situation, and the receptionist on the other end of the line offers to squeeze him into an open slot tomorrow. She makes him promise to take tonight's dose of his antibiotic, despite him feeling like it isn't working.

"Anita sounded kind of worried," Michael says, hanging up then tossing his phone across the couch.

"What do you mean?" I scoot closer him and rest my head on his legs. His arm drapes over me instinctively.

"I don't know. She asked *really* specific questions. The way she urged me to get the soonest appointment was kind of weird."

I shrug. "Hopefully they do a test or whatever and give you the right antibiotic this time."

"Yeah, I hope so."

The worried expression is faint but apparent from my angle in his lap. His shoulders remain tense as my hands cup his cheeks, and his lips press together in thought. After sitting up and searching his face, Michael's expression still shows no sign of peace. I swing myself into his lap and bury my head into him.

"I don't want you to work tonight," I whine. I nuzzle his neck, and his muscles relax beneath my weight. His mood shifts with his posture.

"I don't want to work tonight," he chuckles and pulls me closer.

I cling to his chest like a koala. His heartbeat breaks through its cavity and carries to my ears. Beneath my hands, his muscles grow tense again, and his deep breaths release as heavy sighs.

"Come read upstairs while I work."

"Really?" My head pops away from his chest. Michael usually claims that I'm a distraction when he works late, but it's obvious the stress from the phone call with Anita has left him needing company.

"Yeah, go get your pajamas on and pick out a blanket. Come sit upstairs with me."

"Deal!" Relief floods his expression when I nod in agreement. I kiss him quickly, then race up to the bedroom to change. Michael's laugh echoes up the stairs behind me.

By the time I've washed my face, changed into pajamas, and grabbed a book and a blanket, my eyelids are drooping. I walk heavily, step by step, down the stairs from our bedroom to the loft.

Michael, now only wearing sweatpants, sits hunched over his desk with a blanket draped around his bare shoulders. He doesn't say anything as I walk toward him, which I take as a sign of focus and refrain from interrupting with anything more than a kiss on his temple. His eyes don't move from the paper in front of him, but his cheeks rise with a smile.

I make myself comfortable in the large chair, curling my feet under me and tucking the blanket neatly around me. My plan was to read a few chapters, but I spend more time looking at the back of Michael's head than I do looking down at the pages.

His short, boyish brown hair makes him look younger than he is, and his ears stick out playfully. His thin, muscled arms are bent into a chicken dance posture as he leans into his elbows pressing against the desk. The open laptop casts a pale glow on the creases near his eyes. His shoulders fall heavily, his slow, rhythmic breathing more tired than usual. He shifts restlessly in his chair.

Michael's been pushing through life lately, unable to catch a break. His work is unending, his cough is worsening, perpetual fatigue clings to him regardless of how much rest he gets. He never complains, but his exhaustion is evident in the permanent crease of his brow and his decreasing weigh.

I'm overwhelmed by how much love I have for him. I want to walk over to him, rub his shoulders, lead him upstairs to bed, remind him I'm here. I want to tell him Anita's concern is lingering with me, too. But I don't. I don't want my emotions to be another thing he feels pressured to carry.

Instead, I continue to study his familiar features, wondering how we transitioned from strangers spilling beer at the bar to a married couple sitting in comfortable silence. I trace the curve of his neck, commit the shape of his shoulders and strength of his back to my mind. Memorizing him with a panic, although I don't know why.

I wake up to Michael sliding one arm under my legs and the other behind my back. I blink rapidly, not realizing I'd fallen asleep, but my eyelids refuse to stay lifted.

"Let's go to bed." Michael's hushed, tired voice causes me to melt safely into his arms. I feel his lips press against my forehead before slipping back to sleep.

After letting Butler outside, Michael says goodbye as I brush my teeth, and he leaves for his appointment. Since my first meeting isn't until the afternoon, I take my time scrambling eggs and slicing an orange for breakfast. While eating, I skim my email inbox on my phone. Not seeing anything urgent, I take Butler for a walk, then continue my procrastination by folding myself into a ball on the couch with a blanket and a book.

The sound of the keycode on the front door beeping carries in before the automatic lock buzzes, and Michael's heavy winter Timberland boots appear. The red in his cheeks from the cold makes him look pale as he claps his boots together, knocking off the snow.

Butler, hearing Michael's return, runs to the door and jumps on his leg. Michael bends over to pet him, a smile pulling at his lip.

"Hey babe, how'd it go?" I call across the room, dog-earing my book's page.

"They want me to go get some kind of X-rays or a scan and sent in a prescription for different antibiotics. She said it might be pneumonia or something like that. I thought pneumonia made you bedridden."

"Your version of bedridden is not running. And it's been a few weeks since you've gone for a run."

"The cold air makes my lungs miserable." Michael shakes his head and sits down on the couch next to me. His clothes emit the chill they collected from outside and the sharp smell of winter wafts across the couch. His smile fades and tension returns to the muscles in his jaw.

"So, when do you go for X-rays?"

"They had an opening today. I'll leave after lunch."

"You look stressed," I frown, seeing the thoughts turning through his mind.

"I have a lot of work to catch up on. I don't have time to be sick anymore or to go to any more doctor appointments."

I nod.

Besides a sniffle here and there, Michael doesn't get sick. He doesn't even have allergies. He exercises and has a good diet. He isn't used to having to slow down, especially for this long, and it irritates him.

"I have a few meetings this afternoon, but let's go get dinner tonight. We can go get something spicy that clears out whatever bugs you have in there."

Michael nods, his expression still stiff, and heads to the kitchen for food before leaving for his appointment.

I don't notice the passing time. I'm so submerged in work that I don't even hear the door open. Michael peeks his head around the doorway into my office, which startles me, then goes to work at his desk.

I interrupt my workflow to see how the appointment went and when we'd hear back from the doctor, but Michael is short in his responses. He shrugs at my questions, and I take the hint. I step back, letting him process the weight silently and submerge himself in his work.

At dinner, he's in a much better mood. We get Arabic food downtown and walk by the river afterward. On the car ride home, we call his parents for a quick chat and end the night with a movie on the couch.

The rest of the week passes normally, each day a smooth routine. On Friday, Michael leaves to meet up with Logan and his friends to watch one of the basketball games. I take advantage of the empty house, making popcorn and setting up the living room to binge some trash TV.

Within an hour, I hear the keypad on the door unlocking. My head swivels around in surprise.

Michael stands in the doorway, methodically taking off his winter apparel. He leans over to arrange his boots neatly on the doormat and hangs his hat tediously on the hook. As he crosses the room, he releases a puff of air.

"Hi." He kisses the top of my head from behind the couch, then walks around and sits next to me, legs sprawling out loosely. I pause the TV, then turn to Michael so my whole body is facing him.

"What happened? Did Logan have to go home?" I ask, confused. When he doesn't answer, panic rises, "Is Mason okay?"

My heart jumps wildly in response to the anxiety he's brought into the room with him.

"I got a call from the doctor's office. They want me to see a specialist," Michael nods to himself, accepting whatever it is they told him. The rims of his eyes are red, and his neck is flushed, the color creeping up into his face.

"What kind of specialist?"

Michael's tense posture and held breath are unsettling. It's an uncomfortable feeling when someone so stable emits such a heavy amount of fear. It's tangible in the weight of his voice, obvious in his defeated posture, and palpable in the blandness of his words.

"They want me to see an oncologist."

I feel like I'm bungee jumping. Like I've been pushed off the ledge before I was ready, and my stomach is lurching into my throat without warning. Like I'm spinning in a free fall through cold air, and I can't catch my breath. And then I feel the tug of the rope jerk me up, my stomach tumbling back down with a swift, unexpected harshness.

"What?" I croak.

"They got the results from the X-rays. She said based on my labs, symptoms, and X-rays, there's a concern that it's cancer."

I sit stunned. Michael pauses, his brown irises flashing through mixed emotions.

"On the phone, he asked if I was a smoker, said he didn't see anything in my chart. I grew up in Boston, who didn't smoke?" Michael takes a breath, and his words fall out faster than I've ever heard him speak, "There are thousands of people who have smoked longer than me. I stopped after law school like I said I would. I stuck to what I said."

The room spins as the information sinks in. His increasing frustration manifests in the reddened tint of his cheeks and the anger filling his tone. He rubs a hand hard down his face, letting his fingers sink into the sockets of his eyes.

"You don't even smoke anymore," I repeat after him and shake my head violently, as if I can reject the words of the doctor.

Michael doesn't continue. We sit in disbelief, letting his words absorb like oil in water. There's no way what he's saying could be true. It's impossible that he has cancer from cigarettes that he smoked in a previous decade, cigarettes that haven't touched his lips in over a year. Since he graduated. He quit. He stopped because he knew it was unhealthy. He stopped because he was smart enough to know the consequences of continuing. He stopped because he said he would.

I don't realize I'm crying until Michael's thumb wipes away a tear, and his fingers guide my face to his.

"It's going to be okay, Anna." He declares with pretentious strength, but I can see the fear brightly as it overtakes his dark eyes.

How is he the one acting strong right now?

I don't know what to do to help him. I pull out my phone and open the Uber Eats app and scroll through.

"Edibles and Jersey Mike's?" I ask as Michael's eyes meet mine with the most excitement that can be expected in a situation like this.

We place the order with an expected delivery in thirty minutes. We agree to look up the specialists on the list the doctor emailed to Michael until the food comes. After that, we decide we won't be talking about it anymore tonight.

I lean back, feeling the generous support of the couch cushions. Michael lays his head down in my lap with his nose tilted up toward my phone as we scroll through the results together.

There are about fifteen names listed, either clinic names or doctors. When we plug them into the search bar, a variety of pictures come up. Some old, some young, most men, some women.

We laugh at Dr. Ahmad when his professional hospital picture pops up; a thick-bearded man with a dark blue button-up under his white coat that's tight at his neck, forcing his bobblehead to stick out roundly. Our next laugh comes from Dr. Morgan, a man with a wide drooping nose, curly light brown hair, and glasses that make him look like a mad scientist.

It doesn't take long to sort through the googly-eyed doctors and settle on a clinic. We agree on a cancer center in Detroit. Not only is it close in proximity, but the website holds encouraging pictures that convince us this journey might not be as bad as we think it will be. The doctors emulate genuine happiness in their smiles regardless of the terrible specialty they've chosen. There are pictures of smiling patients in wheelchairs sitting in a colorful hospital hallway and multiple images of adults ringing the cancer-free bell. One patient, despite holding a scary looking mask used for radiation, smiles with a fist pump of victory striking the air. Even the patients without hair are laughing or toasting their apple juice. They look happy. They look like they've beaten it.

I urge Michael to call in the morning, and he agrees reluctantly as the doorbell rings.

"We're going to be alright," I draw out each word with strained confidence. He rests the weight of his head in my hand as I hold his cheek.

It's been two hours since we took the first edible and over one hour since we made the rookie mistake of taking a second round because we *didn't feel anything.* Mac Miller plays on shuffle over the ceiling's built-in speakers. Our bodies lie lifeless and flat on the couch looking up, searching for answers in the white walls. The tops of our heads touch, and, while I'm tucked into a blanket, Michael's long legs dangle off the couch, surpassing the armrest. We reminisce about funny memories of each other while our eyes droop. Our bodies are heavy, but our thoughts are light. We laugh at ignorant things we said early in our relationship, tell honest impressions of the other's friends the first time we met them, share words we hadn't said and take back those we shouldn't have. Almost none of the information is new for either of us, but we enjoy the resurfacing memories as they come.

We've done this a handful of times; usually when big things happen, like getting married or moving to Michigan. We'll make the couch our base, draping it with blankets and rearranging the pillows. We'll order food, compile snacks from the kitchen, and fill up our water bottles. Michael will finish his, then move on to what's left of mine, and we'll play rock-paper-scissors to see who has to get up for refills.

We don't ever go into the night having this idea; it's always a spontaneous decision. Tonight is no exception. Today has met the criteria for a big life moment, but in the most negative way.

We've been allowing the time to pass peacefully. Butler's moved from his food bowl to us and back to his bowl again a dozen times. Michael sneaks him pretzels when he thinks I'm not looking, but he's too high to be sly, so I pretend not to notice. Michael finished his sandwich before the edibles had kicked in, so he's snacking on mine, bite by bite.

Of all the conversations we've had tonight, we successfully avoided the topic of cancer, but it has been lingering in my mind, nipping at my happiness when it rises too much. I'm confident Michael feels the same.

I wonder what tomorrow will look like, or next week, or next month. I don't know anything about cancer outside of the movies, and those never end well. There's always a romanticized portion of the pain that I was victim to, but right now I don't feel it. I feel nothing close to romance—nothing whimsical, nothing quixotic. There is no inspiring joy or hope that runs through my veins. Quite frankly, I feel nothing at all; I thank the edibles for this.

"Hey babe?" Michael murmurs. I don't feel his head move, so I follow his lead and stay still.

"Yeah?"

He hesitates, "Will you pray with me?"

Again, neither of us move.

"Yeah." I nod, the top of my head sliding against his. I extend a hand above my head, and he grabs it intuitively.

"God," he pauses tearfully. We linger in silence. "I know I'm supposed to start out with things that I'm thankful for, but I'm not feeling very thankful right now."

His voice cracks, and I squeeze his hand. He squeezes back but doesn't continue.

I reluctantly jump in. "Bring us the comfort that Michael says You can bring."

"Thank you for bringing this to our attention when you did. I know that it's part of Your plan." He continues with returned confidence. "Thank you for giving me Anna, the only person I'd want here with me tonight. Amen."

"Amen," I repeat with contrived poise. Silent tears stream down my cheeks.

MONDAY
FEBRUARY 13, 2017

THE HOSPITAL IS HUGE, too big to feel familiar regardless of how many appointments we've had over the last two weeks. The hallways are winding, and the elevator system is endlessly confusing.

We walked through the hospital doors for the first time less than a month ago, feeling energized and ready to take on the battle we foresaw. Since then, every visit—scan, biopsy, blood draw, probing exam—has chipped away at us little by little, dwindling what minuscule hope was left. Today, we walk through the hospital holding hands fearfully.

Who picked out these colors? I think angrily to myself as we move up and down the halls searching for a department we've never been to. *Who pays a designer to select gray and silver as the focus colors of the entire hospital and every single piece of artwork, plaque, or award in it?*

The silver-lined frames against the bleak white walls make me feel like I'm walking through an asylum, except I'm too nauseous and aware to be imprisoned and sedated.

The pictures online made the hospital look bright and cheery. They showed sunlight shining down on the hallways and patients smiling as they roamed the floor. We quickly learned there was no truth in those pictures. They lied about the smiling faces of the patients as they walk in and out of the revolving hospital door. The stale smell of sickness sticks to the walls and mourning families gather around every corner.

The hallway signs lead us to an elevator. When we step in, a girl in scrubs is talking loudly into her phone. She's oblivious to the people shuffling on and off each floor. Michael reaches down and squeezes my hand, a subtle gesture that signifies he's perceived my frustrations.

I release a rushed sigh once we've exited, "I understand this is her job, but doesn't she realize this could be the worst day of our lives?"

I look down at the white speckled floors as my eyes begin to sting. Unsolicited anger arises in me from a deeper place than the annoying words of a random, obnoxious employee.

I continue anyway, needing the release of my frustrations. "Doesn't she know this is a hospital where *sick* people come?"

"This is where *we* come when we're sick. But this is her job. This is where she comes to make money," Michael replies.

We turn down a hallway that looks identical to all the others we've been through so far. The only difference is this one has big yellow letters above the walkway spelling out **ONCOLOGY**, and the pictures here display only balding patients.

Reading the sign makes me nervous. Michael's hand gripping mine signifies he feels the same. I look up at him, feeling minuscule in comparison to his towering height and minimized by the impending news.

We check in and verify that we have indeed gone to the basement first to complete the requested blood work. We sit in two of the many open wooden chairs. The prickle of the gray cushioning pinches through my pants.

This waiting room is different from the others. It generates an atmosphere that is less sterile but more bare. The chairs line the perimeter of the room, leaving a gaping space in the middle. The fluorescent lights have a gray hue that illuminates the room.

Once we're sitting, my lungs gasp for air, and my heart pounds against my chest. The speed of its beat is counteracted by the slowness of the passing time. I check my watch every ten to fifteen seconds, but I still jump in surprise when they call Michael's name.

"I'll have you step on the scale outside your room before you go in." A friendly medical assistant leads us down another foreboding hallway. His warm, kind tone stands out in comparison to the dryness around us. Feeling fuzzy and distracted, I forget his command, and my body suddenly halts as Michael comes to a stop in front of the scale.

Once weighed, I follow Michael as he enters the room. The paper crinkles beneath him as he jumps on the patient seat. I take the chair in the corner. We sit in anxious silence, swapping occasional worried glances. Our wait is short, and within minutes, a light knock turns our attention toward the door.

"It's good to see you both. I wish it were under better circumstances." Dr. Graham walks in, rubbing her hands together to spread the foaming sanitizer. She's a tan, thin-framed woman with naturally highlighted light brown hair. Although she doesn't appear to be older than thirty, her smile lines and commanding confidence give away her stacking years.

We'd all met on a telehealth call about a week ago. She introduced herself and explained the testing Michael had scheduled, which all seemed invasive and intimidating. Without being too morbid, she factually explained the details of lung cancer, how it's diagnosed, and the outcomes. She assured us the medical field was rapidly producing improved treatment options if it came to that. She'd said, *cancer is no longer the death sentence that our parents knew it as.*

"How are you feeling?"

Michael hesitates, "I'm doing okay."

"How are the symptoms?"

Michael is again reluctant in his response.

I look at Michael, urging him to be honest. I want to jump in, to hold his hand and give her the gruesome details of what I've been seeing at home. Michael meets my eyes with evident defeat. I wonder if Dr. Graham can see it too.

"The symptoms are getting worse. I'm coughing up blood pretty regularly." Michael sighs and runs his hands through his hair the way he does in the middle of our arguments or after the Patriots lose. "I'm down to 185 pounds. I know you didn't call us in today for good news. It hasn't been very long, but I can feel whatever this is growing."

"We've run a lot of tests over the last couple of weeks. From your MRI imaging, CT scan, sputum sample, and the biopsy, we can make a pretty definitive diagnosis." Dr. Graham jumps straight into it without the same reluctance as Michael.

A thick fog blurs the majority of the next twenty minutes; only bits of the conversation penetrate the haze. The words that do make it to my ears cause me to retreat further.

The room around us spins, the walls tumble, the colors fade. By the time Michael's diagnosis sinks in, I'm confident she's repeated the whole speech at least three times. Even though it's exactly what we expected, the words are no easier to hear, and the prognosis is no less shocking.

Michael has small cell lung cancer.

Dr. Graham explains that this type of lung cancer is primarily caused by smoking. The prognosis is discouraging, to say the least. The five-year survival rate is less than 5%, and this type is the faster progressing of the two types of lung cancer. She explains that they can see that the cancer cells have invaded multiple lobes of his lungs and his liver. This explains his symptoms of fatigue, weight loss, shortness of breath, and coughing up blood. She warns us that small cell lung cancer targets the major organs. It's already spreading, and, if given the chance, it will most likely move to the brain and bone.

"Since it has metastasized outside of the original lobe and gone into another organ, it's considered extensive," she pauses, checking if we understand. She continues when she receives two blank stares in return. "This means that we want to be aggressive with treatment. I plan to speak with the surgical team. I think you could benefit from having some of the tumors surgically removed. You're young and healthy, which is encouraging. Either way, I'd like to start you on chemotherapy immediately."

"I'm sorry, can you explain one more time?" I shake my head in confusion.

"I'd like to start chemotherapy. Treatment would last approximately four months if you're responsive." She looks at Michael as she speaks, monitoring his expression. "You don't need to make a decision today, but I would encourage you to decide if you'd like to proceed with the treatment plan sooner rather than later. I can't stress enough that this is a very aggressive cancer."

"You said that treatment lasts a few months if he's responsive. What if he isn't?" I'm dizzy. Sinking into the corner, pressing myself into the cushion of the seat, I hold my breath.

Before she can answer, Michael looks at me with sorrow—a silent apology as though he has done something to disappoint me.

"Dr. Graham, I want to respect your time, but can you give us two or three minutes to talk?" Michael forces a polite smile, and Dr. Graham nods before disappearing, closing the door behind her with care.

The weight of her words flattens me. It's like the ceiling is caving in. It's common knowledge that life ends at some point, but the doctor's words make the truth tangible. This new looming reality makes the passing time feel wasteful, but silence continues to absorb Michael's limited time.

Michael reaches out an arm, and I take a few unsteady steps over and fall into his chest, letting out the tears.

There is no discussion during the car ride home.

Michael and I both knew accepting treatment was our only option, so we told Dr. Graham we had made the decision to move forward with her plan. She took the time to go over Michael's results, showing us the dark spots that have invaded his body in the radiographs. She reiterated the seriousness of small cell lung cancer as well as the speed at which it spreads.

As she spoke, I saw the cancer's toxic black roots ruling Michael's lungs, its outstretched arms reaching for the surrounding organs. I pictured the inky malignancy spreading throughout his body, the healthy cells choking as the cancer captures the space.

I count the slow-moving seconds, willing the silence of the car to dissipate. I watch the dotted lines between lanes as we rush over them with an urgency that feels draining. I track the mile markers as they increase every

0.1 miles along the grass of the highway.

This is an aggressive cancer, Dr. Graham had said gravely, ensuring we understood the meaning of her words. What was it? Was she trying to tell us there wasn't any hope left? Was she trying to stress the importance of making a decision today? Does she go over the results twice with all her patients?

The questions are innumerable, and the panic is immeasurable. The car is racing while I sit motionless, but time isn't moving fast enough. The walls around me are suffocating.

We pull into the driveway, and Michael asks if I'll stay in the car with him while he calls his parents. Although there aren't any tears, his eyes are bloodshot, and he clenches his jaw. The fear and disbelief he's built up intoxicate the space between us.

Elaine's cry cuts through the phone's speaker, and my breath catches mid-inhale. This is the first time she and Scott are even hearing about Michael being sick. I block my imagination as it pictures their horror, the fear of losing a child. Michael assures her he'll be okay, but the droop of his lips as he speaks promises otherwise. Scott states he'll be praying fervently, then remains silent for the rest of the call. Elaine asks for timelines and promises to stay with us as long as needed once chemo starts.

Amber and Logan are next. He takes a breath and closes his eyes as the phone rings. Again, a weight crashes on my chest when I hear Amber's disbelief. Logan, like Scott, doesn't say much. He apologizes between questions Amber fires rapidly. Michael answers his sister the best he can, but there's a lack of information for all of us. He reiterates that he's trying to stay positive and suggests they do, too. He doesn't say that he's a fighter or that he's going to get through this; he doesn't make empty promises to them.

Our last call from the car is to Kyle, who breaks down as much as Elaine and Amber. Kyle has always been the most emotional of Michael's friends—I would even venture to use the term moody. Today, he displays a full range of emotions. He promises to be there for anything we need, promises to get a flight out with a single call, no questions asked. Michael pinches the bridge of his nose, preventing tears from spilling as Kyle cries on the other side, hundreds of miles away in Boston. I'm surprised at how long the two men sit on opposite ends of the phone without speaking; a childhood friendship that spans three decades revealing itself in sad silence. Kyle says he'll make plans to come visit immediately and volunteers Anita as a medical information source. I hear her offer a reply in the background, but I don't think Kyle does.

When they hang up, Michael doesn't comment on any of the calls as he puts his phone down.

We go inside, the conversation still paused. Without thinking, our bodies lead us to the couch. I keep my toes tucked under his thigh as we scroll through Google, something Dr. Graham advised us against. Nothing comes up that increases our optimism.

...poor prognosis with limited therapeutic options...

...one of the most aggressive tumor types...

...median survival of 10 to 12 months...

...prophylactic cranial irradiation...

We watch queasy videos of surgery removing different lobes of the lung. Sometimes there are little incision points with small camera wires going into the skin. Other videos show the doctor's entire hand in someone's chest.

Nothing feels helpful. I fall asleep with Michael's head pressed against my chest while his thumb continues to flip through the pages of negative outcomes.

WEDNESDAY MARCH 11, 2017

BEFORE MICHAEL WAS ADMITTED, Dr. Graham had taken time to go through Michael's treatment plan in its entirety. She explained what the process would look like, the expected side effects, and the purpose of each medication. Once we had settled into a room on the inpatient oncology floor, she stopped by to go over the details a second time.

This morning, the pharmacist came in and explained the side effects in expansive depth. We waited in our small room for the nurse to bring in the medication while the sounds of the hospital buzzed around us. She returned with syringes full of liquid and a labeled IV bag. Between beeps, she went through the list again: *nausea, febrile neutropenia, bone marrow suppression, anorexia, diarrhea, anemia, alopecia.* A never-ending slew of made-up words neither of us could define. Michael kept a straight face, but I'm confident my panic showed.

Despite the warnings and the nurse poking her head in every fifteen minutes expectantly, the entire bag drains into his body with no complaints.

About an hour ago, a crew of kitchen staff delivered a plate of meatloaf. Michael has been taking slow, hesitant bites. We're waiting for the nausea to kick in, but the more time that goes by, the more naively hopeful we become.

We play cards, laughing together as the sun sinks, and flip through the limited TV channels. When we draw the curtain and flip the lights off to fall asleep, we've started to believe the chemo won't take a toll on him, that for some reason he won't fall victim to its poison. He's untouchable, my invincible superhero.

I wake up after only a couple of hours of sleep. Darkness still cloaks the landscape outside the window. I'm disoriented as I look for Michael from the hospital room recliner. He clumsily reaches out, pushing whatever is on the hospital tray onto the floor in his haste. Being within arm's reach, I rush to pass him the clean plastic bin we'd been given for this exact moment. Immediately, the sound of retching fills the room.

Still half asleep, I call for the nurse. My yell echoes down the hallway while I press the call button on the remote incessantly. Within a few minutes, she's standing at his side, pushing a syringe of medicine into one of the many lines stemming from his arm.

Last night's meatloaf looks less appetizing regurgitated in the bin. Michael shakes and shivers as the acid-filled spit hangs from his lips, dripping down into the plastic. I rub his back gently, unable to think of a better way to help. The nurse's distant voice reassures us that this is normal and expected while setting a handful of clean straws for his water cup on the tray.

Nothing about this is *normal* or *expected.* I've never seen Michael like this; he hasn't gotten anything more than food poisoning since I met him. He's healthy—or at least he was up until a month ago. Since we've met, I've known him to be someone who runs miles every day despite the dropping temperatures outside. He studies the laws of states he doesn't even practice in. He exercises his brain and body so he can brag about feeling young forever.

There's a layer of shock settled into the room around us that, despite the passing time, doesn't fade. The bouts of vomiting don't slow. He looks withered in the bed, crushed under the heaviness of the medications, shivering while wrapped in warm blankets. Each time he bends at the waist over the bedside, the defeat his face holds grows denser.

Michael's still feeling the effects of the chemo hours later. The sun is still rising, but the side effects are at their peak, and the cocktail of anti-nausea medications is failing him miserably. He's shaking, eyes closed with a tight white-knuckle grip on the hospital sheets. I've made an effort to continue touching him in some capacity so that he knows I'm still here. I feel helpless otherwise.

Michael's hand reaches out, signaling the rising nausea that will become vomiting within seconds. I rush to pass him the container, which we have already cleaned a handful of times, and rest my hand on his back. His shoulders are tense, pulling together as his body violently contracts to expel what's left in his stomach, a concoction of bile and water. He coughs and spits into the bucket before falling back against the bed, worn and defeated. His hand extends, and I pass him the water, jumping at any opportunity to be of use.

The nurse brings the bin to the toilet and dumps it in with a loud splash that causes my body to wince. Michael doesn't react, unbothered by the now-familiar sound.

Michael complains all morning and afternoon. His stomach churns, his dizzy head spins, and his mouth salivates constantly to prepare for the next bout of throw-up. His body resumes its deterioration, growing weaker and more withered. He doesn't fall asleep, but he keeps his eyes closed as the hours pass.

The doctors stop by in the early afternoon to approve his Day 2 treatment despite his current state and lack of food intake. He worsens almost immediately, and, for the entirety of the infusion, he's nauseous and fatigued.

The hours creep by; the tick of the clock's second hand echoes with each movement. The beeping of the hospital machines and Michael's sickly groans fill the silence between ticks. By the time he speaks, the sun has passed to the other side of the building, setting into the skyline.

"Hello, beautiful," Michael's voice holds an unrecognizable layer of exhaustion and pain. He squints his eyes, sees me next to him, then lets them fall.

"I'm right here," I squeeze the hand I've been gripping, my arm extending from the reclining chair I've pushed against his bed.

"Can you turn on the basketball game?"

"Yes," I sigh with a chuckle as a wave of relief ripples through me. The normalcy of the request brings a vibrant hope that I hadn't realized had paled.

I fight the hospital blankets wrapped around me to free a hand and click through the channels with the remote hooked onto his bed. The green jerseys of the Celtics appear on the micro-TV mounted on the wall.

Michael keeps his eyes closed most of the game. Periodically, he'll ask me to adjust the sound; increased volume signifies he doesn't have a headache and isn't nauseous, decreased volume is usually followed by dry heaving or grimacing.

"I thought I heard some noise." This shift's nurse, Jeremy, peeks around the corner. He pushes the half-closed door open as he walks in. He's been a good nurse over the last few hours, attentive but allowing Michael space to rest when possible.

"Hey." Michael's eyes flutter open.

"How are you feeling?" Jeremy looks between the two of us. Michael shakes his head and lets his eyes fall closed.

"We're okay," I answer for him. My mouth is painfully dry as I speak, but the thought of food or water makes me feel sick. My stomach twists and knots. I try to focus on the things around me: the hum of the blood pressure cuff on Michael's arm as it inflates, the distant voices of the basketball game commentators, the genuine laughter from down the hall.

"I brought this for you." Jeremy smiles as he holds out a chocolate milk to me.

"Thank you." I return the smile and set it down on the windowsill. I've been living off the contents in the room designated for patient families: pudding, chocolate milk, and crackers.

"And this is for you." He opens his hand up to Michael, whose eyelids lift slightly. Michael smiles too, seeing the ChapStick. His elbow remains on the bed, but the rest of his arm raises to take it, and he brings the stick to his face slowly. After hours of throwing up, mouth breathing, and refusing to drink water, his lips have been chapped all day.

"I just have to record some vitals. Any headaches, nausea, stomach pain? We have some medications ordered in case you need them," Jeremy offers as he logs himself into the computer.

"No," Michael mumbles.

Not long after Jeremy leaves, food services knock on the open door. Michael is sitting in an upright position watching the end of the game. His eyes are heavy, but the straight-backed bed reinforces his posture to keep him awake.

"Is it a good game?" A bald man in hospital clothes carries a tray over to Michael.

"Mhm. Great game." Michael's says hoarsely, but his expression is full of weary excitement. The man stays for a minute talking about basketball, letting Michael go on about the players and the game. I hadn't realized he was paying enough attention to know the players in the game right now.

"Hope the Celtics win it tonight. Enjoy." He winks at me as he leaves, and I'm grateful for the momentary normalcy.

"Thanks, man," Michael replies, shifting his weight.

I'm reminded of what he ordered when the smell of cooked carrots and chicken fills the room. A decent-sized chicken pot pie, a cup of orange Jell-O, chocolate pudding, and skinless apple slices fill his side table.

The more Michael eats, the more my shoulders relax. My heartbeat normalizes, and my breathing slows. I've never seen Michael turn down food, so when he pushes the full tray away from his bedside, signifying he's done, returned panic swells in my chest.

Although he continues to rest throughout the game, he cheers in an enthusiastic whisper when the Celtics win. Jeremy walks past the room when he hears Michael, mirroring my wide grin.

At night, Jeremy comes in at scheduled times to check his vitals. He tries to be quiet, but the movement wakes us both up. It's impossible to get restful sleep. The constant hospital background noise doesn't stop. Machines beep loudly, nurses talk to other patients at an emphasized volume, wheels scrape against the floor, keyboards click, and laughter comes from behind the nurse's station. There's loud, wet, consistent coughing from the patient in the adjacent room that startles us awake whenever we start to doze off.

On Day 3, despite hardly keeping food down, the doctors clear him for another treatment. Thankfully, today is the last day before they let us go home. The hours, again, blend together in a compilation of sleeplessness, back rubs, ice chip refills, and injections of anti-nausea medicine.

After what feels like an eternity, the sun peeks in behind the drawn blinds. Lines pattern the walls creating bright stripes. Snow covers the tops of the hospital buildings around us. I stand at the window, sipping my hot coffee, feeling the cold radiate in from the other side of the glass as I watch the cars pull into the hospital entrance. They circle the building, jutting off in different directions toward the various specialties around the hospital.

I break my stare and turn around when I hear the ruffling of blankets.

"Hi," I smile as Michael sleepily looks around the room, "you finally slept for a few hours."

Although the same distractions existed last night, he was so exhausted he crashed into a deep sleep. I wasn't able to get the same rest. Anytime my eyes began dropping, the fear of sleeping through his painful cries brough a rush of energy through me.

I spent most of the night watching him breathe, scared his chest would stop rising. When I wasn't staring at him, my eyes were fixed on the monitor, tracking his heartbeat count to make sure it didn't dip too low or creep too high. I made sure the blood pressure cuff was cycling through its periodic measurements like it was supposed to.

"Do we leave today?" Michael asks as his eyes wander to the wall clock. He frowns when he realizes it's only 8 a.m. His voice is still the usual mellow tone, but it lacks life. After four nights of loud, terrifying sounds and waves of stress interrupting any chance of REM, he's eager to leave.

"Yeah," I nod and sit up in the recliner, "Yeah, we're going home today."

Thankfully I'm able to keep my promise. The doctors check his labs and clear him for discharge pending Dr. Graham's approval. The team gives us a thick stack of papers to review. It contains a ridiculous amount of information, including a complete list of side effects, prevention and treatment for said side effects, and guidance on when to go to the ER. They advise us to call the hospital's outpatient pharmacy and have his meds brought up before we leave so we don't need to make any extra stops on the way home. While we wait for Dr Graham, I call the pharmacy and gather our things.

We've made a mess of the room in the short amount of time we've been here. I brought a duffle bag for each of us, full of clothes, snacks, card games, books, and chargers. The contents of both bags lie strewn across the room, most of it unused. It amazes me how comfortable we became in such a short amount of time and in the most uncomfortable situation.

"Hi Michael." Dr. Graham's long face pops around the corner, and she clicks away on her tablet as she walks in. "Your labs look as expected. I think it's safe for you to go home, given that you practice the preventive steps to make sure you stay healthy."

"Just get us out of here." I know Michael means it to be a joke, but there's an unshakable desperation that makes it clear there's truth behind his words.

Dr. Graham listens to Michael's heart and lungs while asking questions about the treatment and how he's feeling.

"I have you scheduled for a telehealth appointment with me a week from now. Remember to take your temperature daily. In seven to ten days, the blood cells that fight infection are going to take a drastic dip, and you won't get the symptoms of a fever to tell you that you're sick. Stay home if you're able to. Anna, you'll also play a part in making sure Michael stays healthy by keeping up your hand hygiene and limiting your outings, too."

Dr. Graham reapplies hand sanitizer before shaking our hands, inadvertently giving a sympathetic smile to each of us. We leave as fast as we can; Michael needs quiet rest and consecutive hours of sleep, and he can't get either in the hospital.

Michael stares beyond the window on the drive home. He's quiet and distant. I offer to call Amber and have her bring Butler home, but Michael shakes his head and asks if we can call her later.

"Of course." I don't know what else to say, and we sit in another few minutes of silence. "Are you hungry for anything specific? I can pick up some food after I drop you off or get it delivered."

"Maybe later." Michael's voice is melancholic and fatigued.

Once we're home, I walk next to him through the front door and up the stairs. He's stable on his own, but I can hear the difficulty of each step in his breathing.

On the other side of the bathroom door, I listen to the shower turn on; the rushing sound of water splattering against the tile drowns out his quiet grunts. I wonder if he'll be able to shower by himself after the next treatment, or if he'll progressively lose his independence.

I'm sitting on the bed flipping through movie options when he comes out, rubbing his hair dry with a towel. Although he hasn't gotten any additional sleep, his eyes look brighter, and his posture is straighter. His arms extend energetically above his head, moving the towel back and forth. Seeing his regained normalcy sends a wave of relief over me.

"Are you hungry?" I ask eagerly.

"Mostly nauseous." He sits down on his side of the bed and takes a few sips of the water I left out for him. He slides on a pair of sweatpants before leaning back against the propped-up pillows.

"Can I do anything?" My words are full of despair.

Michael cover himself with the blanket at the foot of the bed and pats his chest as an invitation. I'm careful as I scoot closer to him, wondering if he's breakable, and snuggle up next to him.

"You can lay here with me and watch *Star Wars* until we fall asleep together."

"Only if we start on episode one."

"Deal."

"And skip episode three."

"No deal," he chuckles.

This is how our movie marathons begin. After completing the chemo in each treatment cycle, we subject ourselves to a series of movies. For the first cycle, we choose *Star Wars Episodes I-III*. After that, we watch the Andrew Garfield *Spider-Man* series, then *The Lord of the Rings*, and finally *Harry Potter* for Cycle 4.

Four cycles, four months, and more than forty hours of movies later, we wait for a call from Dr. Graham, recalling the turmoil we've been through in such a short period of time.

It was impossible to heed the warnings about chemo. The side effects have been unavoidable. There aren't words to describe the tsunami cancer treatments cause. Michael was forced to stop most of the daily activities he found joy in. His strong body withered, and his faith was uprooted. There are certain aspects of the treatment process that doctors can convey, but there are more effects that they can't. Unless they've been through it themselves, there is no way of understanding the existential crisis that happens.

For months, Michael has been living on time that isn't his, feeding poison to his body in hopes that the cancer cells die before the rest of him. The chemo caused his hair to thin, then disappear. It gave him endless stomach issues requiring steroids to fix. The steroids altered his body shape and mood.

Despite all the physical changes, the mental deterioration shocked us most. Michael lost his enjoyment of life. He couldn't run anymore, and we weren't told when that would change—if it would ever change. We had to keep visits with Mason outdoors to avoid the germs he brought home from daycare. Michael couldn't join the softball league this year or golf with Logan and his friends. He spent most of the summer inside, too weak to leave the couch and fearful of the photosensitivity we were warned about. Michael's firm allowed him to work from home but gave him only a fraction of cases and sent another lawyer to go to court in his place. Everything he loved to do was taken from him; he felt purposeless.

He's never admitted it, but I think Michael's faith was most affected. I'd hear him pray while in the shower, angry and frustrated and questioning God. His pain and confusion are most evident during Sunday church service, which we've been watching from the couch to minimize germ exposure. Every sermon has the potential to be contorted to fit our situation. It's clear that Michael struggles to follow their simple suggestion to be faithful, find peace, and trust God.

Dr. Graham calls after lunch. Both of us inhale as though the oxygen around us is limited, like there's water rising and this is the last breath we get before succumbing to the flood.

"The treatment isn't doing as much as we hoped it would. Your scans from last week show that the cancer is still progressing aggressively," she opens the call factually. Her momentary pause turns into an expansive period where we all sit frozen, a chill coating the air surrounding us.

"So, what does this mean?" Michael asks, closing his eyes and habitually rubbing his hands over his face.

Seconds ago, we were sitting in the living room with our legs intermingled, both reading silently. Now every nerve stands on edge, our hearts pound audibly, our breath caught somewhere in the space between the past and future. Between sickness and hope.

"I'd like you guys to come in. We can go over the options."

"Let me know when the appointment is, and I'll be there," Michael says, fatigued.

"I'll have Scheduling call you," Dr. Graham says with a straightforward tone. "Don't hesitate to reach out if questions come up in the meantime."

Michael hangs up. Thousands of unspoken words fill the silence hanging in the air around us. Fear is overwhelmingly palpable. I try to shift my thoughts toward something positive, but I can't prevent the tears from welling. We've learned that the request to meet in person is always paired with bad news.

Michael sits with his phone in his hand, suspended between us. The screen has turned black. Discouragement lingers.

Michael, desperate for a distraction, suggests we have a bonfire. After staying in Michigan for about a month, his parents went back to Boston last week, so we only invite Amber and her family over. I don't have the energy to care about the germs coating Mason's little hands or the sicknesses that may be sticking to Amber or Logan's clothes. It's impossible to know how many more nights we'll have. I agree without hesitation.

Being around Mason proves to be nothing short of therapeutic for both of us. His tiny presence brings new life to Michael. He lights up watching Butler chase Mason around the backyard and laughs wholeheartedly as Mason changes direction, taking his turn to chase Butler.

As the sun finalizes setting, the five of us sit gathered around the roaring flames, and Butler lies next to Michael, resting his head on Michael's feet. We pass s'mores, which Michael eats four of, and Amber fills us in on the family drama we've missed. She speaks quickly, bouncing between various subjects, with nervousness embedded in every word.

"Your call with the oncologist was today, right?" Amber finally asks, optimism dancing in her eyes as she wipes Mason's mouth with a wet wipe to remove the smeared melted marshmallow.

I look at Michael, not sure how much information he wants to share. He looks back at me, his brown eyes dark and tired. It seems like he wants me to step in, but I remain silent, knowing my voice will break under the lie.

"Yeah. I think we're going to do a couple more rounds of treatment or radiation. We'll reevaluate after."

"That's good, that means you're getting good effects from the chemo!" Amber cheers, a surge of relief clear on her face. My stomach cramps, and my heart drops down in my chest, feeling the impact of Michael's lie. Because we both know why he lied. We both know the truth.

"Guess you're stuck with me," Michael attempts a grin, but, in the reflection of the fire, I can see the wetness of his eyes. Amber and Logan are distracted by Mason's squirming and fussing and don't catch it.

Amber puts Mason to bed in the guest room while Michael and Logan cheers a beer. When she rejoins the small circle, we're all a little lighter.

The city lights are distant tonight, granting the sky a full display of inky blackness. The sea of stars twinkles above us like glass catching light, and the moon, hidden behind rolling clouds, emits a white glow. Chirps of crickets rise and fall between the popping of the burning wood. With the warmth of the fire allowing Michael to shed his top layer, and all four of our laughs filling the dark summer air, life almost feels normal.

FRIDAY

JULY 21, 2017 - PART B

THE CAR IS EERILY quiet on the drive home. I'm not sure how my foot finds the pedal, how it knows when to press the gas versus the brake, because my mind feels numb. I'm trapped in a haze, my body stuck standing still while the world around me continues to rush by.

I wonder what conversations are taking place in the cars as they pass us. Hundreds of worlds in moving bubbles. People driving to work while listening to encouraging podcasts attempting to heal a failing marriage, or the newest Joe Rogan conspiracy, engorged in the possibility of more beyond this life. There are conversations between best friends, parents and their kids, spouses. In some cars, people play sad music, addicted to the comfort of depression, while others play Disney songs for the toddlers in the back. All oblivious to our world—Michael and me—most not knowing the feeling of a sinking heart when faced with the word *terminal.*

While my foot presses down like lead in a silent plea to get home, the rest of me remains at a halt. As we drive, I see the passing white lines between lanes, but it's as though I'm standing with my eyes closed in the middle, feeling the air from the racing cars pull me left and right, teetering in the threat of being swept up, accidentally pulling me into a lane where I get hit, where it all ends.

Muscle memory gets us home safely, neither of us speaking for the entirety of the drive. I can't move, can't turn off the car, or shift my eyes to look at Michael. I stare at the house in front of us, trying to guess what happens next.

Terminal. The word repeats itself in my mind.

What am I going to tell Butler when Michael stops walking through the door? Who will I share dinners with? How do I live in this house without him? Why do I have to?

The loneliness is overwhelming as I hold the unexpected heaviness of future nights without Michael. My mind puts me into a bed that's cold on his side, surrounds me in the silence of an October to come where football doesn't play on the TV, places me under a vast blue sky in summer that lacks joy without him.

"I don't want you to—" I inhale a sob unable to complete the sentence. Michael's hands pull my head into his chest, and his shoulders tremble. "I can't lose you."

The stillness of the car is interrupted by my thick, croak; the air splits with my weeping. I can't look at Michael, I can't lift my head, I can't unwrap the arm that's curled itself around him. I can't let him go.

Despite Michael being the one trying to ignore the knock of death, he helps me inside and guides me to the couch. Exhausted, he collapses next to me.

"I think," his voice is foreign as it's carried through the small gap between us. He hesitates, his whisper wavering under the weight of the forming words.

Fear grips my throat, holds my breath hostage, knowing the sentence that is about to come.

"I think I'm going to take the next step to get the pills."

Energy rushes through me immediately, bubbling into the saliva stuck in my throat. I'm not big enough to hold the emotions rising, and they spill out of me in a cry. The tears are hot, falling ferociously in a formidable despair.

"We need to be realistic about the future." Michael's words are concise, but his tone is anything but calm.

I'm mad at him for considering Dr. Graham's offer. I'm furious at her for giving him the option. I'm filled with violent anger at the God Michael's claimed as his. I'm pissed at everything, at the sturdy house we've built that feels like it's crumbling under us, at the fireplace that roars and spews warmth that burns my cheeks, and at the couch cushions that I sink into like quicksand.

"No." It comes out as a pleading whisper.

"I know," he repeats and joins my crying. His fingers dig into me, pressing me flush against him. "I know, Anna, I'm so sorry."

Darkness has started falling behind the windows covering the wall, but we're blanketed in the glow of the fireplace. The comfort of his hands gripping me and the steadiness of his rhythmic breathing calms the pulsing of my head.

Michael's eyes sweep over my face, studying me, coated in a glistening wetness. Seeing the fear pull out his tears causes a wrenching, nagging, breath-stealing ache to swell in my chest. The piercing shock strikes through me, reminding me that it never left. He kisses my forehead and tucks my hair behind my ears, letting his fingertips linger against my skin.

"I don't want to forget what you look like," his cry is splitting as it cuts through my body, my stomach turning as his tears fall.

"Please don't go," I whisper.

He shakes his head in submission before speaking, "I think my body made that choice already."

"No," I hiccup.

"I know where I'm going," he says in melancholy confidence as he strokes my cheeks with his thumb.

"You can't leave me here."

"I can't stay." His eyes spill fear. "I can't starve to death, Anna. I can't do that."

"But you can't leave me," I repeat.

"I'm going one way or another. I at least want the choice not to suffer."

Fear sprouts anger and blossoms into rage, then tumbles back into sadness.

"I'm going to take care of everything. I won't talk about it again unless you ask." Michael wraps one arm around me tightly and uses the other to press my head against his shoulder. His fingers entangle themselves in my hair, but no matter how tightly he holds me, it isn't strong enough to change his prognosis.

He lets me weep, lets me cry into him. I switch between screaming and whispers, pleading out of fear and anger. I get mad because he isn't. I get frustrated that he's made a decision without consulting me. I feel pitiful about my selfishness and fall into manic desperation, fueled by the unknown—the darkness that reaches into a life beyond Michael.

Michael watches me wordlessly, his eyes a cocktail of defeat, love, and pity. He repeatedly tells me he loves me, cradles my head into him. We grip one another in desperation, like we might be able to find a life source in the other.

I lay limp, a product of my life's plot, subjected to every twist and turn I've never been able to imagine. Michael cycles between pulling me in tighter, kissing the top of my head and resting his quivering chin on me, and burying his face in my hair to breathe me in.

"I'm so sorry."

MONDAY

JULY 24, 2017

RAINDROPS MAKE THEIR PRESENCE known, echoing a light patter against the glass as I make my way across the wall of windows, closing each of the blinds. The green of the grass and tree leaves has deepened and vibrantly contrasts against the navy-colored sky as the storm's darkness replaces what little light is left.

Butler lays nervously against the couch at Michael's feet. His head rests unmoving on his paws, but his eyes dart around skeptically with every bright flash of lightning and heavy boom of thunder that follows. He's petrified of storms, and Midwest summers are full of them.

I've already charged our phones and spread candles around the living room in case we lose power, leaving a lighter within reach on the coffee table.

"First bad storm of the summer." Michael's voice is withered. His eyes open and close slowly. He's tired; fatigue preys on him ceaselessly, prowling both night and day. I had been so focused on preparing for the storm that I didn't realize he'd woken up.

"Getting ready in case we lose power," I smile.

"It looks like you're very prepared." He moves the tube of oxygen away from his face and pats the couch next to him, signaling for my company.

"I have a surprise for you."

"Please don't tell me it's food." Michael attempts a joke, but there's an honest undertone of nausea in his words.

I run upstairs to the closet in the spare bedroom. The box sits on the floor, out of place in a sea of spare pillows and suitcases. It isn't too heavy as I drag it out, but it's an odd shape, and when I lift it, I have to remind myself to make it look effortless. I don't want Michael to feel guilty for not being able to help.

When I get downstairs, Michael is struggling to sit up. He leans his weight from side to side, inching up, using the pillows as cushioned leverage. I slow my pace, trying to allow time for him to do it himself without feeling embarrassed in the struggle, and place the box at his feet. He leans over, the bones of his spine like spikes under his shirt, and opens the lid. A wide, chapped smile spreads across his paled face.

"It's our first big storm in Michigan, and I want to make it special." I skip over the negative thoughts telling me it might be our last.

In the box is an air mattress, boxes of our favorite candy, bags of microwave popcorn, a bottle of sparkling grape juice, and a battery-operated Bluetooth projector. In Boston, we would set up blankets on the floor during power outages—which happened almost every storm since the electrical wiring was ancient. The big storms had faded out by the time we moved here last year, and I didn't want to miss our opportunity to carry on the tradition this year.

"Well now I hope we lose power," Michael kisses the side of my head, "I love it."

Michael's eyes redden as he tucks his lips together.

I've noticed his emotions have been more outward lately; he has difficulty controlling them and verbalizes how he feels more than he ever did. Being an arm's length from death can soften any man.

I spread out the air mattress's shell and plug the long cord into the wall, then give Michael the task of inflating it. While he watches the mattress rise, I grab us glasses for the sparkling juice. I only pop one bag of popcorn, worried Michael might not do well with the smell overtaking the living room. When I get back to the couch, hands full of goodies, Michael is pulling the sheets across the mattress. I put the snacks on the coffee table and add a layer of couch pillows behind our regular ones for extra support. Butler sneaks closer to us, tail wagging with so much excitement that his whole butt wiggles.

We're about thirty minutes into the movie when the power flickers a few times, then gives in entirely. Even though we were expecting it, the darkness surprises us, and we're subdued by silence. The buzz of the electricity cuts out, the hum of the fridge drops off, and the hushed white noise from beyond the walls becomes quiet. Only the sound of the small projector's fan purrs.

Michael's been awake the whole time, laughing with me at *The Wolf of Wall Street* as it lights up the living room, but I can see his eyes getting heavy.

"I'll light candles," I say in a whisper.

Michael squeezes my hand, then releases it with a smile.

The cracks in his lips have become more prominent. I make a note to get the Aquaphor we've been keeping on the kitchen counter; we've flooded the house with the gel and spray versions. The chemo has dried out his hands and lips to the point of cracking and bleeding. I'm thankful it's a humid summer, I can't imagine how much worse it will be in the harshness of winter six months from now.

Six months. My stomach sinks at the thought. Six months is a long time for a terminal cancer patient.

Michael hasn't gotten any chemo in about a month. Besides requesting a home nurse, I'm not sure what Dr. Graham's plans are now that he's on palliative care. What an ugly word—*palliative.* My mind wants to spit it out; the bitterness is all-encompassing and drenches me from head to toe.

I notice Michael has opened the candy boxes when I pass him the tube of Aquaphor to smear over his lips and a can of the spray for his hands. *How bad can the cancer really be,* I think in shades of blind positivity, *he's eating and laughing.*

"Are you hungry for any real food?" I ask, slipping back under the blankets next to Michael as he responds with a reluctant groan.

When I turn toward him, I notice his stiff pose, an Aquaphor in each hand. His lips twitch and contort as though he's speaking, but no sounds come out. A few mumbled words expel but they're gibberish—sporadic words not fitting any pattern, like an involuntary glitch.

I reach out and touch his hand, understanding that his body is failing him, a painful realization. His mouth continues to move as if searching for words on a blank page. Every few seconds, a word slips out incoherently. His eyes stay fixed on mine in a helpless panic, and a redness infects them as he restrains his tears.

This is the first time something like this has happened, but I know what this means. His slurred speech is proof that the cancer is spreading to a previously untouched part of his brain. A wave of sickness passes over my already clenched stomach, and my jaw tightens, holding back tears of my own.

I am useless. I can't do anything for him. He sits struggling to communicate. His breath grows heavier as his frustrations rise, and his head shakes with defeated fear. He can feel his tongue's lack; his thoughts are clear, but his words refuse to form. I hold his hand in mine, trying to soothe him, but I can't come up with any words to speak over him. I take his face in my hands, cupping his jaw, willing any hopeful words to come to mind. I'm taking too long, the despair is building behind his lost eyes.

I close my eyes and pray. Not because I know what I'm saying, not because it's what Michael is trying to communicate, or because I believe that my words are going somewhere higher, but because I don't know what else to do.

I rub his arm and lie down on the pillow. The words pour out of me as he follows suit. I mumble strings of words the way he does, repeating the things I've heard him say before bed. His hand begins to relax in mine, and his eyes flutter closed.

We lay quietly while Leonardo DiCaprio's voice and the dim light from the candle flames fill the air around us. Butler's head rests under Michael's left hand while I curl up to his right one. Our hands stay interlocked as his thumb rubs back and forth, so I know he's still awake regardless of his closed eyes.

I don't take my eyes off him until his jaw drops as he falls asleep. His breathing deepens as it pours out from his open mouth, and his thumb slows in its movement before stopping altogether. I study Michael, absorb his breath, memorize the angle of his jaw, the creases in his ears, the feeling of the thin bones of his fingers wrapped in mine. I find myself studying him often; the unknown that holds us in its grasp is daunting. I live in a bubble of fear that I'll forget, and, in death's permanence, I'll never be able to identify the things that I missed.

"I love you," Michael mumbles in a decipherable slur. We lose light in the living room as the end credits roll, and I reach up to click off the projector. The darkness encompasses us fully, and I draw closer into Michael's warmth.

"I love you so much."

WEDNESDAY

SEPTEMBER 6, 2017

THE THIN, WITHERED, REFLECTED version of me only takes up a small portion of the bathroom mirror spanning the wall. A layer of steam frames the outline of my body. My hair is frizzy, even in its dampness, from months of neglect. My paled skin is rough, both stretched and wrinkled, and lacks the vibrance it carried for over two decades. I can feel the life draining out of me each morning as I stand behind the closed door hunched over the sink. My stomach churns turbulently. The veins on the sides of my head throb.

This has become my morning routine: standing with my arms spread across the counter, struggling to support my body as it threatens to collapse. After my shower, I stand naked and timid behind the locked door, counting the seconds of each breath until I can muster the courage to open the drawer next to Michael's sink. My mind creates horror movies of how this could end, plays them on repeat until I can open the drawer and prove myself wrong.

In one swift motion, I gasp a quick inhale of air and pull open the drawer: toothbrush, toothpaste, deodorant, three pill bottles. I count them, *one, two, three.* Two orange vials and one amber colored bottle containing a liquid. *One, two, three.* Then I count them again. And one more time for good measure. My exhale bursts out, and my shoulders drop in relief.

The girl in the mirror looks no more hopeful, no less betrayed. She ages by the second, fear pulling spare minutes from the end of her lifeline, eating them away with the promise of a timely death.

Tears well as my emotions surge like a storm. Dread and self-pity collide with relief and freedom. I'm filled with the agony of a heartbreak that hasn't happened yet.

When my heartbeat can no longer be heard, I brush my hair and then my teeth. I slip a sweatshirt over my head in hopes of shaking the fear-induced chill.

He didn't choose today.

I know that I get another day with him.

WEDNESDAY

SEPTEMBER 20, 2017

CARD GAMES HAVE BECOME uncomfortable. Michael's tailbone presses into the wooden chair when we play at the table, causing him to ache and bruise. When he's feeling stable enough to leave his oxygen tank, we go upstairs to the loft where we play on the heavily padded, plush carpet. Tonight, we have two decks of cards combined for a game of line rummy.

"You can't let me win every time just because I'm a cancer patient," he teases, laying down a four-card run. Michael is winning, as he usually does.

"I wouldn't have a clear conscience if I won," I roll my eyes.

Even though Michael doesn't truly get competitive, he never holds back on smack talk with me or anyone else. It doesn't matter if we're playing basketball or Uno.

"You're totally cheating. Are you counting cards? Can you see my hand in a reflection somewhere?" I scowl when he lays down his last cards.

He tallies his points, then mine, while I shuffle what remains of the deck.

"I thought you were letting me win."

Sometimes the changes in his facial features are more noticeable. Michael's skin looks ghostly under the recessed lights. As he smirks, the skin pulls firmly over his chin exposing small veins. He has patches of dry skin staining different parts of his face, and his eyelids are often crusty; distinctly noticeable today.

We play a few more rounds until I have to admit defeat. Michael shakes his head when I ask to play another round, and I assume he's in pain.

While we were playing, I noticed small grimaces and picked up on slight body readjustments that indicate discomfort.

Selfishly, I've enjoyed the last few hours of Michael without the oxygen tube that reminds me of his sickness and the pain meds that envelop him in a blurry fog. The old silly and witty version of him started to peek out.

We mindlessly shuffle the cards while we toss out ideas on what to eat for dinner. This is one game that I actually do always let him win. I can find something that sounds appetizing anywhere, he can't. Since he stopped the chemo, his hunger has become depleted by the tumors growing throughout his body rather than the poison itself; a lose-lose situation altogether.

"I'm sorry babe, all that sounds good right now is Leo's Coney Island."

"Cheese fries and chicken lemon rice soup it is," I smile and pull out my phone to place the same order we've had for the last eight days. I contemplate going to pick it up but decide against it, realizing I'm in sweatpants from yesterday, and I haven't washed my hair in at least four days.

My boss gave me permission to work from home. I spend the mornings in my office and the rest of the day soaking up as much time with Michael as possible. I don't have enough time to add selfcare into my days, meaning I've neglected myself completely.

"Order is placed. Should be here in thirty minutes. I'm going to take a quick shower, go pick out something for us to watch over dinner!" I jump up and skip upstairs.

It's impossible not to notice the changes in my appearance as I slip out of Monday's pajamas and into the shower. I look a lot thinner; my natural rosy-red cheeks have faded to be as pale as the rest of me, and my hair has knotted itself into clumps.

The water's hot as it runs off my shoulders, down my chest, pooling inside my belly button. Outside the sound of the water pushing through the showerhead, the bathroom is silent. My fingers work to massage the shampoo through my hair and into my scalp. I breathe in the steam, then release the thick air with a heavy exhale as I rub soap down the back of my arms and across my chest. I soak my face in the falling water, closing my eyes to surrender myself to the stream.

No one warns you of the permanent tension that resides in your chest when you're watching someone wither away. The unending shortness of breath caused by the fear of losing the person you love. The manic checking of your phone for emergencies. The challenge of maintaining a positive mindset.

A caution would have been helpful. I would have spent less time wondering if my constant panicked state was normal or if I was unintentionally allowing myself to implode.

I check my phone once I'm out of the shower, verifying the food is on its way. After I towel-dry my hair and wipe down my body, I put on a clean pair of sweatpants and a tank top.

My bare feet pad down the stairs, but when the wall breaks, Michael is still on the floor, his back against the adjacent wall. He looks up at me, a darkness in the sunken skin beneath his eyes.

"I need your help." His voice is thick like syrup, but his words are bitter as they hang in the air. I walk toward him, staring with a blank expression, confused.

"What's wrong?"

"I—" his sentence breaks, and I see his Adam's apple bob up and down as he swallows his pride.

He doesn't attempt to finish his sentence; rather, he shows me.

He reaches his hands out in front of him and presses them into the carpet as he tries to shift his body weight. His arms shake as he makes a failed attempt to push himself up. His bones are heavy, his muscles brittle, his lungs lack air, and the physical and mental strength have been sucked out of him.

The answer comes in a rush of adrenaline as I watch him. I reach for him quickly, holding his arms firmly in my hands. I use my weight as a counterbalance to pull him upwards in a silent beg for him to stop.

Once he's on his feet, the struggle ends, but its dagger remains pierced through me, tearing through any residual joy from playing cards and destroying any peace brought by the shower's warmth. The man who was strong—who carried me on our wedding day and many nights after, who ran for miles with ease—can't even stand up on his own.

"I'm sorry," Michael says gloomily. He looks at me with flat brown eyes, hollow and pleading as they stare into me. They beg me for an answer, for a better life. Or maybe they're hoping for an end to this one.

I want to express confidence in return, but I know my expression is one of helplessness.

He holds my shoulder, the last of his energy straining through his gripping fingers. He hesitates here, allowing himself to regather a patterned breath before dropping his hand.

"Don't ever apologize. I'm sorry I didn't understand." My heart breaks as the words tumble out. If I didn't go upstairs, he wouldn't have struggled. If I didn't leave him alone, he wouldn't have had to go through that. My guilt is overwhelming.

Michael lets out a stuttered breath, "Let's go downstairs. I still have to pick out a show."

I allow him to lead the change in topic, unsure what else to do. Together, we walk downstairs, Michael leaning into me. Each step he takes is unstable, and I pray to his God that we get down the stairs without him falling. While he hobbles to the couch, Butler barks at the door, signaling the delivery of our food. I bring in the Leo's bag and unpack it at the living room coffee table. Michael adjusts the pillows behind him to provide needed support and positions the nasal prongs of the oxygen tank, shifting it until it feels comfortable.

Like his speech episode, we don't reflect on his incident upstairs. For the rest of the night, we avoid the topic. I don't need to ask to know we will be sleeping on the couch tonight, close to the oxygen tank.

"Do you think," Michael shifts his body on the couch so he's looking at me through the dark, "that God will use me to show people He can heal the sick?"

We turned the TV off a while ago and are lying head-to-head on the

L-shaped couch covered in blankets, ready to sleep. There's a blackness in his eyes, an obscurity that scares me.

"What do you mean?" I mimic his movement and scoot closer to him.

"Do you think God is bringing me to my lowest point so He can heal me? Do you think I'll be the miracle that everyone talks about?"

I take a deep breath in, feeling my eyebrows knit together, concentrating on the best way to respond. I want to tell him that if God was as good as he claimed, He wouldn't bring him down to the lowest point and induce so much suffering to prove Himself as good.

Michael's question feels different, and as I look into his lifeless eyes, an emptied well of hope, I know I have to lie.

"I think God can do anything."

SUNDAY

SEPTEMBER 24, 2017

MICHAEL IS ON THE couch with ESPN quietly creating white noise as I walk down the stairs. His eyes are closed, but his hand moves habitually across Butler's head, who leans into the couch enjoying the gentle scratches. Without even glancing in their direction, I head to the kitchen, craving a cup of coffee. The sound of my bare feet padding against the wooden floor gives my presence away.

"The leaves changed overnight," Michael calls out into the emptiness between us. His voice is frail, almost unrecognizable in its weakness.

I glance out the window. He's right; the chilly nights have convinced the leaves to change early this year, not able to wait until October. What was once greenery has now faded into bits of cool yellow and dull orange that pop between branches. The singular tree in our backyard looks lonely with its muted colors, stray leaf droppings on the grass, which is also losing its vibrance.

"Want any coffee? Decaf?" I ask, coated with bits of residual sleepiness.

"Not decaf."

Our mornings consist of small talk or silence until Michael finds the energy to sit up. Usually, he's motivated by coffee.

I brew a pot and reach into the cabinet for mugs. Rather than picking the two front ones, I sort through looking for ones that match my mood. There's a large dark blue one with the Patriots symbol on the front; I select this one for Michael knowing we'll be watching football all day. I choose a plain white mug with *Boston* scribbled on the front in cursive.

I used to not notice how much I missed the city until there was a reminder. Now, I ache for the life we had there. It haunts me in the way Michael says "draw" instead of "drawer," in the strangers at the grocery store wearing Red Sox hats, and in the poorly caffeinated coffee. I miss walking the streets with Harper on cold nights, bundled in countless layers. I miss the sound of the lapping ocean on an empty beach once the crisp air has scared everyone else away, the smell of salt that stuck to my hair. I miss when Michael was healthy.

The loud gurgling of the coffee machine has stopped. Its silence interrupts my stirring mind. I fill our mugs, add sugar to mine, then carry them over to the couch where Michael attempts to sit up.

"I'm sorry we spend all our Sundays like this." Michael shakes his head as I sit down next to him.

I place his coffee on the table and, seeing that he's still struggling, offer my hand to help him sit up. He graciously takes it but averts eye contact in embarrassment.

Once he's situated with supporting pillows on either side, I hand him his coffee. He wraps his hands around the mug, his cold fingers absorbing its warmth. Before taking his first sip, he inhales the bitter smell. Butler notices the shift in attention and repositions himself near the burning fireplace.

"Michael, this is how we've spent almost every Sunday since I met you. Coffee, church, and football. Nothing's changed."

I say this, but everything's changed. I heard his words, but I felt the pauses between them. He's not sorry for the Sunday activities, he's sorry he isn't energetic. He's sorry he doesn't get to take me out to eat at a new lunch spot. He's sorry my head has become too heavy for his chest, and he has to sit next to me instead of lying wrapped around me.

I look down, silently grieving for both of us, blowing on my coffee. Once it's cool, I curl my legs up to my chest and switch the TV from the generic commentary to YouTube.

Our Sunday morning routines still start with church, but now we watch from the comfort of our couch. Michael may feel like he's missing out, but I hold no animosity toward the change. We skip through the opening music and jump straight into the sermon.

I find this morning's message to be relatable, talking about peace and hope, kindness and graciousness. I guess it isn't hard to prey on our lack of faith, understanding, and optimism right now.

When YouTube live stream ends, Michael wants to talk about the message. He asks me to reread the passages pulled from the Bible: James 1, focused on verses 12-15. He's too weak to do it himself, so I oblige. I read the section allowed, then sit in the shared silence of Michael's thoughts until he speaks.

"Do you think this is a trial?" Michael surprises me with his heavy question. His eyes are tear-filled, and the corners of his lips are pulling down.

He's tired. Not only physically fatigued, but the driving life behind his eyes is gone. Over the last few weeks, he's lost his upbeat positivity and his desire to keep moving. He's let go of the portions of this journey that were in his control.

"What do you mean?" I ask.

"Do you think I'm supposed to prove something or that this is a test I'm supposed to pass somehow?"

I'm paralyzed. I don't know how to answer that question. I allow my thoughts to form freely on my lips without filtering them.

"I think a God that would make you prove something through cancer isn't a God worthy of worship. Based on what you've said about God, I don't think He's expecting anything more than your trust right now."

I surprise myself with my answer, and I must have shocked Michael too because he nods thoughtfully.

The screen loads an array of recommended videos, but rather than changing the channel, Michael and I both remain still.

"We should talk about what will happen when I die."

His words cause us both to flinch; even Butler's ears perk up at the harsh syllables. My eyes fill with tears, a drop falling straight down into the puddle of coffee at the bottom of my mug.

I nod and sniff my emotions back.

There's a long pause, but neither of us puts in effort to continue the conversation. Eventually, Michael gestures toward the remote, and I hand it to him so he can change the channel to the football game. We place a delivery order from our favorite Chinese restaurant without either of us circling back.

Michael talks about the score and his fantasy team, flips between the channels of the different games, fills me in on recent injuries, texts Kyle to trash talk because their teams are playing each other this week. It's encouraging to see some light pulled to the surface. The curl of his lips pulls his eyes in to join the smile, his voice rising as much as his current energy allows to yell at the players through the TV. I lay curled up next to him with my head on one of his supporting pillows. When he isn't gesturing to the TV, his hand takes its usual place on my thigh.

Michael's hungry when the food arrives. I'm glad he has an appetite, and, despite his comment, I can tell he's feeling positive today. The scent of thick grease and warm soy floats up as I open the bag. I unpack the contents onto the coffee table and get two plates from the kitchen. We open boxes of fried rice, white rice, almond boneless chicken—with no almonds—and orange chicken. There's a bag of crab rangoons, a container of steamed dumplings, and a large quart of egg drop soup. Clearly, I wasn't sure what he would be hungry for today because the table is covered in more food than the two of us eat in a week.

Full of fried rice and exhausted from his interaction with the one o'clock games, Michael sleeps through most of the next round of games. He wakes up periodically, checks the scores and his fantasy team, and drifts back to sleep.

The light from outside has disappeared before the end of the games. I let Michael rest while I attempt to clean up the leftovers and straighten up the kitchen. I haven't finished putting the dishes in the dishwasher when I hear Michael getting up, followed by Butler's nails against the wooden floor.

"You're sexy when you clean the kitchen," Michael says as he walks over to me, a slight limp in his step.

"Yeah," I scoff, "right."

"I'm serious," he laughs and kisses me once he reaches the sink. He leans against the counter next to me for inconspicuous support.

I roll my eyes, wrap my hands around his waist, and lean a small portion of my weight into his chest. His arms engulf me, and I feel his bony chin rest against the top of my head. I remain relaxed until the tension building in Michael infects me, too. I pull away to look at his face, but the purpose of the conversation is clear before he speaks.

"We need to talk about when I die."

"You're not going to die," my voice cracks.

Pain rolls through his brown eyes screaming loudly. "Let's go sit down."

"But I don't–"

"We have to talk about this."

His steps are slow, methodical in movement, as I follow him back to the couch. My legs move mechanically behind him, my mind too far off to focus on the steps I'm taking. There's a blankness that consumes me as if in shock; the world whited out around me. My lungs are frozen, unable to intake any air, but I'm not suffocating. Michael gives me life in the strange calmness he emits. He grounds me; he's my foundation. I scoot close to him on the couch, desperate for serenity.

I lose track of time as Michael presents the information he's gathered. He spends time explaining the process of transferring the car and house to my name. He tells me that he has added me as a beneficiary on all the bank accounts we don't share, including his retirement accounts. He goes over a stack of documents, some that he put together himself and others from banks and legal websites.

"Everything I've told you is in this folder, so you'll have it as a reference. You won't have to think about what's next or search for answers or help."

He passes me the thick envelope with the documents we've discussed. My weakened hands break under its heavy pressure and begin shaking.

I reach across the coffee table to set it down on the opposite side, fearing that the papers may materialize into truth if I keep them too close.

"There's an extra copy of everything in my desk," Michael says, his eyes following the folder as I slide it away, "in case something happens to this one."

"Okay."

"We have to talk about life insurance."

I look at him, confused, as my brain attempts to process what he's saying. I don't have a chance to ask any questions before he continues.

"If I die naturally, you'll get enough money to cover all your expenses for a very long time."

"What do you mean?"

"If the cancer takes me from you, you'll be taken care of."

"What's the other op—"

"If I take the pills, I don't think you'll get anything. I've put together a list of lawyers who will try to get the insurance claim accepted. But I don't think you'll win. There's enough money in my 401(k) to pay down the house and refinance to something more affordable. Take it out within the year so there's no penalty. Only take what you need; leave the rest for retirement."

"No," I cut him off, "there is no second option."

We haven't discussed the pills in the vanity, at least not out loud. One day, they just appeared, a bag with three vials left on the bathroom counter to let me know he picked them up. I put them in his top drawer as acknowledgment.

"Anna, we've talked about this." He speaks calmly, but his tears overflow, leaving wet streaks of defeat on their way down.

"No." I stand up from the couch, unable to remain still, "No, *you've* talked about it. I've listened."

"Anna." He looks at me with sad eyes and a hunched back, a tired posture.

"No, Michael."

Michael says nothing. My feet express my racing thoughts, and he watches me move from side to side across the living room, pacing in an attempt to self-comfort. I stop only feet from him as my mood shifts from wounded to furious.

"You told me you'd never leave. You don't get to choose when you fucking leave me!"

My hands fly up to cover my mouth, hearing the harshness in my words. We don't talk to each other like this.

But we don't break promises either.

Michael stares at me. He's given up. It's so easy to read on him, and yet I can't accept it. The tears are free flowing now, dropping onto the living room rug.

"You promised you'd always be here," I sniff in desperation. "You promised you'd never leave."

My hands rub harshly over my face before taking their position on my elbows again, cradling myself as my body bends over with a wail.

"I know." Michael's hands hold my arms as he guides me to the couch. He sits, then pulls me down next to him. He doesn't say anything more. He holds me against his chest, letting my tears soak through his shirt. When I begin to feel calm, a wave of fear crashes over me, and the cycle starts again.

"Why now?" I ask through tears I've lost control of.

"I just need you to know I've taken care of everything. I will always take care of you, Anna. It doesn't mean I'm not still fighting."

"Are you?" I sit up so we're eye to eye, gripping his fragile arms in my hands roughly. "Are you still fighting?"

I search his face for an answer, but I already know the truth.

THURSDAY
OCTOBER 12, 2017

I WAKE UP TO an empty bed. The pillow next to me has gone cold in the absence of Michael's heavy head. Panic strikes, and my anxiously pumping blood jolts me awake. In a swift, visceral reaction, I spring up and rush toward the bathroom, assuming I'll see Michael's thin figure curled up near the toilet. With a stomach-churning vivid imagination, I picture his body shivering and alone, shifting to escape the pain of the tile while resting his head on a rolled-up towel between bouts of coughing up bile. But when the bathroom door swings open, he isn't behind it.

"Michael?" I repeat myself twice more in the absence of an answer. The embedded alarm in my mind grows louder with each passing second.

"I'm down here!"

My mind creates the worst possible scenarios, and the thoughts take off sprinting.

Did he fall? Did his weak bones give up on his way downstairs, and he's lying helplessly on the carpet of the loft? The thoughts are horrifying because these aren't made-up scenarios; all have happened in some capacity.

I rush down the stairs with an urgency only fear can produce. When the wall breaks, I see his familiar figure in a large black sweatshirt hunched over the desk. The chair swivels toward me, revealing Michael's smiling face.

"You scared me." Tension escapes my shoulders, and my grip on the railing loosens. The breath I didn't know I was holding releases in a sigh. After a pause to reset my nervous system, I cross the room and place my hands on his shoulders, squeezing them. I glance down at the bright computer screen, trying to decipher what he's working on. My eyes look into the blue light of the screen, but the protruding bones under the gentle pressure of my hands absorb my thoughts.

"I didn't mean to. I'm sorry, babe." Still at waist level, Michael leans his head into my stomach to be cradled. I kiss the top of his drawn hood and rub his outward-facing ear between my fingers.

"You cold?" It's a rhetorical question. The answer is in his thick sweatshirt, warm flannel pants, and blanket draped across his lap.

We were warned about this at the start of chemo: how the anemia would result in Michael feeling dizzy and cold, that the hair covering his body would fall out, slowly at first then all at once, adding to the constant chill. We knew it would happen, but it was still a surprise when his shampoo-filled fingers began pulling out clumps, covered like magnets. Since stopping the treatments, his hair hasn't grown back, and his bones are no less brittle. His eyebrows are thin, his eyelashes almost obsolete. His skin and lips are a single shade of pale.

"I'm a little cold, but I turned up the heat already." He shrugs, then turns his attention back to the computer, ending the cancer-centered conversation as he often does.

"What are you doing?" I ask, eyeing the undecipherable document on the screen and the immeasurable tabs open.

"Being a second set of eyes on the Kane Garrick case."

"You don't have to help. You don't even work there anymore."

"It was my case, Anna. I was supposed to be there."

I drop it and change the subject, "Do you have an appetite this morning?"

"I could eat a little bacon." He shrugs indifferently, but I light up in excitement, kiss the top of his head again, and race downstairs to the kitchen.

I make a conscious effort not to overdo it, but the kitchen ends up filled with plates of toast with cinnamon butter, turkey bacon, scrambled eggs, fresh-cut fruit, and pancakes. I take the time to arrange it like a fancy buffet across the island countertop, adding glass cups next to bottles of apple juice and orange juice.

We've been keeping the fridge overly stocked. Most of it goes to waste, tumors causing Michael's appetite to be obsolete and stress inhibiting mine. But days like today, when Michael wakes up ready to eat, make all the trash bags filled with whole chicken pot pies and uncooked steaks worth it.

I catch Michael watching from his desk, wearing a grin of appreciation. I make a fresh pot of coffee and call to him, signaling that breakfast is ready. I try not to watch as he walks down the stairs. He grips the railing, taking caution with every step, fearing that his weak bones will crumble under his weight.

"Smells delicious," he says solely out of gratitude. I know this because I watch as he puts only one slice of toast, one piece of bacon, and two chunks of fruit on his plate. He recoils when he reaches past the eggs and pancakes. Regardless of how much space remains on his plate, I'm happy to see him eating.

"What time did you get up?" I ask from across the table, sipping my coffee and munching on bacon.

"After the sun was up for once," he smiles halfheartedly. "Figured you deserved to sleep in too."

"I needed it, thank you." I refrain from scorning him for not letting me know when he got up. He isn't in control of much, so I do my best to allow him to make inconsequential choices where he gets to.

"Paul called me about the Garrick case. It's nice to be needed at work, even if I'm not on the case officially."

He reviews the case with me, going over the first few days in court and all the details they missed. We enjoy indulging in the fictitious normalcy of everyday conversation. I missed this version of Michael.

As he speaks, I meticulously watch Michael, looking for signs of sickness. I can't pinpoint when I started doing this, only that it's now a constant internal battle not to. I focus on his lips as he talks, checking his teeth and gums when the words allow. I follow his darting eyes, looking for subconscious pleas for help and analyze the movement in his brow, searching for grimaces of pain.

After breakfast, Michael sits at a counter stool while I clean up. The plates of food look untouched. While I pile leftovers into containers, he brings up going to church in person on Sunday. I'm reluctant to agree. My hesitancy no longer comes from my disinterest but rather stems from my worry of Michael's weakened immune system. When we run simple errands, I spiral into worry, checking his temperature with fervent diligence until I'm certain he's in the clear. I can't imagine what my reaction would be after being submerged in a large congregation of germs. We don't stay on the topic of church, but every few minutes he pushes me to promise that I'll go. I scrub the dishes harder to suppress my overactive imagination and promise that I will without giving any verbal pushback.

"You're a lot more awake today." I glance over my shoulder from the sink to see Michael sitting up straight. His eyes follow my hands as I stack the hand-washed plates into the dishwasher, a habit I picked up to ensure the dishes are sanitized.

I hear his unspoken words: *you're not doing it right, that's not how you load a dishwasher, you won't be able to fit all the dishes in there if you do it that way.*

"Yeah, I haven't taken my pain meds. I need a day that isn't foggy."

"How are you feeling about Mason's birthday?"

"Is that today?" Michael rubs a hand over his bald head.

"Amber will understand if we don't go. And Mason won't even remember it," I say as I put down the towel and lean on the island across from him. I don't say anything more, giving Michael the space to think it over. The pain conveyed through his expression is palpable.

"I'm just tired," he sighs, rubbing his face.

"We don't have to go." He takes my outstretched hand in his and neither of us move as he contemplates.

"No. No, I want to. I want to see Mason today. It's not until tonight, right?"

I nod, and we both turn toward the microwave clock. I've lost track of time since I've started working from home. My boss gave me permission to skip most meetings and take on fewer projects without a pay change as long as I didn't miss any deadlines.

Michael's grown extremely weak, and I get worried about him being home on his own. I worry about the accidents that would happen if I were to lose track of time, secluded in my office. He's forgetful and sometimes does things that don't make sense, like turning on the sink and walking away or leaving the freezer door open for hours after getting ice for his water.

We spend the day lounging around the house until 3 p.m., when we start to get ready to head to Amber's house. I had completely forgotten to order a gift this week, so we stop at the store on the way there. Michael ignores my persistent request for him to stay in the car and insists on picking out the gift.

There's a renewed excitement in Michael as we pace up and down the aisles, scanning the toys. He looks like an oversized kid, standing in his ankle-length navy jogger sweatpants, hunched over the action figure boxes. He stops to pick one up and inspects it with curiosity. When he decides against it, he sets it back in its place and moves to the next one. He bounces over to the Lego section and stops in front of a large box that shows big, chunky, Marvel-themed building blocks. His face lights up as he digs through the selection, pulling out a different set for every superhero. Michael studies the sets of painted blocks spread across the store's floor. His eyes drift over each with indecision, then to me with hope. I agree to get them all with an eye roll, and he loads one of each into the cart. We find an extra-large gift bag to fit all four of them—Spider-Man, Black Panther, Captain America, and The Hulk.

When we arrive at Amber and Logan's, the house is already full of family, friends, and food. People greet Michael with caution, hesitantly shaking his hand or waving uncertainly while standing a few feet away. He's patient as he answers the repeated questions of how he's feeling in various adaptations of the truth.

Despite the number of people, there's an emptiness without Scott and Elaine. They came up last weekend to celebrate Mason's birthday. We've been avoiding seeing them in person as much as possible. It makes it harder to hide Michael's deterioration. He made the decision not to tell his family that he'd stopped chemo, a decision I chose to support despite my disagreement. I wouldn't want to look my family in the eye and tell them I was giving up either. That I was dying.

We spend time picking at the fruit and cheese trays while catching up with those who have been too nervous to come visit us at the house. I watch Michael from across the room as if waiting for something to happen. He remains on the couch most of the time, with people coming to him for conversation.

Michael was quickly integrated into Logan's group of friends. Since we moved here, they made plans together at least one night a week. Summer was spent on the golf course having a few beers and going out to dinner after. Wives and girlfriends joined them for UFC and football watch parties. But none of them have come over since Michael got sick, most haven't even called.

There's a strange feeling that manifests when someone becomes unrecognizably sick. Embarrassment is my best guess. No one has ever vocalized it to me, but I've seen it in friends and coworkers. It's as though they don't want to see someone they care about in their deteriorated state, like they don't want that to be the memory they carry with them.

Some people forgot how to interact with Michael entirely, feeling like he's a different person now that his cheekbones protrude under chalky dry skin.

I haven't been able to make sense of it over the last six months. It feels so conditional to me, like the love they have for him depends on his normalcy and ability to partake in their activities. As though he's useless without his golf swing. Like he's a different person if he doesn't have a beer in his hand.

After pizza, Amber begins corralling the small crowd into the living room. Many people choose the floor instead of sitting next to Michael on the couch. His loneliness is visible even from across the room. I'm sure he was expecting one of the men to take the free seat next to him, but they sit at arm's length, so I take the spot.

After a handful of presents, Amber passes our heavy gift bag to Logan, who has Mason on his lap. "This one is from Uncle Mikey and Auntie Anna!"

Michael sits up with the same excitement that he had in the store. An oversized smile takes up most of his face, and his eyes crinkle. Logan pulls out the boxes, opens one, and Mason bangs the blocks together in his hands. He runs over to us, waddling across the carpet, and wraps his tiny arms around each of us in a hug.

After a tough battle with his short attention span, Mason finishes opening his presents. We gather to sing "Happy Birthday" and watch Mason spit all over the cake as he blows out the candles before proceeding to each have a slice. When he gets his, he laughs and smears bright blue frosting across his face. As the night progresses, the party lulls, and people start to trickle out, concerned about their own kids' bedtime.

"We should probably head out soon," I say to Michael, loud enough for Amber to hear. Michael's begun shifting his weight restlessly on the couch and rubbing his shins, unspoken signs he's in pain. I've been happy to have a day where Michael is present, uninfluenced by narcotics, but I can tell the pain has surpassed tolerable discomfort now.

"Mason, come say goodbye!" Amber calls out. A quick response of two little feet pounding against the tile comes from the hallway. Michael lifts Mason into his lap and holds him in a hug. He whispers something into Mason's ear that makes them both laugh.

"He's so good with Mason," Amber whispers to me as I help her organize the gifts against the wall.

We both pause and watch them. Thin, brown-eyed Michael beams as he partakes in a tiny conversation with Mason, who mumbles random strings of mispronounced words. His little hands flail, mimicking Amber's movements while conversing.

Michael beams as he looks down at the small body in his lap. His wide-eyed grin mirrors the one he had the first time he met Mason.

"He looks so alive," she adds. I hear the catch in her voice but don't take my attention off Michael. I love seeing him so joyful, it's been an uncommon occurrence in the last few months and only comes in small doses. Amber's words are perfectly descriptive; Michael looks *alive* and *happy.*

We mindlessly move gifts of toys and books, both of us entranced by the two boys.

"Ready?" Michael asks me as he puts Mason down, struggling to do so smoothly. I nod as he slowly stands up from the couch.

I hug Amber and Logan goodbye at the front door.

"Take care of my little man," Michael says, pulling Amber away from their hug. He holds her shoulders, studying her face. There's a chill in the seconds he looks at her, unspoken words pouring into the space between them. She looks puzzled for a moment, then nudges him.

"Take care of my girl," Amber nods in my direction.

"She'll always be taken care of." He squeezes her shoulders then drops his arms down.

"Thank you both again for having us over!" I wave as we walk outside to the car.

Michael waves as Mason blows us a kiss.

When we get home, Michael's exhaustion is obvious. I change upstairs, bring a clean pair of sweatpants down for him, then go to the kitchen to get his pain meds together.

"I think Amber knows you're not getting chemo anymore. When she looked at you today, she seemed more sad than usual," I say hearing Michael's knees crack as he walks into the kitchen.

Two hands wrap around my waist, and I smile, feeling the familiar body against me. I reach out for the glass of water I've gotten for him, but Michael guides my arm back down.

"Just a few more minutes morphine-free," he says.

I close my eyes and let his arms encircle me. Michael's warmth tonight leaves cancer feeling distant. We sway from side to side silently, letting the stress of the day wash out like we used to.

"I miss dancing in the kitchen," I say.

"I don't miss your music at all."

We both laugh and allow time to pass without care. The heaviness of our bodies sinks into the other's. When we're this close, I can feel the stress dissipate; the beating of his heart removes my worries one at a time. I hope Michael feels the same, that I provide a comfortable safety for him, too.

We drift carelessly into the freedom of the moment, forgetting about the active battle of lost minutes banging on our door and the fear of living on borrowed time.

"I love you," Michael says tenderly.

I keep my eyes closed and let his words absorb into me, "I love you."

"Let's stay like this for a while."

FRIDAY

OCTOBER 13, 2017

THE FAINT SMELL OF a breakfast buffet spills over from my dreams into the bedroom. My arms stretch over my head, then to Michael's side of the bed—except he isn't there. My eyes flutter as they open, adjusting to the light pouring in from behind the curtains. When they dart to the empty spot next to me, I notice the comforter is made up on his side of the bed.

When I realize the smell isn't from my dreams, I inhale the aroma to wake up my brain. I slip on one of Michael's sweatshirts, softened by years of use, and bounce down the stairs, still groggy.

Michael's in the kitchen with his back to me, standing over the stove in a shirt that falls off his shoulders and pants that slip down despite being tied tightly around his waist.

As his thin arms shift a wooden spoon around a pan, his head hangs strenuously; I can't tell whether it's out of fatigue or concentration.

"Morning." I sneak under his arm, sticking myself between Michael and the stove, and breathe in the greasy smell of bacon.

"Hey sleepyhead." Michael's lips push into my tousled hair.

"What's all this?" I point to the array of food on the stove. There are eggs and bacon cooking simultaneously, and fresh-squeezed orange juice on the counter.

"I had extra energy this morning. I haven't cooked for you in months." Michael shrugs when he says this, but he blushes, and I kiss his arm—the only part of him at eye level—in gratitude. He puts the spoon down and spins me around with more strength than I thought he had.

"Breakfast with my husband two days in a row," a grin takes over my cheeks. "I'm spoiled."

Michael and I spent months watching his health rapidly decline, but lately it's been on the rise. Dr. Graham's prognosis doesn't fall on deaf ears, but it's impossible not to hope that his unexpected increase in energy and appetite suggests that he's getting better.

Maybe he will be the miracle everyone talks about.

"I'll set the table." As I go to step away, he holds me for a second longer.

Michael is chatty over breakfast, his face lighting up when we talk about Mason's birthday last night. He tells me repeatedly how much it meant to him that Mason loved his presents and that he had so much fun picking out the perfect gift. I bring up the presents we can get him for Christmas, but Michael changes the subject; I assume out of fear that he'll be missing it.

"You have that meeting at work today, right?"

"Yeah, it's in the office later this afternoon. I was thinking about picking up dinner after work if you're hungry."

"That sounds like a good plan." Michael's smile disappears, and he dips his head down.

"I can stay here though. They're recording it, so I can watch it later tonight."

"No, you go in. You need to see your coworkers. I'll think of what to eat for dinner."

"Are you still helping on the Garrick case?" I try to turn the conversation.

"I sent Paul my notes yesterday. I think he's got the rest."

Michael's mood is somber while we finish our meal, and his sentences are short. I can't help but feel like it's my fault for having to leave, but he urges me to go to the meeting multiple times. I cling to the hope that after a nap he'll be peppy again, the old Michael.

After cleaning up what's left of breakfast, I don't have much time before I need to leave for the office. Michael wants to sit with me while I get ready, so I use the guest bathroom off the loft to limit the number of stairs he has to go up.

I end up applying much less makeup than I used to, just a light neutral shade of brown eyeshadow and a little mascara and blush. I skip foundation and eyeliner completely. It's been a while since I've worn makeup, and it looks different than I remember.

Michael sits quietly in his desk chair, watching me as I lean closer to the mirror for inspection. Mascara dots my eyelid and the eyeshadow looks forced.

From my periphery, I watch Michael smile, but it fades quickly. I wonder if he's remembering the way I used to look when I had the energy to make myself more presentable.

"I really don't have to go in," I sigh. Michael looks so frail. The chair swallows his shrunken frame.

"You can't stay here," Michael replies. I hold out my hand as an offer to help him down the stairs. He accepts it with a defeated expression.

Michael leans into me. I'm surprised how light he's become every time I bear his weight. We take each step one at a time, my heels clacking together when we drop down to the next one.

"I can if you want me to."

Guilt bubbles up from my depths as I watch him shuffle to the couch and reattach his oxygen cannula. He's too weak to be left alone, even for a of couple hours. What if something happens? What if he needs me?

"Come here." He pats the cushion next to him.

"Hi," I whisper. I plop down and lean into him for a kiss. He takes the oxygen tube away from his nose before kissing me slowly. His lips are weak against mine.

"Hi," Michael repeats with a smile and holds my face in his palm. He kisses me over and over, pausing to look at me between each one.

"What's that for?" I giggle, enjoying his extra affection.

"You're just beautiful. I'm so lucky." Tears begin to form, but he regains his posture before they fall. "I love you."

"I love you," I say, kissing him one last time. "See you later."

I'm exhausted from the meeting by the time I get back into my car. Hours of listening to upcoming changes in the new year left us all nervous as we walked out of the office. Did the changes mean they'd be letting people go? Would I be the first to get laid off since they'd been so lenient with me for so long?

I'm craving pizza, my comfort food, and my mouth waters the whole drive home thinking about it. I debate stopping to get takeout but decide against it. Michael's appetite is so unpredictable, and I'd rather we get whatever he's in the mood for tonight.

"Babe?" I call into emptiness from the front door. I lean my weight against the wall as I slip my shoes off. "Do you want pizza? I'm starving!"

The lack of an immediate greeting by Michael and Butler worries me. I haven't been leaving often, but, when I do, Michael never fails to meet me at the door with a welcoming kiss and open arms that fold into a tight embrace. Butler is always quick to follow, bouncing up my leg, trying to get between us in an adorable fit of jealousy.

"Hey, you in the shower?" I call louder.

Silence.

"Michael?" I check my phone to make sure he didn't go out with Logan or Amber to run errands. No calls, no texts. The silence of the house fuels my fear. I rationalize that if Butler isn't greeting me, they must have gone out.

He's okay, I repeat in my mind. I force a swallow, pushing down the storm of spiraling thoughts, and let out a slow, shaky breath. *He's probably outside.*

I walk toward the back door to check if he took Butler outside for fresh air, but I stop short after noticing it's locked from the inside. I do a quick sweep of the loft and my office before climbing up the wooden stairs to the third floor, thinking he must be in the shower.

"Hey babe, I–"

The minute my foot crosses the threshold into the bedroom, I can feel the overtaking chill of stale air. A bone-penetrating cold fills the space and sends a shiver down my spine, raising the hair on my arms. Despite the daytime sounds that stream into the house from the surrounding streets, the room is silent—a vacuum for sound, a void that swallows everything except the heartbeat pounding in my ears.

My other foot crosses over into the room. I don't freeze or halt dramatically. My body comes to a gentle stop. The air expels from my lungs without refilling. My pulse slows. I can feel every second as it passes. The clock on the wall lets me know time is still moving: *tick, tick, tick.*

Michael is lying flat on top of our tan comforter, a Bible placed at his side and a cross necklace threaded between his fingers, which are interlocked on his chest. A mostly full glass of water and three empty medicine bottles sit on the nightstand, their lids placed next to them.

His feet splay to the side, unopposed gravity pulling on his legs so they fall apart. He lies motionless—lifeless, too still to be breathing. His chest doesn't rise and fall. It creates a concave shape in the absence of air. There is no blood pumping under his skin. It's faded of color now and taken on a pale, grayish-blue hue and is pulled tightly over the bones in his cheeks and chin. His mouth has fallen open, leaving his appearance zombie-like. His eyes are closed, and his face lacks the familiar grimace that clung to him like a parasite even while he slept. He looks more peaceful than I imagine he felt.

If my stubborn mind has any reservations, Butler convinces me of the truth as he sits at the end of the bed, resting his weight on Michael's feet. His eyes wander up to me, but his head doesn't move, and his tail doesn't wag.

I can see Michael, just a few hours ago, smiling over breakfast, his toothy grin pushing on his cheeks. I can feel the hug he gave me this morning before I left, the tightness of the embrace that lasted a minute longer than usual.

The facts sink in slowly, like film flashing in bursts across a projector screen. Their intensity crushes me, and I catch myself against the wall before stumbling forward. I fall into him when I reach the bed. His arm is like soft, pitting ice against my sweating forehead. A shock rushes through me when our skin meets, but there's a tugging exhaustion that prevents me from jumping away.

Reality is inhaled in thick breaths, and sorrow is expelled in heavy tears. I dig my face into his chest and cry loudly, wailing into the chamber of silence. Butler doesn't respond; his eyes remain closed, and I know that he understands what I still can't.

I burrow my head into the space beneath his chin and sob with no restraint. At some point, I unfolded his hands because one of them is now clutched in mine. I rub his wedding ring with my free finger, whispering helplessly that I love him.

Maybe I should, but I don't rush to call 911. I don't want him to leave yet.

I'm not sure when I pick up my phone, who I call first, or when I walk downstairs.

The moon is high in the sky. An ambulance is pulling into our driveway with no siren, without the bright flickering lights.

There's a lapse of distorted time as strangers rush past me carrying a stretcher up the stairs. Amber cries in my arms while holding me to provide solace for both of us.

I remain an iceberg, immobile but melting in the heat of the pandemonium that moves in a fast, colorless blur around me. Police cars arrive, illuminating the street in blue and red; neighbors flick on porch lights as they peer out their windows and step into their front yards; Amber's broken voice pierces through the haze as she hysterically makes calls to all the people I can't. My phone floods with calls and texts from Michael's parents, Miller, Harper, Kyle, extended family, and friends. I answer none of them.

A hand on my back escorts me to the front yard while people in uniforms go inside.

I make no choices in the passing hours. I'm pushed around by the outcome of Michael's actions and move only when directed to. My cheeks are wet, but I can't feel the tears fall. I can't look around, can't take in what's happening. I only see the things that pass in front of my direct field of vision as I stare blankly at the front door. Part of me still waits for Michael to walk out.

There's a blanket around me; I don't know if the paramedics put it there or if it was something Amber did. Police officers ask me questions with yes or no answers. My head shakes or nods.

Michael rests securely on the stretcher as two men carry him toward the ambulance's open doors.

Suddenly, life is clear, the haze lifted, and my stunned silence breaks as I let out a raspy cry. My legs give up, collapsing my body, dropping down to my knees. They sink into the cold dirt. My fingers dig into the partially frozen grass, but I feel nothing. A visceral whine wails through the night, both familiar and unrecognizable, screaming out the name I've spoken in so many different tones, seeped in countless emotions. All of them except this because his name was never supposed to be coated with so much pain.

After the knees of my pants have soaked up the ground's dampness, I feel familiar hands attempting to pick me up. Amber's messy brown hair falls over her face as she grunts to lift my limp body. I throw myself forward out of her arms, lunging and screaming for Michael and falling back into the mud, my nails finding their place in the dirt.

Michael had those medications for months. There had been no recent talk of picking a day, no admissions of struggling with the idea of death, no signs that he wasn't doing okay, no mention of the orange bottles hiding in his drawer at all. His mood had improved; his demeanor had lightened; glimpses of his radiant, positive spirit I'd missed had started to return.

My mind flashes to Dr. Graham's caution. Patients who pursue physician-assisted suicide frequently have a burst of energy and joy. With the control given back to them, they feel free. There's a sense of false hope. She warned that although the medication provides regained control and the fear of death is temporarily lifted, it doesn't eliminate the original reason for seeking it.

I forgot to heed the warning.

MONDAY
OCTOBER 23, 2017

I STARE INTO THE wooden casket, the room's suffocating silence broken only by the sound of the stale air blowing from the vents above.

The walls, an off-white color that makes them look dirty, provide a void that absorbs any exterior sounds, allowing my heartbeat to pulse in my ears. I can hear each unevenly spaced breath as it enters my expanding lungs, muffled as though I'm underwater, internally loud but still disconnected. I keep sinking.

The room feels small, and the illusion that it's shrinking messes with my head. There is a slew of outdated furniture spread across the room. The decorations would feel archaic in any other setting, but they're fitting here.

I keep my eyes focused on the cold body lying level with my waist.

Joy has been pulled out of me, and my heart writhes out of beat in its absence. Between the waves of gut-wrenching sorrow and the seconds that I remember he's gone, my body is numb in a way I've never had the horror of experiencing. The air has been sucked from my lungs. I'm gasping for breath, drowning in an overly oxygenated room, feeling suffocated by my life source.

When I lost my mom, I knew my life would be permanently changed; I knew there would be no day comparable to the ones before. As abnormal as it was, under self-injurious and detrimental addictive circumstances, losing a parent is the natural progression of life. It happened sooner than what's natural, but I continued to grow and moved out when I turned eighteen like I would have regardless. A striking pain rooted itself in me with the loss of her, an active pain that still haunts me. But nothing is comparable to losing the person you chose to spend your life with. I have nowhere to go that Michael hasn't touched because he's all over me. I have no home to go back to without him.

I stare down, unsure what I'm supposed to feel. Tears hang like weights behind my eyes, and I know I will remain forever paralyzed in this moment.

I stand with both hands firmly gripping the edge of the wood next to Michael, willing the tears to freeze with me. I can feel myself applying unwarranted pressure to remain poised, but Michael would have stayed composed; he was so good at being strong for everyone else.

Was.

It's just me and him in the big, empty, echoing space that dozens of other bodies have been displayed in before him. I'm grateful for the time we get, the two of us. There's so much I want to say, and I cover myself in loathing when the words refuse to form on my lips. It's the last time I'm ever going to see Michael, have him in front of me physically where he's within my reach to touch and hold. But he took the opportunity to hear me while he was alive by not warning me.

"Hey, Anna?"

I don't move at first. Completely overtaken by exhaustion, I'm convinced I haven't heard anything.

I turn around when I finally register my name and process the gentle, familiar voice.

"Anna, sweetie, can I get you something to eat?" Harper stands patiently in the doorway, looking at me with the only expression I can't find fault in. There's no pity, but it isn't nonchalant either, no pretension that the world hasn't changed.

I manage to shake my head. I want to respond but I'm too scared to shift the focus of my energy away from my feet working in conjunction with my legs to keep me standing.

"Anna, you've been standing there for two hours." Harper allows time for me to absorb her sentence but continues on when she receives only a blank stare in return. "I'll be back with a water and some food from the buffet."

Outside of immediate family, Harper has made the biggest contributions to the funeral. She took on the role of director at the funeral home owned by her dad about a year ago. Without anyone asking, she volunteered the building, located right outside of Boston, and a catered buffet free of charge. I was thankful someone thought to provide a place where people could share memories of Michael. I never would have thought of food, and even if I had, I wouldn't have gotten enough. There's an insurmountable difference in the number of visitors for someone young and full of life compared to someone at the natural end of theirs.

Harper disappears. I continue to stand, doing my best to organize my thoughts into a cohesive string. It's like merging the spaghetti bowl of highways into one lane.

I check my watch. It's close to 8 p.m.

The viewing ended after six hours, around 4 p.m., and Harper closed the doors at 6 p.m. once everyone had trickled out from the service—which she also arranged with the help of Scott and Elaine. She escorted Michael's family to their cars, and I'm sure provided a level of relief when promising to take care of me.

And now I have been standing here for almost two hours, she was right. I haven't said anything or moved or allowed myself to cry. In an sudden realization of exhaustion, my legs give out, and I slide down the table that holds the casket. My body stays in shock: at the time that's escaped, at the now empty room that was full of people just hours ago, at my cold husband who lies inches from me.

What have I been doing for two hours?

Harper shuffles in with a plate of food, a water bottle, and a can of ginger ale. She notices my new position and seamlessly moves from the doorway to sit cross-legged next to me as if that were her plan all along.

Saying nothing, she picks a cucumber off the top of the salad on the plate and extends it to me. I take a bite, letting it disintegrate in my mouth, lacking motivation to move my jaw to chew. After forcing myself to swallow the slice, I reach for the ginger ale to wash it down. My mouth is dry, almost metallic tasting. I fear this is what death tastes like.

We sit together in silence for a very long time.

"Remember when we went to Michael's parents for the Fourth of July? Michael came up to me panicked and drunk, telling me you weren't going to like the ring, but he refused to show it to me. He knew I couldn't keep it a secret. He was totally consumed by it. I think that's the only time I'd ever seen him frantic."

I say nothing, picturing the holiday she's referring to. I'd spent enough time at his parents' house by July to extend my invite to Harper. There were plans for Amber to fly into Boston even though Logan couldn't make it; she was more than halfway through her pregnancy at that point. Michael, Harper, and I picked her up from the airport, and we spent the night indulging in too much alcohol, playing card games that are easier sober. Amber, the only one out of the four of us not drinking, spent hours trying to teach us euchre before we all gave up. Elaine and Scott made beds for everyone around the house, so we didn't have to go back home. They didn't let Michael and me sleep together, as if they didn't know we shared a room almost nightly.

"Anyways," Harper interrupts my close-eyed imagination with a pinched voice, "it was so early in the relationship, but I didn't question it. You guys had only been together for like six months. He didn't tell me when he was going to propose but I knew the two of you would end up together. I don't think I ever told you that."

Sometimes I forget that other people loved him, that they're mourning him too. Despite the never-ending sea of crying people who had come to the funeral, today has been one of those times.

I lean my head against Harper's shoulder and grab her hand from her lap to interlock fingers.

"I'm sorry for your loss." I squeeze her hand, letting the tears fall unrestrained. She takes a big breath in, attempting to muffle her crying.

We sit unmoving, palm in sweaty palm, for a long time.

My head slips forward off Harper's shoulder suddenly, and I'm jerked awake without even realizing I had fallen asleep.

"Shit," I gasp.

Harper's still awake and gives me a melancholy smile as I rub my face. Flakes of mascara fall onto my fingers, and I'm reminded of the entirety of the long day, almost forgetting for half a second. I close my eyes again, hoping that maybe this time I'll wake up to Michael, or maybe I just won't wake up.

"I'm going home. Do you want to come?"

I contemplate her offer for a minute, then shake my head.

"Okay, these are the keys. If you leave, make sure you lock up. I'll leave the side door at my place open."

I nod, noticing her choice of words, using *if* and not *when.*

I come up short trying to think of something to say that expresses how thankful I am not only for today but for the hours it took her to plan the funeral. For her hours of preparation and for taking care of all the minuscule but important details my brain never could have been decisive enough for. For choosing a picture for the small remembrance cards and a second one for the thank-you cards, picking out a casket, and putting together a slideshow of pictures that highlighted Michael's liveliness. For selecting the most beautiful flowers and placing them in an even more eloquent arrangement. For taking care of his transportation to Boston, scheduling his cremation, and picking out the perfect urn.

As much as I try, I can't find the right words. Nothing is heavy enough to describe the gratitude I hold in this moment.

"Thank you," is all that comes out, spoken with a tired, wavering voice and a head shake. I don't even try to smile.

I watch her from my spot on the carpet as she stands and collects the untouched plates she brought me. With the best attempt at a smile, she places a kiss through the hair on the top of my head. When our eyes meet, she gives the same faultless expression she wore earlier. Harper doesn't say anything more. She scoots the unopened water toward me before disappearing through the doorway.

The door closes, trapping the silence again, taking up monstrous space in the still air around me. My stomach drops and a cold sweat drains the blood from my face as the quiet of the room allows thoughts of reality to sneak in. I jump up in disbelief; Michael can't be the body that lies in the casket.

I close my eyes only to see the memory of Kyle's bright blue ones, contrasted against their red protruding veins. He approached me today with arms wide and folded me into a heavy hug, unable to contain his tears. He held onto me, his whole body shaking. I think of his desperate need for me to comfort him while he was attempting to do the same for me. I'm not sure which of us was holding the other up under his profuse apologies, brokenness flooding his voice. I can't forget his swollen face, his cheeks more flushed than when Michael and I stood next to him at his own dad's funeral. I don't know if he pulled away or if someone interrupted us, but I never wanted to let go.

I picture Mason's two little legs running around the feet of his mourning parents, between the legs of weeping family members. I can hear the questions repeating from his innocent lips, heavy on Amber as she grieved her brother—*Is he sleeping? Why are people crying? Will Uncle Mikey come over for Christmas? Where will Santa leave his presents?* I can hear Amber's answers, lying with the truth, before Logan took it upon himself to be Mason's distraction. I think he found relief and control in having a tangible task. Because how do you explain death to a toddler?

I can see the four men from Michael's golf league who flew into Boston. They walked with their heads hanging, waiting their turn to be next to him, to see him for the last time. The tall one, Jim, reached into the pocket of his dress pants and pulled out a ball to place next to Michael's shoulder. The way he paused over Michael's folded hands, hesitating before grabbing them in his own. How he came to me and held my hands, shaking them in disbelief, saying a million words of support through tight silent lips, too shocked to part them. The other saddened faces prevented their eyes from finding the casket, too pained to look at Michael as they passed.

I open my eyes now to look down at the discolored version of my husband, realizing that I haven't looked at him all day. I may have stood beside him, referenced him in conversation, and thanked his people for the roles they had played in his life. I referred to him all day, socialized as if it were a work party, as if he were standing there beside me engaged in another conversation or he'd gone to get a drink, as if he'd be right back.

Because he lacks enough hair for the style he used to have, shaggy but poised, his forehead looks more square than it should be. His skin is flush against his cheekbones but not quite as tight as the last time I saw him. He droops the corners of his mouth, forming a frown I'd never seen him wear, with lips thinner than they're supposed to be. His posture is so still and inaccurate, it looks unnatural. His arms are tucked in tightly, and his hands sit on top of one another in the center of his chest. He looks uncomfortable in a dark gray suit I've never seen before, placed in such an awkward position. I scan my eyes from his waist, disappearing in the closed half of the coffin, up to his lips, which lie unmoving.

Despite everyone attempting false positivity by saying otherwise, he doesn't look good. He doesn't look like himself, not before he got sick nor after.

The agonizing cry piercing my ears surprises even me. It comes from deep inside, leaking out into a guttural howl that's harsh against the silence.

My mourning rises and falls like waves, getting louder and more desperate before drifting into hiccups drawn out by pain.

I lean into Michael's body and bury my head in his chest. Part of me instinctively waits for his hand to reach up and caress my head, to pull me into the safety of his embrace. I long for his comfort, will him to promise I'll be okay, that he's okay. The thoughtful begging becomes verbal pleading between sobs that grow deeper.

But I am the only breathing person in the building. Never again will he hold me together, protect me in his arms, breathe comforting promises over me. His cold body in front of me is proof of the inevitable. Silence is my new assurance.

I exhaust myself and curl into the fetal position on the carpet below him. I cry until I drain myself, until I don't have energy left to cry, then remember I will never hear him say my name again. The cycle restarts, then repeats.

THURSDAY
OCTOBER 26, 2017

BOSTON IS A CITY PLAGUED by Michael's ghost. Years of memories soaked into each neighborhood, every street infected. The last week has flown by, despite every minute dragging on. It's been days since the funeral, and although I nodded along to many one-sided conversations and accepted ample food drop-offs, it's hard to recall where all the time went.

Harper housed me for the majority of my time in Boston—she insisted, and I didn't push back. As much as I wanted to be there for Elaine, I couldn't stay with her and Scott. Being in the house Michael grew up in felt unbearable—sleeping on a pillow that once held his face, sitting at the table where he ate countless childhood dinners, sipping coffee while memories of him echoed off the walls.

Harper owns a house about twenty minutes outside of the city. It's small, but the structure holds beautiful architecture. She's spent a lot of time and money modernizing what she can, adding granite countertops and large beams scaling the living room ceiling. The yard is small but well-kept, and the grass is surprisingly green for this time of year. There's a vegetable garden on the side of the house that shows signs of a successful summer crop.

Harper had shown me the upgrades on FaceTime throughout the process, but, in the year she has owned the house, I've only been out to visit once. Despite the circumstances, it was exciting to see the improvements in person. I loved hearing stories of the many mistakes made during the reconstruction process.

Harper provided good company but acted as an even better distraction. She would put on the most recent season of whatever trash TV she was keeping up with. Without fail, we would talk through the episodes about nothing in particular, an act of normalcy I wasn't expecting with grief cemented to me. She told me stories about Jonah, the man she started dating seriously about six months ago. I had heard about him over phone calls, but my mind was always focused on Michael, so I remembered little to nothing about Jonah. She told their story from the beginning; I assume she knew I'd been distracted the first time. She shared his cute quirks and funny habits as we filled ourselves with popcorn and red wine.

After a couple of nights of just Harper and me, we included Jonah. His presence brought peace with a masculine energy. He was attentive and responsive to Harper's needs and, in turn, mine as well.

He wasn't as energetic as Harper, but he listened with the same deep intensity and easily kept up conversation. He was responsible, cleaning the kitchen or restocking random foods when he noticed them missing. He'd sneak coasters beneath cold glasses on her soft wood coffee table and put leftovers in containers rather than leaving them out on the counter.

The small things didn't go unnoticed by me, and there was a comfort in knowing Harper was being taken care of.

Jonah's gentleness acted as a reminder for me that Harper was also feeling affected by Michael's absence, although she hid it well around me. Clouded with intense brain fog throughout the duration of the day, it was usually Jonah's visits that reminded me to reach out to check in on others.

When Jonah wasn't there, Harper made a clear effort to take care of me. She refilled my water glass anytime she noticed it was low and always made breakfast despite having left it untouched the day before. At night, she would crawl into bed with me, hearing my cries of desperation seep through the walls. I'd see the light from the hallway spill into the darkness and feel the bed move before her hand met my back, rubbing side to side in silent comfort.

When Elaine and Scott volunteered to drive me back to Michigan, my first thought was to say no, feeling a pressure to remain positive the whole drive. The idea of this expectation fled when I realized their emotions likely mirrored mine, and I agreed to be their passenger.

With the valid excuse of helping Amber out with Mason, Elaine and Scott reserved a hotel room in town. It was reasonable that they would want to be close to Amber right now, and I assumed they'd be checking in on me, too.

Although I didn't want the company, I knew I would probably need it. So would Elaine.

After spending last night loading up the car and eating a quick, early morning breakfast in silence, the three of us began our venture to the Midwest.

The car has been quiet for most of the drive. Elaine and Scott make casual conversation with each other but give me space in the back seat. I spend most of the ride with my eyes closed or distract myself with games on my phone. Every so often, I ask them to turn up the radio and hum along as we cross state lines.

I search my memories, looking for fragments of forgotten moments from the last time I made this drive. Michael's arm drooping across the van's empty center to keep his hand on my leg. The food stops, stretching our aching legs, Michael yawning loudly with his back arching dramatically, my body warming with his goofiness. Breaks for Butler when it was so dark he'd disappear at the end of the leash into the unlit grass patches of the rest stop. Conversations overflowing with the excitement for the life we were building—so much hope in the future ahead of us. So many promises left empty.

I miss the feeling of his fingertips pressing into my thigh. I miss his laugh. I miss our silence.

This road is now tainted. The hours of the route drenched in sadness where life, hope, and imagination once flourished. I never want to make this drive again.

Sometime after the third stop, somewhere in Ohio, Elaine attempts to fill the darkened car with conversation.

"It would be nice to get dinner this week, once we're all settled in. There are so many good Lebanese restaurants near you."

"That sounds like a good idea," Scott encourages, reaching for her hand.

I'm not in the mood to talk. My thin body is curled up beneath a heap of blankets in the back seat, struggling to find warmth. I'm exhausted at the thought of conjuring words to keep up a conversation. I wish I had closed my eyes earlier so I could pretend to be asleep, but it's too late now.

"Amber has so many recommendations. Do you have any favorites, Anna?" Elaine turns toward the backseat where I stare back at her, drawing a complete blank on the names of the restaurants we frequent.

"Amber knows the places we like," I sigh.

We. If Elaine catches the slip, she doesn't acknowledge it.

Elaine turns back, catching Scott's eyes momentary, then stares out the windshield.

"Do you have any plans for when we get back?" she attempts to continue the conversation as she fiddles with the silver bracelets on her wrist.

Mourning my husband.

"No plans."

"We're happy to fill in any free time you have. We can bring Mason over to give Amber and Logan a little break."

I say nothing.

"She doesn't live too far from you," Scott chimes in, mirroring Elaine's endeavored optimism.

"Maybe you and Logan can take Mason and let the three of us have a spa day," Elaine suggests, turning her attention to Scott. She looks back at me, "That could be fun."

Fun.

The car goes silent.

"Amber always brags about the apple orchards. I think it will be good to stay busy," Elaine continues, filling the space to mask her discomfort.

I, again, remain speechless.

"Anna, you can show us around. We haven't gotten to spend much time in Michigan."

Anger rushes to my cheeks. I take a deep breath only to inhale more frustration.

"We should put something concrete on the calendar. It would be good to have something to look forward to."

"I don't want to make plans, Elaine. My whole life has changed!" I spring up, hearing the echo of my anger bounce off the inside of the car.

Scott flinches, and Elaine closes her mouth.

I take a deep breath to erase the disrespect from my tone before continuing, feeling Michael's nudge even in his absence, "My whole world is different. I don't want to go to the apple orchards. I don't even want to be alive."

Warm beads of sadness streak my face. My words become desperate, pain overwhelming me.

"Hasn't your life changed? How can you even think about going out to eat? How can you think about fun? Hasn't your world changed too?"

"My whole world was taken from me," Elaine's voice cracks.

My jaw drops in preparation to apologize, but she cuts me off before anything comes out.

"Anna, you're all that's left of my world. You're all that's left of him."

Scott's hand crosses from the steering wheel toward Elaine, and he wraps his fingers around hers. She bows her head, accepting his hand, and looks to the window. Although I can't see from the backseat, I assume she's hiding her tears.

Of course, her life has changed too. How selfish to think that it hasn't, that Elaine's attempt to make plans is genuine and not a coping mechanism to cover up the pain of her own. I feel terrible. Michael would be so disappointed.

I reach forward, gently resting my fingers on the shoulder of Elaine's sweater.

"We know," Scott says before I can even open my mouth, "Anna, we know."

Forgiven before I can even ask.

I wake up with the slow roll of the car as it turns down a familiar-sounding street. I sit up and lean on my side with one weak arm holding me high enough to confirm the houses through the window.

The streetlights illuminate the road in the absence of the moon and paint stripes across the stiff leather of the back seat.

Scott has two hands properly placed on the wheel, but his knuckles are white; his grip gives away the intensity of his emotions. Elaine extends a hand from the passenger side, gripping Scott's arm.

As we slowly drive toward the end of Bird Avenue, the passing streetlights highlight the dampness of Elaine's cheek.

We pull into the driveway of the third house from the end. The car in the driveway deceives me momentarily, and, for a fleeting second, I think Michael may be home. Grief quickly reminds me that he's not.

What was once considered home, an accomplishment to be proud of, now towers eerily, reaching toward the sky. There are no lights on to brighten the daunting darkness behind the windows, and the emptiness is evident.

Scott turns off the car once it's in park, leaving us all sitting in still, quiet air, holding our breaths. Memories flicker through my thoughts, picturing Michael standing at the front door, tall and strong, the version of him that was full of life.

I imagine that in the front seat, Elaine is picturing him as he once was—a sweet, loving boy, no taller than her hip. Scott is lost in a distant scene of a hot summer evening, tossing the baseball to a teenage Michael. Maybe Michael's older, growing stronger and challenging Scott's athleticism in a way that makes a dad quietly proud.

I have no way of knowing what images are passing in their minds. I don't have access to those memories. And now I won't ever hear them from Michael's perspective.

"I don't think I can do this alone," my voice catches. It hangs in the still air, dangling freely, waiting to be rescued. My words pull Elaine from her daydream, a parallel life where her son lives. She removes her hand from

Scott, releasing her grip, and wipes away tears I hadn't noticed falling.

"I didn't realize you had woken up."

"Will you come with me?" Desperation and exhaustion cover my question.

"Of course," Elaine shakes her head, letting go of whatever was replaying in her mind. She looks at Scott, his unwavering stare glued forward, hands still fastened to the steering wheel. His red eyes brim with tears that threaten to overflow.

Neither Elaine nor I move immediately. When I find the courage, I inch across the back seat and push the weight of the door open. I hear Elaine's car door open as mine shuts.

"One step at a time," I say to myself. Elaine takes my hand in hers.

We both stop short of the front door. Less than a week ago, a new, angry reality hit us as we stared down into a casket that held Michael's body. But somehow, opening this door seems to finalize the truth. I wonder if this feeling will go away. Will my life ever feel real, or will each new day without him feel like a surrender of defeat?

"One step at a time," Elaine repeats back, meant to encourage us both.

I rub my thumb over the keypad where Michael's fingers lingered just a week ago, then enter his birthday: 0619. The lock groans as it retracts.

The door swings open, letting the crisp October air flood into the stale space. The first step feels impossible. My subconscious holds onto the idea that if I don't go in, I won't have to step into my new life without Michael. As though he can still live within the walls of the house if I leave it undisturbed. The rolling tears burn my eyes, anger bubbles in my chest, and confusion stems from a fleeting reality I can't catch.

I look to Elaine, who continues to stare straight ahead. I imagine she's facing the same invisible wall. Crossing the threshold of the doorframe, the very first step, takes us both time. We do it together, not needing to look at each other or do a countdown; we can feel when we're both ready.

My knees give out immediately. I collapse on the rug in the entryway. My mouth drops open and releases an animalistic cry which echoes up the empty floors and boomerangs back down to us. The brokenness of my own scream sparks an internal pain, unlocking compassionate self-pity within me.

Elaine flinches following the booming echo, and her hands fly up to her face in the same level of despair. Within the minute Scott is there, holding Elaine, pulling her close to his chest. The sound of them crying is foggy, jaded, and buried in space as though I'm underwater, a world away.

The absence of Michael fights back, screaming evidence of his presence in a pair of slippers tossed near the door, the iPad that holds his fantasy team lineup set neatly on the coffee table, and a pile of court documents on the counter from a case he reviewed. Two dirty mugs sit next to the sink from the hot chocolate we had what feels like only nights ago.

The air filling my lungs feels toxic. I start heaving, the breaths passing in and out too quickly to catch. Panic flows through my blood, overwhelming my system.

Scott closes the space between us. He lifts me up on my feet, holds my weight in his arm wrapped around my waist, then grabs Elaine's hand with his free one. He leads us both to the couch, where we fold into the cushions.

The night becomes a blur of tears cried in front of the fireplace, flipped on to ease the unshakable chill that has set in. Elaine and I weep while Scott cares for us with selfless sympathy. He brings us toilet paper rolls for tissues and provides as much support as he can between his own painful, tear-ridden exhales.

I jerk my head toward him with every movement. His mannerisms are almost identical to Michael's as he rubs a single hand up and down his reddened face. This reignites my crying, leaving a once-happy memory scarred.

I've crossed the threshold of the door without him.

THURSDAY
NOVEMBER 16, 2017

"I'M ON MY WAY over," Elaine says through the phone, "I'll be there in a few minutes."

"See you soon," I reply and end the call.

I pace across the hardwood with bare feet, hearing my steps echo throughout the lifeless house.

Elaine volunteered to help me write the addresses on the envelopes for the thank-you cards. Harper sent us back to Michigan with prewritten cards to mail out and the large book signed by anyone who attended the funeral. I didn't realize we'd need to send thank-you cards. I wasn't prepared for the funeral to be so drawn out.

Elaine lets herself in, carrying a reusable grocery tote filled with fresh fruit, various cheeses, and crackers. She sets the bag on the counter then removes her jacket and scarf and trades her shoes for the house slippers she keeps here.

When she's shaken the November chill, she greets me with a tight hug. While I unbag the groceries, Elaine sets a cutting board and knife on the island countertop. She washes her hands, meticulously lays out the cheeses, then slices them purposefully. I set up the dining room table, placing Michael's urn on the far side opposite where we'll be sitting.

Elaine takes time to arrange the fruit, cheese, and crackers on platter but there's a bleakness in her posture. Usually she's a bright presence, but today she's dulled.

"I was only planning to get a cheese and cracker tray, but the fruit looked too good to pass up, especially for this time of year. And I've been craving brie, so I thought we'd make one of our own."

"It looks great," I say, trying to sound appreciative.

Elaine brings the tray to the table, and we sit across from each other in silence at first. Her hands shake as she opens a couple of the card boxes, placing two sets of fifty on the table in front of us. The cards have crosses on the front and Michael's picture with a couple of verses from Micah 6 printed on the inside. Elaine flips the cards between her fingers, inspecting the top few.

"Harper did a good job."

"She did," I agree.

"I'll take the first half of the book and start working on those," Elaine speaks unevenly, and her chin quivers as she takes the pages out one by one.

We get through all the cards in a single sitting. Conversation is limited to moments when we ask for help deciphering poor handwriting—addresses or last names blurring on the page.

Elaine adds stamps to the envelopes while I finish labeling the last chunk.

"I didn't think I would be doing this for him," Elaine says.

I catch a glimpse of a tear before she's able to wipe it away.

"Did you ever find …" Her words trail off but her question finishes in the silence.

"No," I shake my head, "I haven't found a letter."

Elaine nods. Her questions haunt me too. Why wouldn't he leave a note? Did he hide it? I've searched everywhere, but Michael didn't leave any words for us to cling to. I can't imagine him not planning it in advance. Maybe he had nothing more to say.

"Do you ever wonder why?" My eyes don't stray from the finished pile in front of me, feeling ashamed for having asked.

"Every day."

"Really?" I look up, surprised by her answer.

"Of course. I ask God daily why Michael had to leave us. I'm only human," she shrugs.

"Does He answer?"

"Who, God?" Elaine chuckles genuinely, "Not in words."

"How does He answer you then?"

"Through scriptures that pop into my mind in the middle of our conversations and giving me peace through what feels like an earthquake. Sometimes I have dreams about him and wake up with refreshed confidence that he's okay. I have to remind myself that I know where he is."

"What kind of dreams?" I'm intrigued. Elaine and I haven't had conversations like this before. I'm grateful she's being so open.

"All different kinds. My last dream was of Thanksgiving. We were all sitting around the table talking and eating. Michael was there sitting in the corner, not at the table. He was smiling and watching us all be happy together. He looked happy, too."

I go get tissues for her forming tears. Elaine bought them for me to keep on hand after telling me that paper towels and toilet paper are too rough for the nose. She uses her shirt sleeve to pat the tears dry until I hand her the box.

"Do you think He'd answer me if I asked?" As the question tumbles out, hope and anxiety fight for the space in my chest in a rush of heavy flutters.

"I think it's very possible," she pauses. "The hard part is we have to know His voice and be quiet enough to hear His whisper."

I nod. I don't know God's voice, couldn't decipher it from anyone else's even if He was screaming at me. But this is the first time I've been told I have to be quiet to hear God. Although I don't fully understand what that means, I don't ask any more questions.

Elaine smiles, "But you better tell me the answer He gives you."

We sit in silence, picking at the fruit and adding stamps to the rest of the envelopes. When we're finished with both, Elaine kisses my cheek and says goodbye.

Hours later, I find myself still sitting at the kitchen table, begging in heaving screams.

"Answer me!" I shout, "If you exist, fucking answer me!"

I slam my hand down on the table, grief muffling the pain as my hand tingles and warms, then slump back in my chair sobbing in defeat.

Since Elaine left, I've been bargaining with God, hoping for an answer. I've whispered and screamed, prayed respectfully and in a tantrum. But all my conversations have been one sided and I'm becoming convinced there is nothing more than the roof and sky beyond the ceiling. The only voice I hear is mine, bouncing back to me, ricocheting between the lonely walls.

My knuckles have become white over the balled cloth of Michael's sweatshirt, gripped firmly between my fingers. My mouth falls open, but there are no words left to escape.

I keep thinking of one of the verses Michael had read to me. He would read the Bible out loud while in bed, and I would listen until sleep took over. In the story, there's a man tearing his clothes, overwhelmed with the grief of losing his son. I can imagine the man as if he's standing before me in my kitchen, looking crazed and filled with frustration. His outrageous cries cannot calm him. Pain exudes from his chest in the form of sweat. I picture his eyes squinted tightly together, his jaw extended more than what should be possible. I can see the droplets of spit that are flung out of his mouth in his powerful screams. His fingers would be balled around the neck of his shirt, and his knuckles would be pale as the muscles in his arms flex, struggling to pull it apart. Two uneven pieces of cloth would lie on the floor, and still, this would not feel like an adequate release for the pain he holds inside.

Sweat has soaked into the cotton of my shirt, causing it to stick to my back like a magnet. I move from the table to the living room and undress in the light of the fireplace. I wrap myself in a thick blanket before lying on the floor. The chimney sits inches from my face, and I stare at the bricks in hopes that the monotonous pattern will blur my thoughts.

"Please. Please just give me an answer." My voice is jagged as it echoes through the silence that cloaks the house.

For hours, waves of agony crash over me. I drift between holding my chest in a silent, open-mouthed cry and lying lifeless on the floor, completely numb and exhausted. The whole time I think of nothing but the man tearing his clothes.

"Please answer me."

He doesn't.

THURSDAY
NOVEMBER 23, 2017

IT'S THANKSGIVING TODAY. I can't even remember holidays before Michael. Memories of the last couple years with his family, Boston with his parents then Michigan with his sister, have been antagonizing me all week.

Miller's coming over. Despite explaining that I didn't need her to uproot her schedule, she insisted that the drive was easy, and she wanted to visit. I'm grateful she pushed back. Despite rejecting Amber's invitation, I can't imagine spending the day alone.

My liveliness ebbs and flows. There are days I welcome visitors and appreciate their company. Other times, like this week, I can't even get out of bed. I can't make myself shower or eat. I wake up and spend all day waiting until the sun drops again so I can crawl back into bed and sleep.

My phone was endlessly busy for about two weeks. People sent constant texts and called often, hoping to be helpful. Countless homemade dishes were left on the doorstep; fruit platters and meat and cheese trays stocked my fridge. Food delivery gift cards were sent, and flowers were delivered.

Then things got quiet. People moved on. Michael popped up in his friends' minds less frequently. My absence at work became less obvious to my coworkers. Family returned to their daily activities that never involved Michael to begin with.

But I can't forget. I can't move on. There isn't a minute that I don't think about his grayed skin in the casket or stare at the boxed vase that holds what remains of his body.

When the holidays started creeping closer, family started checking in more often. Friends began calling again to extend their empty offers.

Let me know if there's anything I can do.

Just know I'm always here for you.

Remember, you can reach out anytime.

I don't reach out because no one actually means they'll do *anything*, and I don't know what they can do. Instead of voicing my frustrations, I thank them politely. I assure them I'm feeling the best I can be, make counterfeit promises to talk soon, and ignore their nonspecific proposals.

Elaine is the only person who is direct and clear. She sends me dates and times of when she will be coming over. She doesn't present it as a question, so there is no room to decline. She does laundry and lightly cleans. Sometimes she'll cook dinner, separating it into single portion-sized containers. She knows I won't waste any energy making myself a plate.

I appreciate her quiet company. Elaine's accepted that she'll end up disappointed if she's seeking conversation. We've come to understand that our grief looks different. Most days we chat while folding laundry or while she does the dishes. She tells me animated stories about Michael, and we both cry the whole way through.

A call from Miller lights up my phone, interrupting my warranted sulking. She tells me that she's an hour away and that she plans on stopping at the grocery store to rummage through what's left on the shelves. Neither of us thought to plan ahead.

I drag myself off the couch and walk zombie-like to the pile of clothes Elaine had put on the dining room table. I've never admitted to Elaine that I no longer go upstairs to the third floor, but she quickly caught on. One day, she started leaving folded clothes on the table instead of upstairs. The next day, she brought down a small basket of supplies—my toothbrush, toothpaste, hairbrush, and a box of pads—and left it on the kitchen island.

The clothing pile has a constant inventory of sweatpants, tank tops, hoodies, and socks, since that's all I've been wearing for weeks. I pull out a mismatched outfit and a pair of socks and step by step make my way up the first flight of stairs into the bathroom attached to the loft. Without Elaine's routine clean, it would show ample signs of my disorderly use.

My body looks starved as I slip out of my clothes. My ribs poke out, allowing each bone to be visible as it wraps around the circumference of my chest; the fat of my breasts has dissipated, leaving little more than budding nipples; my shoulders are bony squares attached to an overly visible collarbone; and the once-cute gap of my thighs has grown into a disturbing cavity. Rather than radiance shining from under my skin, there's a gray tint that has taken its place.

I tug at my hair and study myself while I wait for the water to warm, then step inside, letting it pour down my face like a rainstorm. Goosebumps prickle my skin as I soak in the heat. I pour shampoo into my hand, massage it in with my eyes closed, then repeat with the conditioner.

I spread soap across my body lazily. When it's all rinsed off, I allow my legs a break from standing and sink into a sitting position. Droplets of water ricochet off the knees I've pulled to my chest. The fiberglass feels hard against my exposed tailbone. I block out the pain of a forming bruise and hang my head in the hot water.

After I'm certain a large portion of the hour has passed, I get out and towel-dry my hair. I slide on oversized clothes that drape over my frail frame and sulk downstairs.

Within a few minutes, I get a text from Miller letting me know she's almost here. After two minutes of watching the hand of the kitchen clock tick, there's a gentle rhythmic knock at the door followed by the beeping of the keypad. It creaks open without me having to move, and Miller's head pops through the crack. She looks down, then side to side wearily.

"He's still with Scott and Elaine," I say blandly from the couch, knowing she's looking for Butler.

Miller swings the door wide, and a gust of crisp Michigan November air overtakes the warmth of the room. As the breeze pushes in, I realize inside the air's gone stale, gotten thick with dust. The house has remained stagnant—lifeless and marred, like a pond left to grow algae and cattails. Windows shut, doors closed, nothing moving.

The plastic bags in her hands crinkle as she wiggles her shoes off. Once she's fully inside, she sets down her duffle bag and too many groceries for the two of us.

"You get enough food?" I ask sarcastically, hearing the sharpness as the words fall from my lips. As an apology, I will myself off the couch and help bring the bags into the kitchen. We empty the food onto the counter: rotisserie chicken, ingredients for a green bean casserole, salad fixings, and an oversized pumpkin pie.

"I got the essentials," Miller nods with a genuine smile, unaffected by my negativity. "I'm happy I can be here and spend Thanksgiving with you."

Miller searches the cabinets for proper spices and cookware while I bring her duffle bag upstairs to the guest room. I make an effort to pick up the towels and clothes I'd left on the bathroom floor in hopes of portraying the facade that I'm fully functioning so she doesn't worry.

When I get back to the kitchen, she's already turned the oven on and is in the middle of mixing the ingredients for the casserole. Knowing she doesn't expect any help, I take a seat on the stool at the island like Michael did so many times toward the end, his body too weak to stand.

"How was the drive?"

"Not too bad, typical holiday highway driving." The wooden spoon in her hand moves vigorously through the mixture. "I'm starving, though. I thought I would be here earlier."

"The chef is never late."

"And thankfully I missed the Lions," she laughs, "What are Amber and Logan doing today?"

"Celebrating with Michael's parents. They still haven't gone back to Boston. I'm starting to wonder if they ever will." I give a halfhearted chuckle.

"Well, I'm glad you chose to be with me." She empties the contents of the bowl into a casserole dish and slides it into the oven, then turns back to me with a smile. "Even if you chose me because you refuse to leave the house. Do you have any wine?"

"I'm in no shortage of alcohol," I say, reaching for an unopened bottle from the tall pantry cabinet and uncorking it.

"A little motivation, even if driven by alcohol, is better than none." Miller takes a full glass from me, raises it in a motioned cheers, and takes a sip. I wonder if she made that up now or if that's been her motto throughout grad school.

Miller catches me up on her life as she finishes the meal prep, and I listen more intently than expected from across the counter. She tells me about her roommate's job change and their celebratory dinner, petty arguments within her friend group, and how difficult this semester has been. She talks with a normalcy I haven't heard recently, as if nothing is different. Where I would have expected anger and a hardened heart, there's a surprising relaxation that shows up in the familiarity of Miller and her drama. I remind myself to thank her for visiting over the anticipated cheesy dinner toast.

Miller slides the chicken into the oven to warm when there are seven minutes left on the timer and sets the table while the countdown continues. I attempt to be helpful by bringing the silverware to the table, but I'm lethargic and slow-moving. Miller has already brought most of the food over by the time I've gotten the napkins.

We sit across from each other, passing dishes of food back and forth. The sound of spoons clinking against our plates overtakes the quiet space.

"It's weird being here without Michael," Miller says staring at the untouched food in front of her. She moves it around with her fork but doesn't take a bite.

"It's still weird for me too," I nod as my eyes dampen.

Dinner is comprised of sullen silence. Neither of us bring up Michael again.

After we're done eating, I help clean up by putting the food in small containers as Miller cleans the used pans. Once we're finished, I offer a wine refill, which she rejects politely. I remind her where the bathroom towels are upstairs and watch from the kitchen as her dark curls bob in synchronization with her steps.

I assume my position on the couch while Miller finishes her shower. It's just past 10 p.m., and, with a big exhale, my body relaxes, feeling the anticipated end to the day.

I wish Miller could stay longer, but I make the decision not to ask, knowing she would leap at the opportunity. I'm not the kind of company she needs right now, especially as finals approach.

"Hey, Anna?" Miller calls down into the dark from the railing of the loft. "Do you want to sleep with me tonight?"

"Yeah, that sounds nice." I give her an honest smile, "I'll be up in a few."

I head upstairs after changing. Miller's in bed scrolling through her phone. I turn on Michael's desk lamp in the loft and flip the main light switch off. With little more than a sliver of light coming in from the cracked door, I use the blue light from Miller's phone to find my way into bed. Once I'm done fidgeting, Miller plugs in her phone, tosses one of the pillows behind her onto the floor, lays down, and rolls over to face me.

"Will you tell me a story?" she whispers in the dark.

The inflection of her hushed voice mimics her younger self. In my mind, we travel back to our shared bedroom, Miller asking if I'd tell her a fairytale, too scared to fall asleep in the silence. I'd tell her fables of storybook princesses and evil monsters that turned good. As we got older, she'd ask me to tell her a story from my day, still scared of monsters but the ones who no longer hide in the dark, bold enough to make themselves known at all hours.

"What kind of story?"

"Will you tell me a story about Michael?"

Even in the inky dark, I can see the shimmer of her eyes. Mine reflect the same glint, and the warmth of a tear trails down my cheek, dropping onto my pillow.

After a short collective pause, a memory of Michael, joyful and vivacious, comes to mind, and I chuckle before beginning.

"This one time, when Michael was living in the basement apartment, I was staying the night. We'd gotten the blandest Mexican food possible to cater to his spice sensitivity. It was so plain I felt like I was eating cardboard. We'd smoked while waiting for the delivery, so not only was this still the beginning of our relationship when I wasn't super comfortable at his house yet, but I was so high."

In my mind, his face is full and pigmented—free from the hollow, bony features that were prominent toward the end. His walk is tall and confident, the bounce in his step young and goofy. Slightly crooked white teeth shine through his familiar smile. Behind my closed eyes, his head is colored by rich, deep brown hair. It's thick and full. Matching brows draw attention to his lively brown eyes. I can feel his joy. I can feel the love that surged from his gaze to mine in the small moments, when the world would stop. When he'd pause everything, just to look at me.

"Was this when he was living with Kyle?"

"Yeah, it was that super rundown apartment. I can't remember if you came to Boston while he lived there. I probably wouldn't have taken you there either way," I smile, remembering that apartment. His dirty, damp room; the tile that always felt cold on my feet even with socks; the parties and drunken game nights that led to us giggling closely under sheets, using the need for warmth as an excuse to be close.

"Okay, keep going," Miller says eagerly, nestling deeper into the comforter.

"I asked him if he'd go get hot sauce from upstairs. Michael was still trying to impress me, so he was like, '*of course, babe.*' He was gone for like five minutes, and I was waiting awkwardly downstairs the whole time. It was way too long to be grabbing hot sauce, but I figured he got distracted talking to his roommates. When he came back, he had two glasses of water and no hot sauce."

I pause to wipe away tears composed of both happiness, as I relive the memory, and sadness, knowing new ones can never be made. Miller encourages me to continue by squeezing my hand over the blankets. Another reminder of Michael.

"So I'm confused at this point, like where is the hot sauce? And when I ask him, he bursts out laughing. With no explanation, he goes back upstairs and again, he's gone for way too long. Then I hear his feet running down the steps, and his head pokes down, and he goes, '*what was I going upstairs for?*' and

I couldn't help it, I started cracking up. He completely forgot why he'd gone to the kitchen both times. And my laughing caused him to laugh, and we both fell out. I made fun of him for years. Not only was it the most stoner thing on the planet, but his face the whole time was hilarious."

"I can't even picture him not having his shit together," Miller laughs along with me, and I wipe the tear clinging to her nose.

"It was the first time I saw him like that. He was *so* punctual and always had a plan for everything. I had never seen him *relaxed*."

"I blame the weed."

"I blame myself."

We laugh again.

Eventually, Miller's eyelids get heavy, then fall shut. Her breaths deepen and steady as slumber takes hold.

"I miss laughing," I whisper to sleeping ears.

Her patterned breath brings me comfort. Besides when Harper climbed into bed with me after the funeral, this is the first time I've slept next to someone since Michael left. I'm brought back to memories of him through the sounds of someone else's breathing. Careful not to wake Miller, I move two pillows to the edge of the bed. I tuck them in under the blanket and flip around. Even though I know it isn't real, I pretend the pillows are Michael sleeping behind me. With Miller's steady breathing and the pillows in place, in the blur between sleep and wake, there is a small moment when it feels real. My last conscious thought is Michael, and I'm filled with somnolent serenity.

In the morning, I wake up to an otherwise empty bed and the smell of frying bacon. I lie on my back, the reality of life hitting me heavily as it does in the mornings. I look forward to waking up one day without the feeling of an elephant crushing my chest and the uncomfortable breath-catching churning of my stomach. But when that happens, it means I'll wake up being okay that he's gone, and I don't want that either.

Miller and I sit at the island stools for breakfast. She stacks her plate full and finishes easily before helping herself to seconds. In the same amount of time, I finish my orange juice and eat a couple of pieces of bacon.

I'm struck by the desire to beg her to stay as she finishes repacking her duffle bag, but I hold my tongue. I stand in the bedroom doorway with my arms crossed, fighting the tears so they don't become noticeable. Miller zips up her filled bag and walks toward the stairs, pausing next to me to squeeze my shoulder. I walk her to the front door and give her an extended hug. She holds the full weight of my head on her shoulder as we stand in an embrace.

"I love you," I whisper into her curls.

"I love you, too. I'll be back soon," she promises before walking down the porch steps toward her car. She waves as she puts it in reverse, and I give her a tight-lipped smile and a dimpled chin. Even after she's driven away, I continue standing in the open door's frame. The cold air washes over me like a detox.

I spend the rest of the day sitting in front of the fireplace; the gas-induced orange and yellow flames dance over imitation logs.

The TV remains black, and the room remains silent with the exception of the slight hiss of the fire and the ticking clock hands that echo from the kitchen. I anticipate the falling darkness as I count the passing seconds indicated by each *tick*.

Once the sun sets and dusk's navy blue has almost completed its transition to deep indigo, I fall onto the couch with a glass of water and two sleeping pills in hand. I allow myself to melt completely once the Ambien floods my system and pulls me into a happier world. I spend my last thought hoping I never wake up.

FRIDAY
DECEMBER 13, 2017

MY BOSS EMAILED ME earlier this week to let me know I've used most my grievance time and will soon dip into my PTO, which will dwindle quickly since I don't have any days to roll over. He said he doesn't have a timeline in which he's requiring me to come back to work but explained that my paychecks will stop in about a month.

I've felt the change in seasons, the devastating beginning to the new year lurking, but I hadn't processed it's already been two months. I can't keep track of the days. All I know is I'm somewhere on the other side of October. I'm in the valley between a life where Michael laughs joyously and one where he doesn't exist.

I refuse to accept that I'll be leaving Michael behind, that he won't be moving forward into the new year with me. I beg time to stand still.

Despite today's unseasonably warm weather, it's undeniably

December. The pavement has traded its shade of black for a salted gray. The bare tree branches and brick buildings blend together to form an ambiguous, colorless landscape. The sidewalk and grass touch the sky, mirroring the dreary lack of color, making it impossible to differentiate where one stops and the other begins.

I sit behind the steering wheel of my parked car, glancing between my eyes' reflection in the rearview mirror and the large wooden entrance to the coffee shop.

Amber recently called and told me she's worried I've become a recluse. To appease her, and because a tugging feeling told me she may be right, I've made it my goal to order something at a coffee shop I once frequented.

I've been parked in the same spot for more than half an hour waiting to gain the courage to go in. Every time I think I'm ready, the feeling is retracted before my hand can reach the door handle.

Between attempts, I've been people-watching behind the tinted car window. Michael and I loved to people-watch.

Various groups of teen girls come and go through the revolving door. None of them wear coats as though the forty-degree weather is a sign of spring approaching. They all smile and laugh jovially as they pass their phones to each other, then giggle some more. I imagine the phones display texts from their crushes or social media posts from classmates they use as judgmental entertainment. The naive, giddy joy that they exude is infuriating.

There's a cluster of moms in long Canada Goose jackets guiding a herd of children into the coffee shop. The adults drag the kids by the hand across the parking lot mindlessly as they trade gossip. There's nothing I wouldn't give to be able to share work drama with Michael one more time, to partake in stupid gossip. To spend one day clueless of the depth that pain can root itself. Where I'm not forced to understand the thick opacity of depression's cloud—the one I've become so familiar with. To have days filled with laughter again.

A headache begins to brew as I vehemently hold tears back. I'm not a bitter person, but my heart continues to harden. I'm so angry for the life we missed out on, the life with Michael that was taken from me.

How can everyone go on like nothing is wrong? How can they walk through the gravel parking lot like the world isn't covered in a layer of darkness? How can they rush through the day, taking advantage of the lives around them?

How do they not realize that the world has changed? That everything has changed.

It's a supernatural experience to feel the heaviness of the world from behind glass. Looking through a muddy lens, wearing skin that doesn't quite fit right, feeling like a sponge for the gloom of the world. It's like I'm standing with my feet in cement while everyone else runs the race of life, not knowing that everything is different now.

I shift the car into drive, zip out of my parking spot, and head back home.

I'm somewhere between three glasses of wine too deep and two glasses too little. I can still feel the heavy burning in my chest as it grows from a glowing flame to a roaring fire, but I've lost the sober control of my emotions.

I fail to find words to give to the emotional and physical trench I'm trapped in. No two- or three-syllable word can capture the invasion my nervous system is at war with daily or depict the thickness of the burn that rips down my throat and into my chest.

From the living room, trapped in the glow of the fire, I scowl at the box on the kitchen table. Inside is a blue urn filled to the brim with every piece of my happiness. I twirl my wine-less glass in contempt as I pace back and forth with indecision.

I don't want to put up the Christmas tree without Michael. For days, I've told myself that I'll do it tomorrow, then repeat the phrase when tomorrow becomes today. But the twinkling lights wrapped around the tree have always been my favorite part of the holidays.

Michael and I had made a tradition of playing Christmas music, filling mugs with hot chocolate, and dancing as we decorated the house in green and red. Last year, after finishing the tree, we sat snuggled on the couch admiring the vast juxtaposition of the colorful bulbs against the darkness of the room.

I put down my glass and begin unpacking the tree.

"You picked out this stupid tree and you aren't even here to help put it up," I say through clenched teeth to the unassembled pieces I've scattered across the hardwood floor.

Once I've sorted through the different parts of the tree, I begin moving furniture to clear a spot for it.

Already out of breath, I sit on the arm of the couch and stare at the vacant corner. The tightness in my chest flares, triggered by the incessant reminder of Michael's absence. I don't move for fifteen minutes, and when I do, it's to get more wine.

One by one, I stack each prickly piece, fluffing the branches of each layer before adding the next one.

The outside light is becoming limited. The setting sun signals the production of melatonin, causing my eyes to get droopy. I still look forward to sleeping more than any other part of the day. When I'm asleep, I'm allowed to drift into an alternate reality where a version of Michael still exists.

I take one more lip-staining sip and contemplate the best strategy to circle the tree with a string of lights.

"How would Michael do this?" I ask the emptiness.

I start from the bottom and make a few laps around the tree before I need to drag a stool from the kitchen. I shift it in a circle, inch by inch. It doesn't take long for me to give up on this strategy. The pattern evolves into a sloppy zigzag that stops before the top of the tree, where I can no longer reach.

After the lights have been strung, I slide the green and red box labeled **ORNAMENTS** across the floor next to the tree. One by one, I hang the small collection of bulbs in a disorganized pattern that mirrors the pandemonium of the lights.

Memories fill me as I pull out the ornaments: a Patriots football, a caricature of Michael and me on a glass bulb, a square wooden block with *Block Island* written in large defined letters ironically, and a Millennium Falcon that connects to the lights for effect. I can feel the pressure of tears as the ornament ribbons twirl between my pinched fingers.

After another pour of wine, the Christmas bin is empty except for one last rectangular box. I'm not sure if the ornament has my eyes stinging, or if it's because it signals the completion of the Christmas tree: proof that Michael is no longer here. It'll be the first of many years to come that I'll have put up the Christmas tree by myself, without the help of my husband.

I lean over, lift the small white box from the holiday-colored bin, and pull the ornament out by the short-looped string. Two Minions, Bob and Kevin, wearing Santa hats on the beach, are each lounging in their own hammocks. Kevin has his arms lifted behind his head with his one eye looking up dreamily. Bob is gripping his teddy bear, smiling, mimicking Kevin's stare.

Of all the gifts Michael ever surprised me with, this one is by far my favorite. He'd gotten it last Christmas, shoving it at me the minute he got home. He'd bolted across the hardwood from the front door, apologizing profusely, knowing his boots were leaving snow prints with every step. His smile was contagious, stretching from ear to ear.

It holds the memory of us sitting in the movie theater, barely dating at the time, high and hysterically laughing at the kids' movie that we'd convinced ourselves had a targeted audience of adults. It represents all the times he got me out of self-made trouble in the same way Kevin does for Bob.

With tears, I hang the Minions on a branch facing the couch. It looks pretty, the sandy base of the ornament illuminated by one of the red bulbs creating a pink hue. I breathe in the warmth of our sandy vacations: Fort Lauderdale, Charleston, the shorelines of Rhode Island in the summer.

To complete the tree with the Yoda angel, I have to use the kitchen stool again. Once I've gotten down, wobbly from the wine, I step back and admire the tall green plastic pine tree proudly. I sigh as my fingers intertwine on top of my head as if I'm an athlete trying to catch my breath after a marathon; the fight between accomplishment and loneliness leaves me struggling for air.

I stumble toward the kitchen to make our traditional hot chocolate, flipping the light switch off. As I pass the front door, the flicker of my reflection in the hanging wooden-framed mirror startles me. My feet jerk to a stop, allowing me to study the woman staring back at me. I fail to pinpoint a day since Thanksgiving that I have brushed my teeth, washed my face, or even looked in a mirror.

One hand drops to my protruding hip. My mousy brown hair looks like knotted fishing string. My face is drained of all color except my green eyes, which pop in contrast to the dark rings beneath them. I look malnourished—which is more true than not considering my intake has been little more than toast, coffee, and alcohol for the majority of the last eight weeks. I slide my hand up from my hip to my ribs, each one so prominent I can outline the bone through my shirt. The girl staring back at me looks drained of life. She looks like Michael did.

I slip back into the familiar numbness, directing both my thoughts and footsteps toward the kitchen robotically. With a mug of hot chocolate in hand, I return to the living room and stand in front of the tree.

My eyes keep floating back to the Minions ornament. I take it down and set it on the coffee table. My body finds the comfort of the couch, curling into the safety of the familiar beige blanket as I wrap it around me like armor.

The subsequent hours are spent on the couch bathed in the hue of the red, green, and blue Christmas lights. Waves of despair rush through me, coming out in heavy sobs. The agony expels in wails that fill the silent voids of the house. I yell out to God in anger, bitter that Michael and I's life was cut short.

Sobs become whimpers, and cries to God become whispers.

The last thing I see before my eyes close is an emptied wine bottle and two small Minions.

SUNDAY
FEBRUARY 18, 2018

I WAKE UP WHEN IT'S still dark to the sharp sound of a scream. I lie in a stagnant haze until I realize it was my own.

Most of the time I can wake myself up before the night terror sets in. They're all the same: seeing the shock overtake his face after the last doctor appointment, reliving the cold of Michael's hands in the casket, the lonely echo of my footsteps as I walk to the front door without him for the first time. My mind doesn't need to be creative; it has enough horror to build off of without putting in effort. All my subconscious needs to do is simply remember Michael's absence.

Butler lies at the bedside, undisturbed by the now-familiar scream.

I'd go back to bed if I could, but the nightmares have a way of kickstarting my heart and sending my sympathetic nervous system into hyper speed. I sit up in bed, allowing my eyes to adjust to the dark room. It isn't even sunrise yet.

I rub my face in frustration. The disconnect between my mind and body is evident as they both fail to self-regulate. My sleep is inconsistent and unrestful, and if sleeping helps with healing, then I'm left hopeless.

That's only the beginning of my paradoxical life. I need to keep my body nourished, but the food I have at the house makes me nauseous. I'm lonely, but also intolerant of company. I need Michael's presence, but I reject his family's offers to come over.

I desperately need just one night that I don't have to hold my chest closed in fear of it ripping open because the visceral pain tearing from the inside feels too real.

If I cry now, I won't get up for the next twelve hours, and, as much as I would appreciate lying lifeless in bed all day, time drags on when I don't expel energy. Feeling apathetic, I slide my legs off the bed. Butler follows, his unclipped nails tapping against the wooden stairs a few paces behind me. He stops at the bottom and curls into a ball on the hard floor.

"I know, buddy. I miss him too," I sigh, and he copies me in a long exhale. His head remains on his paws, but his doggy brows are lifted as he watches the door, waiting for Michael.

After my first cup of coffee, I have an unfamiliar, renewed level of energy. As the light folds between the living room blinds, I enjoy the temporarily lifted fog.

With a deep breath, I stand up from the couch. The effects of the restless night are evident in my lower back as I walk to the kitchen, where silverware and an assortment of mugs rot in the sink. The smell rises and coats the space in a thick, rancid odor of decomposing vegetables. The same odor wafts up when I open the dishwasher: wilted lettuce and burnt plastic. I rinse off dishes, scrubbing the scabbed food pieces, then stack them on a towel splayed across the countertop.

When I get to the fridge, an equally repellent stench forces my nose into a scrunch.

How long has it been since I opened the fridge?

The question answers itself in dishes of moldy baked ziti and soup that has a layer of solidified fat floating at the top. I try and fail to remember the last time someone dropped off a meal, but it doesn't matter—the smell tells me more than a calendar could.

Deeming it unsalvageable, I take the container of fungus-filled pasta and throw the whole thing into the garbage can without opening it. Dish by dish, I dump sour-smelling food, rinsing the empty containers. The water's hot against my fingers, which are starting to prune. Steam rises off the glass mug in my hands and fogs the silver faucet.

I look down at the dishwasher, crammed with strategically organized dishes.

Memories of Michael's laugh flood the kitchen. He's so deeply engraved in my mind that I swear I can hear him, and his face is almost tangible behind closed eyes. I can see his arm reaching out to me, grabbing at the dish in my hand.

My lips part, ready to talk to him. The thought of him fills my lungs with air for a single breath of joy before retracting. I suffocate under the realization that I will never again hand him a sudsy dish from the sink in our makeshift assembly line. A daily habit that I took for granted.

The rushing water suddenly feels too loud. Its forceful splatter against the bottom of the sink is overstimulating. I push the tap down. The water swirls into the drain, a small whirlpool spinning faster until it vanishes with a slurp, swallowed by the pipes. Silence follows broken only by a lone drop falling down into the shallow pool left behind.

Butler's cold, wet nose presses into my ankle, pulling me back from the lost time of my mind. My palms rest on the on the smooth, cool surface of the counter. My wrinkled fingers stretch, clinging to the soapstone. Fading soap suds burst softly, popping against my skin. I hear the soft whistle of my breath as it's pushed through pursed lips, steady and soothing.

My senses hum to life, my heart's furious beats soften, and the overwhelming build of anger and frustration melts away like ice. In its place, sadness returns, numbness enveloping me in its shadow.

When I don't respond, Butler nudges me again. He doesn't jump on me or wag his tail. He simply sits in shallow contentment at my feet and allows me to scratch the top of his head while he mirrors my own emotionless expression.

I crave the detachment that comes with a warm fire and whatever rerun is cycling through the TV channels. I sink into the couch then scroll through the channels, finding a *Friends* marathon. I use the repeating theme song to measure time as it passes.

Hours in, a knock at the door startles me. The depression-infused cloud around me has thickened into a fog.

The keypad on the door beeps. The lock hums as it retracts. Elaine's face pokes around the opening door. Seeing me on the couch, her face lights up, and she lets herself in. Scott comes in behind her carrying a bag of takeout food.

I'm in tattered sweatpants and Michael's oversized shirt that extends mid-thigh, making me look like a messy balloon. I can't remember if I brushed my teeth today or if that was yesterday.

"Hi," I say, my head peaking over the back of the couch. I turn down the TV as they take off their shoes and coats. Butler runs over, greeting them both much more cheerfully than I do.

While Elaine greets me with a warm hug, Scott looks at me as though I'm a wounded dog. I cross my arms and trace the pattern of the vines behind my elbow timidly.

Elaine walks to the kitchen and Scott and I follow, "We brought some food. I know it's not much, but–"

"It's perfect, Elaine. Thank you," I cut her off, grateful for their company.

Scott pulls small, white takeout cartons from the paper bag and places them on the dining room table, releasing the warm, greasy scent of Chinese food into the air. He's silent, but the bag crinkles as he moves. As he snaps the lids off the plastic trays, another wave of scent escapes. It's comforting but heavy and overwhelming, slightly nauseating. I haven't eaten much lately. My stomach grumbles, but I'm unsure if it's out of hunger or disgust.

Across the room, Elaine pulls three plates from the cabinet. The glass clinks together as she stacks them. She sets them in front of us and passes us each a napkin.

"Did you make it to church today?" Elaine asks as she settles into her seat at the table. Her eyes flicker over me—my tangled hair, the baggy pajamas—before she offers a casual wave of her hand. "Did you watch from home like you and Michael used to?"

"I didn't realize it was Sunday," I reply honestly. Blood rushes into my cheeks.

"It's so hard to keep track of the days," Scott empathizes as he passes me the container of orange chicken. The more time that's passed since Michael was here, the quieter Scott has become.

"Did you guys go?"

"It was good. We'd love to have you come with us one weekend," Scott speaks up with a bit more enthusiasm.

"Maybe," I nod.

"How have you been? We haven't seen you much lately." Elaine looks at me with kind sympathy, seeing nothing more than my empty shell looking back at her.

"I had a good day today. I cleaned the kitchen a little bit."

I look around, briefly proud, then deflated. The clean dishes are piled in a disheveled heap; the sun shines through the window, catching every water spot on the counter; and a jumbled stack of papers clutters the island.

"The morning felt productive," I shrug and drop my gaze.

"That's great, Anna," Elaine smiles, ignoring the lack of evidence.

"We wanted to wish you luck back at work tomorrow." Scott clears his throat as he exposes their reason for visiting.

"Thanks." I offer a smile back, not sure what more to say.

We eat and fill silence with talk of church and the weather. Elaine tells me she's been spending a lot of time with Amber and Logan. She updates me in on Mason's life: fun activities at daycare, all the little friends he's making, how good he's gotten at singing lullabies, and the upcoming spring soccer camp they've enrolled him in. I listen courteously but sit with a clenched jaw to hold in the forming tears. I can't think about Mason without thoughts of Michael following.

After a couple of hours, Scott acknowledges the darkness of night falling and uses it as an excuse to leave. He starts packing up the leftovers knowing they'd go to waste if he left them, and I walk Elaine to the door.

"I miss you, Anna."

"You're welcome over anytime," I say.

"I miss *you*. I miss the Anna that Michael loved."

Her words pull a heat wave over me, reddening my eyes. I don't have a response. I look at her, searching her eyes for something solid that I can cling to, hoping to find a life raft to save me from sinking.

"I miss her too."

Scott walks over to us and says a brief goodbye, then goes out to start the car while I let Elaine hug me. Her arms cocoon me, seeking comfort in our closeness. Her sobs are felt before they're heard. Her body shakes against mine as she clings to me.

"I miss him so much," she cries. We stand in an embrace we both need. Neither of us says anything else.

Once her breathing steadies, she pulls back. Her hand cups my cheeks, and she tucks my hair behind my ears with a motherly tenderness.

After giving me a sad smile, she walks out, leaving the house empty again.

The sun has mostly set, signaling to my body that sleep is now acceptable. Although my intentions were to sleep upstairs in our bed, I stop outside the guest room, feeling as empty as it looks.

Before Michael left, I wasn't a daydreamer. But I don't have a foundation to lock into anymore, so I make up realities in my mind because they're more bearable than the one I live in.

As I study the guest room, my mind colors kids into the bed that takes up the majority of the room. Two or three, their blurry faces don't hold a shape. I don't know what our kids would have looked like, but I find myself constantly wishing Michael had left a piece of him behind with me.

I imagine little brunette toddlers running around the room frivolously, giggling and joyously calling *daddy, daddy*. Little bodies jump on the bed and leap off into the safety of Michael's outstretched arms. Little feet in a onesie patterned with cartoon dinosaurs or Disney princesses. Crusted toothpaste in the corner of small lips, and late-night snacks on children's plates picked up by uncoordinated hands.

Tears burn in my eyes, forming a pool before escaping.

This pain is different from the one that fills me daily; this isn't mourning what I had, it's the grief of what I won't. The house fills with weeping for the child I didn't grow, for the life Michael didn't value, and for the memories that we can no longer make. For the light and joy that will forever be missing from this house.

I fold myself between the white sheets taut over the guest bed. I imagine crawling in next to a small child, kissing the top of their head, burying my face in their hair, Eskimo kisses on a nose that matches Michael's. My imagined family is so vivid I smell the baby hair and feel the softness of toddler pajamas.

Butler sulks into the room. I pat the bed, and he jumps up.

"It's just me and you, Butt," I bury my head in his. The tears are free-flowing, and after a few minutes, there are small wet patches painting Butler's neck.

The positivity that found me this morning remains lost. In its place is guilt. How could I have been happy, even for a minute, without Michael?

Time continues to pass, but I can't fall asleep. I toss and turn, weighed down, buried beneath heavy layers of sorrow.

The quiet house reminds me I'm alone.

MONDAY
FEBRUARY 19, 2018

THE OFFICE HASN'T CHANGED. The open concept desks haven't been rearranged, the walls are still a shade of eggshell, and the white noise that plays on the overhead speakers is still the same volume. The same receptionist greets me as I swipe my badge, except today he looks at me with a face full of sorrow.

I'm joined by a stranger as I get into the elevator. We stand the appropriate distance apart, but there's an intensity in the space between us, a lingering sadness that I know she doesn't feel. Today is a normal day in her department, no different from last week. She doesn't know me, doesn't know that I haven't been here in months or that I'm now a widow.

Widow. The word plays itself over in my mind distastefully. I reject it like poison.

A soft chime and the slowing of the elevator signal my floor is approaching. When the doors open, the woman offers a courteous nod as I step off and into a jungle of people who *do* know me.

I walk self-consciously past the rows of desks, certain everyone's eyes are following me. At the far end, behind a row of glass-walled offices, my boss sits hunched over his computer. His eyebrows furrow in contempt as he focuses on the screen, unaware of my approaching footsteps.

Rhett has been my boss since I moved to Michigan. When my six-month contract ended, he offered me a position as a full-time employee. I've never seen him deny a request for time off. He's compassionate and generous with his team—quick to let someone leave early for a sick kid or a dentist appointment. He manages with the understanding that life is unpredictable. This is something he vocalizes to all new hires. He explains that he will trust them unless given a reason not to but makes it clear that if the trust is broken, their employment agreement will be too.

He is a traditionally good-looking, tall, corporate-styled man. He has salt-and-pepper hair that he attributes to his kids who are in their twenties now, and although he wears a suit daily, I rarely see him in a tie. He has a masculine build and sharp facial features worn down by age, but he's well-kept and never sports more than a five o'clock shadow.

I've enjoyed working with him, and he's been a great teacher and mentor to me. He has decades of experience with residential properties. Like me, he started his career on the commercial side, so he enjoys coaching me as I step into this realm of design.

"Hey Rhett, thanks for allowing me the extra week off." I knock on the glass and attempt to smile, but it isn't genuine.

Being back in the office feels like stepping into a world that kept turning without me. Memories of work parties I brought Michael to resurface, freezing my mind, while cheerful, carefree laughter floats in from around the corner. I can't believe how much my life has changed since the last time I was here—and how much everyone else's has stayed the same.

"I'm sorry we couldn't give you more PTO." He stands up from his chair politely but remains behind his desk. His demeanor is kind and gentle, reflecting genuine sympathy back at me.

"I know our meeting isn't for another thirty minutes, but I got here early and realized I don't have any work to do until then." I blush down at my feet, feeling wilted in a place I once thrived.

"Come in, close the door behind you."

"Thanks for the food tray. It was all I ate for a while."

"Don't thank me, it was from all of us." He waves his hand, downplaying his generosity. "I don't know many grieving people who have an appetite for much more than cheese and crackers."

"How have things been around here?" I ask as I settle into the seat across from him, shifting from side to side, unable to shake my discomfort.

"We've gotten by, but I'm happy you're back," Rhett shrugs with a telling smile. "We've kept you in our thoughts and prayers for the last few months."

"Thanks," I never know how else to respond to that. He picks up on my apprehension and sits back in his chair, ready to talk business.

"I have a few builders that need sketches in the queue. Deadlines aren't set for another couple of months. I also have a commercial building request that came in from an old friend last week that I saved for you. I don't think anyone here has as much experience with commercial properties as you do."

"I appreciate it." My shoulders fall as I relax.

"What do you think you're ready to take on?"

"I'm not really sure." As I speak, the corners of my lips droop down, "I'd like to take on the commercial building, but depending on the deadline, it may be better for me to take on one of the residential projects to get back into things."

"I appreciate your honesty. I'll send an introductory email, and we'll work on a timeline as you ease back into business. All I ask for is transparency, so I know whether to hand the commercial property off to someone else."

"I can't tell you how thankful I am for your flexibility. It's made a really big difference."

"I lost my first wife to ovarian cancer," he says with instantly glossy eyes. His gaze drops to the picture frame angled inwards on his desk. He clears his throat before continuing, "I credit my success to my boss at the time, who was more than understanding. I'm trying to pay it forward."

I hesitate, not sure what the right thing to say is. "I'm sorry."

"Me too, Anna."

A quiet pause settles between us. I'm grateful for the rare kind of understanding that doesn't demand words.

Rhett wiggles his mouse, and the screen lights up, a subtle signal the moment has expired, but his expression remains soft. He promises to send an introductory email between me and the builder by the end of the day.

I thank him as I step out of his office, back into the commotion of a life I'm forced to continue to live. The office hums productively—white noise crackles from the speakers above, soft voices review timelines, keys tap, mice click, the printer spits out page after page—the low buzz of everything moving forward.

I set my bag down on an open desk. My fingers dance restlessly as I fidget with my things, shifting them to different spots on the desk, forgetting their usual arrangement.

The eyes of my coworkers burn into me with the knowledge of my loss. When their gaze feels too heavy, I retreat to the elevator, bowing my head to avoid making eye contact with them.

The doors open, and I press the button for the main floor. I give the receptionist a weak smile as I walk past the entrance, down the hallway, and into the bathroom to cry.

TUESDAY
MARCH 6, 2018

I'M POINTED TO THE coffee on the opposite side of the room by a long flannel-covered arm attached to a man with a thick beard and close-mouthed smile. I give him a tight smile and nod in return.

As I cross the room, I admire the smooth, expensive wood that lines both the walls and floor of the barn-shaped structure. In the far corner, a white plastic folding table holds a few boxes of donuts, and a scant coffee cart sits beside it.

Steam rises from the styrofoam cup as I fill it with decaf. Feeling awkward in the space, I grab a donut to keep my hands busy as I join the circle of chairs set up like an AA meeting. I venture a soft *hi* to the two people already sitting in the arrangement. They greet me briefly then turn back to one another to continue their conversation. I pick a small piece off the donut and avert my gaze.

I don't want to be here. After sending me grief groups through text and every social media platform with no response, Amber signed me up against my will.

She informed me with a phone call.

"I've already paid in full, so you can't say no," she said, leaving no room for argument.

"It's just a bunch of lonely, hopeless, sad people," I retorted. I had no interest in sharing my story with strangers or being sad on purpose. I felt like I was getting better, and I knew that submerging myself in a pool of depression would be taking steps backward.

"You'll fit in fine, then." Amber, much like Michael, inherited the stubborn trait, a gene carried by both parents.

I groaned.

"Harper gave me the idea, so there's no fighting it."

That was the extent of our conversation.

There's no way to prove that I'm not wasting their money with Harper being in Boston and Amber busy with Mason, but here I am willingly sitting in a fold-up chair.

Men and women, the majority between thirty and fifty years old, slowly trickle in. Most of them mimic my awkward demeanor, some looking more comfortable than others. Almost all of them pursue the same self-conscious donut grab, pretending to look busy.

Two women walk in seconds apart, then smile, hug, and enter the circle together, chatting like old friends. No coffees, no donuts. Their comfortability makes me feel more out of place.

"Good evening. I'm glad you all could make it. I'm going to give it a few more minutes, then we can get started." The taller of the two Chatty Kathys says before making her way around the circle. She greets us one by one, repeating to each individual that she's happy we chose to come tonight. When she gets to me, I politely introduce myself.

Her name is Carol. She's older than most of the people here, although not by much, but she's less weathered. The corners of her eyes are crinkled from smiling, a good wrinkle to have, one earned from kindness. Her forehead shows lines of natural aging but nothing indicating she furrows her brows often.

Her steps are soft, leading with her toes, and she brings a quiet calm that settles over the circle. We can feel it radiating off her, a comfort that wraps around each chair settling nerves and inviting openness.

She's in plain jeans and a mauve ribbed sweater. Her golden blonde bob falls to her shoulders. Up close, I can see the coarseness of her hair revealing that it's dyed, likely covering greys. Carol wears no jewelry, not even a wedding ring. She looks plain, almost bland, someone who blends into crowds rather than stands apart.

I learn that she's a highly qualified therapist and serves as the head pastor for the church's grief meetings, AA, and addiction recovery program. Thankfully, I don't plan on participating in the latter two.

I watch her carefully as she walks around the room, greeting the people at the coffee table and those standing awkwardly against the far wall. Carol strolls back into the filled chair circle as I'm picking at the last quarter of my donut. She puts a notepad on one of three empty chairs, places a water bottle and tissue box on the floor in front of it, and stands skimming the group silently.

"Hello again, I recognize a few familiar faces. I'm happy you're back," she says, pausing again to hold the individual gaze of three or four people in the circle. "For those of you who I didn't get a chance to introduce myself to, or for those who may have forgotten, I'm Carol. I run a lot of the church's self-help programs, including this grief group. We like to introduce ourselves before speaking by stating our name and who we've lost. You can then say your response or comment. And please, be respectful of each other. Anything said here stays here. Who wants to start?"

After a minute that passes like an eon, a curly-haired boy breaks the tension by raising an unsteady hand. If he's older than eighteen, he doesn't show it. His face is round and smooth, and although his deep voice surprises me, his instinctive hand-raising gives his age away.

"I'm Andrew," he says shyly. "I lost my brother two months ago."

I half expect the group to repeat *Hi Andrew* like in movies, but his introduction is followed by silence.

"How are you feeling today, Andrew?" Carol leads.

"Frustrated." The muscles in his jaw are visible as he grinds his teeth.

Pause. I count the passing seconds: *one, two, three, four, five* –

"I guess I'm frustrated that everyone else is living like normal. Like people are talking about prom dates and the girls are complaining about not having a dress for graduation, like they have nothing more to live for than a date or shoes."

Pause. *One, two, three –*

"What was it that triggered these feelings?" Carol asks, her face filled with a warm concern that makes the entire group noticeably relax.

"There's a girl in my chemistry class who is so loud and complains about everything. Like, sorry you don't like the color of your car, but is it really that important?"

"If you could say anything to her in complete honesty, what would it be?"

"I'd tell her to shut up." Andrew rests his elbows on his knees and buries his head roughly in his hands, visibly shaken. "Just shut up. That some of us have bigger things to worry about than these stupid high school events. I don't need to hear about stupid things that make no difference in life. No one cares. None of this actually matters."

"You're nodding convincingly," Carol states. Andrew, across the circle, runs his hands through his young curls. Two or three seconds go by before I realize she's looking at me.

"Oh," I say, startled, taking another second to organize my thoughts. "Um, yeah, I am, I guess. I've felt like that before. More recently than not."

"Can you introduce yourself to us?"

"Hi, I'm Anna. My husband left about five months ago."

"What do you mean when you say left?" Carol asks, already attempting to pry—which I guess is what I came here for.

"Michael, that's my husband's name, had lung cancer. If he made it, I probably wouldn't be here." I fail at making a deflecting joke. Carol, like the rest of the group, remains straight-faced as I chuckle uncomfortably.

Pause.

I fidget in my seat, my hands falling into my lap, and pinch the skin above my wrist inked with tattooed vines.

Breathe, Anna. Breathe.

"Anyway, I've felt that too. I mean, I've been mad at others for living daily life."

"That's a good way to put it." Andrew's eyes rush to mine with a renewed hope that only stems from someone else feeling as bad as you do. I've felt that before, too.

"I spent a lot of time angry that people could continue life as if nothing had happened. Like the world didn't change." I shake my head and look up, annoyed at the tears blurring my vision. Carol extends a box of tissues, but I wave my hand in rejection. She nods, saying nothing, allowing my words to hang.

One, two, three, four –

"You say this in past tense, Anna," Carol breaks the silence.

"Well yeah. I guess I realized that their world didn't change. My life changed. It felt like the world changed, but in reality, it was only my world that fell apart." I continue holding back the tears, determined to keep them in. A few heads nod in agreement, and Andrew cries. Carol again extends the box of tissues, leaning into the middle of the group. Andrew takes one. I refrain.

A couple more people chime in, and, for a few minutes, open argument exists over who heard the shallowest complaint. Carol allows the conversation but eventually reins it back in to guide the group through topics of pain outlets and healthy daily habits. We discuss showering, brushing our teeth, eating at least once daily, and drinking water. The conversation would have seemed ridiculous to me before Michael left, but it's a needed reminder when stuck in survival mode. I didn't do most of the things she mentions for weeks after his funeral. I assume most of the circle still struggles with these activities.

I don't add anything more to the conversation, but I listen to others as they share who they've lost, how long ago, and where they are in the healing process. It's a reminder of both where I was and where I have to get to.

Their compiled stories guide me like a lighthouse. A bright light in the raging storm that signals safety, promising things will get better. Eventually. I wonder if I'm a lighthouse for Andrew, a sign that the world won't stay dark forever, the next step in his healing.

Once we're finished, I don't rush out. I don't want to talk to anyone, considering the one thing we have in common is loss, but I'm not ready to go back to an empty house.

"Want to help me fold the chairs?" Carol asks, noticing my lingering.

"Sure." I put down the empty styrofoam coffee cup I've been indenting with my nails and start collapsing the plastic chairs. Carol shows me the closet in the hall that connects the barn-like room to the church. The hallway's white tile reflects the two lights shining down, but beyond that, it's dark.

"It's eerie here at night. I've been working here for almost a decade, mostly after dark, but I'm still not used to it." Carol follows my gaze into the thick, inky church air. "Not super comfortable in churches, are you?"

"Religion was more Michael's thing," I step in front of her and empty the chairs I've been holding while she propped open the door. I help her with the stack currently leaning against the wall, then the remaining chairs left in the room.

"Will I see you back here Thursday?" Carol asks once we've put the chairs away. I shrug and follow her as she walks across the room to the coffee cart.

"Maybe. I think so, at least."

"What's causing your hesitation?"

"I don't want to commit and not show up."

"What would stop you from coming?" Her simple question cuts sharply.

The bottles of wine sitting on the counter waiting for me. The endless stream of Xanax my doctor prescribes for me to abuse because she feels bad. Any substance that stops my thinking and, in turn, my driving.

"I've gone back to work recently, so I've been busy." My stomach turns with unexpected guilt from lying in a church.

"What do you do?"

"I'm an architect."

"That's a unique job. Do you enjoy it?"

"Yeah, I do, actually."

"How long did you take off after Michael left?" she asks, mirroring my language.

"A few months. I was planning to go back after New Year's, but I wasn't ready," I say solemnly, forming a thin, straight smile. Although I know that doesn't leave an exact timeline, I still feel ashamed when admitting that it took me so long to function even at a basic level.

"Were you ready when you went back?"

For months I felt each individual second of every day as time ticked by, but, looking back, it blends into a blurred stretch of days, and I can't remember how I felt.

Was I ready?

"Yeah, I think I was as ready as I was going to be. I think I hit a plateau and wasn't feeling any better, so I figured I should go back whether I was ready or not."

"That takes a lot of strength."

We've moved to the entry, and I trail behind Carol as she locks the doors to a now-empty room. When the lock clicks into place, she straightens her posture then remains still.

"Thanks for hosting this," I fill the silence not knowing what else to say.

"Thanks for paying." She winks in the way an aunt would after giving you a cookie before dinner, and it makes me chuckle. "Hopefully, I'll see you Thursday."

"I hope so too. Goodnight, thanks again."

Carol and I part ways. I walk to my car, and she walks to hers on the opposite side of the lot.

I text Amber and Harper separately once I get in the car, thanking them for their pestering. I stop for a McDonald's milkshake on the way home and decide to go on Thursday.

TUESDAY
MARCH 20, 2018

"REALLY, ELAINE," I PACE back and forth across the bedroom as I sigh into the phone, "I'm doing okay today."

"I'm happy to come make you dinner, or I can take you out somewhere," she offers with a pinch of hope. "I can make a cake with candles."

"Amber's meeting me for a drink, and Miller's on her way up to join us." I'm sure she knows this since she's in constant communication with Amber, and I question whether she's hoping for an invite. "But if I feel like I need more company or if I change my mind, I won't hesitate to call."

"Promise?"

"I promise."

"Happy birthday, Anna." There's a strain and a hesitancy that drips as the words fade, as though there's more to say, but on the other side of the phone, she remains silent.

"Thank you," I try to hide my own voice's rasp.

We say goodbye and I slide my hands over my face, attempting to wipe away the sadness everyone has been covering me in all day.

Before this morning, it had been a good week. I've been feeling relatively optimistic lately. But my phone has been ringing incessantly today. When I answer, it's one more person wishing me a melancholy happy birthday, a gloomy call to remind me what I'm missing today. Each text pulls me down a little more and every *thank you* I say with pretentious cheer into the speaker adds a little more weight to my shoulders.

I should have suggested celebrating my birthday tomorrow. I usually go to grief group on Tuesdays and Thursdays, and I could use Carol's soft words today. I'm in need of the guidance and maternal comfort she provides. She would help me change my outlook on today, help me see the blessings in having friends to celebrate with but would provide the space for me to accept the negative emotions provoked by Michael's absence.

The temperature of the curling iron rises causing a sizzle as the droplets of water splattered from the sink evaporate. With my back against the bathroom counter, I sort through various texts.

Happy birthday! I hope you can find joy in the day.

Happy birthday girl! Hope your day feels special despite the circumstances.

Wishing you a happy birthday, you are in my thoughts and prayers all day!

Happy birthday! Thinking of you and Michael today, let me know if there's ever anything I can do for you!

I wanted to send a long thoughtful text but I'm still speechless. Love you girl, happy birthday.

I send a few more replies of appreciation before I set my phone on the counter screen side down, exasperated by the fluctuation in my mood. Butler lies at the edge of the carpet, as close to me as he can get without feeling the cold of the bathroom tile under him. His head moves from side to side attentively as I shift around the bathroom. I brush then curl my hair, rummage through the drawer for perfume, unzip my makeup bag, and lean toward the mirror to inspect my face.

I touch the small wrinkles that crease my forehead. There are fine lines that reach out along the sides of my mouth, and the veins below my eyes are more noticeable than they used to be as they shine through transparent skin.

I apply a thin layer of makeup that brightens up my cheeks and some light eyeshadow to highlight the green of my eyes. I finish with thick mascara and slip on the black skirt I've laid out for tonight. It glides over my hips with ease. The two stick legs that poke out from the bottom look awkward, disappearing into overly wide boots. My body used to be so feminine, now I look famished.

My last birthday was spent caring for Michael after his first round of chemo, not yet prepared for the side effects that I'd only seen on paper. I hadn't learned how extensive the weight loss could be, didn't know what Michael looked like bald, when even most of his eyelashes had fallen out. I was still naive to the lifestyle changes we'd make to avoid opportunistic infections. I was wide-eyed and bushy-tailed, desperately optimistic about the prognosis. At the time, I'd never imagined life without Michael.

Everything has changed so much in twelve months. Every aspect of my life looks different.

I wonder what I would look like if Michael hadn't gotten sick. If I hadn't neglected myself to care for him—malnourishment, a sedentary life, crying daily, my body in a state of constant panic, only to end with a broken heart.

"You'd tell me I look beautiful," my voice trails off into the emptiness around me. Maybe Michael can hear me where he is.

When Miller arrives, she changes into something nicer than the sweatpants she wore on the drive and refreshes her makeup before we get a ride to the bar in Birmingham where we're meeting Amber.

With Michigan finally shifting into the next season, snow has softened into a light drizzle of rain. Spring is close enough to taste, but the sky is still dulled from winter, and the trees still lack signs of life.

"Dang, this is nice," Miller mutters under her breath when we walk in, shivering from the layer of rain clinging to her shoulders.

We're immediately greeted by the hum of light laughter and the smokey smell of wood-fire pizza.

The restaurant is upscale nautical, drastically different from what Miller is used to in Toledo. The floor is plank-like, covered by creaky dark wood, and the dim lighting casts shadows on the ceiling shaped like pirate ship wheels.

Amber has already put our name in for the next open table. She greets us each with an all-encompassing hug once the door closes behind us, preventing the chilly wind from following us inside.

I'm not sure if I'm feeling whimsical because I know I've aged a year, or if there has been an actual change. As the waitress leads us to a table in the back, I *feel* older. I used to feel young around Amber and the rest of their family. The hierarchy was clear, and I fit in with Michael, the youngest kid. At some point during the transition from my boyfriend's older sister to my sister-in-law, the years disappeared. I still look up to Amber, but it's different now. She became my best friend, her family became my family—Michael's family became my family.

We each order a glass of wine before even opening the food menu, setting the tone for the night.

"I can't believe Mason's gotten so big. I remember when he was first born." I shake my head, shocked at the passing time as I swipe through the pictures of Mason from this past weekend. A tiny body going down the playground slide and his little self in a swing that looks oversized in comparison. It feels like months ago that Michael and I were flying to Michigan to meet him.

"I wish I got to see him more," Miller chimes in with a pouty lip, "Every time I see pictures of him, he looks like he's aged a decade."

"He kind of does look like a little old man," I say as I pull the phone closer. I dramatically squint, inspecting the little buttons on his jean overalls and his tall white socks extending from his mini Adidas.

Amber swipes the phone from my hand and sets it on the table next to her. She glares at both of us. "Anyways, have you RSVPed to Kyle's wedding?"

I shake my head and look down at my drink, tapping a nail against the stem. I haven't even opened the envelope yet.

"I'm sorry..." Amber trails off, feeling as though she hit a sore spot.

"It's fine," I shrug brushing it off, "I plan on going. I'll have to respond eventually."

"Understandable," Miller nods, "but I'm banking on being your plus one, so do it soon."

The truth is, seeing Kyle get married without Michael standing by his side feels impossible. Kyle officiated our wedding; it was the one thing Michael insisted on. But Kyle had to pick out a ring, strategize a proposal, sit through wedding planning, get fitted for a tux, and choose a best man all without his best friend. I can't imagine the bittersweet feeling he'll have on his wedding day.

I know I'll go to the wedding despite the associated sadness. I would never miss it. He was such an important part of Michael's life and, in turn, mine. I'm still navigating how to look at Kyle as he stands at the altar, on what's supposed to be the best day of his life, only for him to see everything he's missing when he looks back at me.

After placing an order for another round of drinks, we surrender to the inevitable and ask for a bottle to split instead. When we've finished all the appetizers we ordered to munch on and the bottle is almost empty, I notice the chatter of the restaurant fade. The lively buzz dims in an instant and all sound becomes warped and distant, like I'm trapped behind glass. The cloudy voices are overlaid by the sound of my heart pounding.

Amber and Miller, deep in conversation about something trivial, cut their laughs short. My eyes trail from my phone screen up to the two of them, who are looking at me intensely, their faces frozen mid-expression.

"You look pale," Miller says cautiously, as though the breath in her words could blow me over.

The three of us sit at the table, makeup done and dressed up, smiling and talking about meaningless things. Miller has stained her lips an unnatural pink color, and Amber has applied enough makeup to cover the tired shadows that haunt her face. We have scraps of a delicious meal in front of us as proof of a good time.

All I can feel is guilt building in my chest, tugging at my stubbornly beating heart. All I can hear is the echo of my cry that repeated back to me in the funeral home.

How could I be happy today?

"It's 11:30."

Amber and Miller stare sorrowfully at me, now seeing my stirring emotions.

"He isn't going to call. He isn't going to wish me a happy birthday." I move my shoulder up in an attempt to mimic the motion of a shrug. "It's silly."

"No, it isn't." Amber reaches across the table and rests her hand on my wrist. My fingers remain tightly wrapped around my wine glass. My whole body begins shivering, quaking under the weight of reality.

"I think I'm ready to go home."

Someone gets the tab and calls an Uber. Amber walks Miller and I outside to send us off safely, waiting for a ride of her own.

The rain, falling more heavily than when we arrived, has pulled the temperature down and stained the sidewalks a deep gray. It soaks into the fabric of my shirt and falls into my boots. My clothes become weighted, cold as they cling to my skin like a claustrophobic extra layer.

I wonder if my birthdays will always be like this, if Elaine's birthday was like this, or Amber's. Did I even wish them a happy birthday? How will Scott feel when his comes along?

When the night ends, I'm in bed alone. Miller's gone downstairs to sleep in the guest room. I skip past the unread texts and scroll through old voicemails. I find the one I'm searching for and replay it until I fall asleep.

4:57 a.m. March 20, 2015
26 seconds

Hey Anna, it's me. Just wanted to wish you a happy birthday before my run. Hopefully you're still sleeping. I'm sure you are. I don't know why I thought calling you before my run was a good idea. Anyways, I'll be studying for the rest of the day so if you want to give me a call and let me know how you're doing. But, um, let me know how the night goes with your friends and I hope they treat you good, I think they always do. So, uh, happy birthday.

TUESDAY JUNE 19, 2018

I MUST HAVE FALLEN asleep because when I open my eyes I'm greeted by darkness. I'm not late for the dinner reservations, but my comfy couch cat nap now leaves me with only twenty minutes to get across town. I glance at the urn shining back at me under the dining room light fixture as though to remind me not to leave it behind. If it were up to me, I'd leave it on the table forever, too scared to pick it up, thinking if I do, I'll feel the weight of Michael inside.

My phone rings from inside the purse on the kitchen counter, and I sluggishly drag myself off the couch to answer it.

"Hey Amber," I say as perky as possible, trying to cover any remnants of my recent nap.

"Cut the crap." Annoyance seeps into her words, "I'm calling to make sure you're on your way and not backing out."

"I'm about to leave."

"Anna, I'm serious," Amber says firmly, using the same tone she uses with Mason.

"I *know*. I'm sorry, I'm going to be there. It's taking me a minute or two longer than I thought it would."

I check the clock: fifteen minutes to get across town.

"I'll see you no later than 7:45." Amber says harshly. She hangs up before I can respond.

This is the third time we've attempted to meet up and spread Michael's ashes. I've been the reason it hasn't happened every time, so she has a right to be mad. Earlier today, Harper and Kyle flew in from Boston. Miller, who is driving up, agreed to pick them up from the airport on the way. With so many people traveling for the occasion, I've been backed into a corner with no option to escape this time.

I breathe in the biggest inhale I can manage while my tight chest fights back, trying to restrict my lungs. After straightening out my black dress nervously, in one purposeful motion, I pick up the urn, stick it in a box, and fold the cardboard flaps in.

Before stepping out the front door, I check my reflection in the mirror. The bags under my eyes have lightened and the gentle splatter of freckles across my nose have come back after some time in the sun. I don't quite look healthy, but my eyes hold more life than they did a few months ago.

"You're lucky I love your family," I mutter to the box tucked under my arm as I lock the door behind me.

The drive takes me longer than expected, but I make it to Laleh, Michael's favorite Lebanese restaurant in Detroit. I arrive before 8 p.m., which I view as a success.

Amber loses her worried expression once she sees me and the box I'm carrying. She says something to the group, then waves to me. They all look in my direction. Gathered around the table are Michael's parents, Amber and Logan, Kyle, Harper, and Miller.

I greet the table as a whole, then thank Harper, Kyle, and Miller individually for their travels. I take the open seat between Amber and Miller and place an order for a glass of wine.

After everyone has a drink in their hand, we give the waitress our food orders.

The table makes small talk, and I join in periodically. It's hard to make conversation when I can feel the urn at my feet under the table. It screams to make its presence known, radiating its gloomy energy loudly.

I listen as Harper talks about her family. Elaine asks about Jonah, and Harper gives cheerful updates on their relationship. She promises to have Scott and Elaine over for dinner when they get back to the city. At this, Amber and I raise eyebrows at each other, questioning if they ever will go back to Boston.

Kyle tells us about work, wedding planning, and his upcoming move from Boston to Newport. He shrugs as he speaks and offers no more than a tight-lipped smile when explaining his new need of a change of scenery, but I hear his unspoken reasons, and I know Michael's memories haunt him too.

Scott and Elaine make the announcement that they'll be staying in Michigan through the rest of the summer, although no one looks surprised.

I watch as the conversation breaks off into smaller ones. We pass appetizers and get refills on drinks. The voices around the table remain cloudy as I take small bites of the food I've spooned onto my plate. I want to listen, but resurfacing memories drown out their words. My body is blanketed in storm clouds, while the rest of the table faces only an overcast.

When the waitress has cleaned up the dishes and dessert has been ordered, the energy at the table shifts.

"So," Harper states loud enough to halt any ongoing conversations, and we all draw our attention to her as requested. "I brought presents."

We wait for her to continue while she buries herself in a large tote bag sitting on the ground next to her chair.

Her head pops up like a jack-in-the-box, full of energy. "There's one for everyone. I'll pass them around, but don't open them yet."

She calls out each name, and we collectively work to pass the various-sized bags to the appropriate person. The waitress delivers the dessert silently as Harper passes out the last two. The plates sit in the center of the circular table, untouched.

"You were clear about wanting to spread Michael's ashes, so there is a chance that you're all about to be upset with me," Harper starts.

"What did you do?" I mumble and run a hand through my hair.

"Just listen," Harper hisses back, then redirects herself to the table, "With Elaine's permission, I requested a portion of the ashes to be set aside before the urn was shipped to Anna. I loved Michael, he had become my family too. I wanted to show my love for all of you and my appreciation for Michael."

Harper's eyes are running and she's having trouble continuing so she nods to indicate that we can open the gifts. The crumpling of tissue paper fills the space as we all dig into the little bags, equally nervous and excited. Stillness washes over us one by one, and silence spreads across the table. No one remains dry-eyed as they analyze their individualized gifts.

My bag holds a small box. I open it with shaking hands and pull out a silver-banded ring. The outside of the ring is studded with small diamonds.

"They're memorial diamonds. Each one is made from Michael's ashes," Harper says no louder than a whisper.

My hand moves to my mouth, and a sob catches in my chest with a hiccup. I examine the ring and slip it onto my ring finger. It fits perfectly.

"I know you've been struggling with wearing your wedding bands." She has tears in her eyes. "I wanted you to know Michael will always be with you, regardless of what you do with your rings."

I remain too absorbed in my gift to notice everyone else's immediately, but I assume they're all transfixed since Harper's is the only voice at the table.

I rub the silver wrapped around my right ring finger, ball my fist, and cover it with my left hand. I hold the ring to my lips and cry without constraint.

I feel closer to Michael than I have in a long time. As I look around at the table, I see everyone's unique items. Amber and Harper have necklaces, each with a different pendant holding a small bit of ash; Elaine has a journal with the ashes in the binding; Miller has a bracelet; and Logan, Scott, and Kyle have folding knives with ashes embedded in the handle.

"I made a knife for Mason too." Harper hands a bag to Amber and Logan from across the table. "I figured you two could decide when to give it to him."

We tell repeated stories of Michael through watery eyes, wiping wet cheeks over shared plates of baklava and sorbet. The small slice of cheesecake ordered by Elaine remains untouched in the middle of the table.

"Happy birthday, Michael," Elaine whispers as she pokes the middle with a candle. Scott flicks on a lighter, and Elaine puts a hand on his arm. We sit in silence watching the flame dance, lost in memories we don't share. Elaine passes the plate to me and motions for me to blow it out. My breath catches on my first attempt. After taking a deep breath, I blow out the candle. The family erupts, clapping and crying all at once.

I had refused to bring the ashes to Christmas like Amber originally asked, then avoided Scott's birthday, still unable to let go. There were many monumental days over the last eight months, but I agreed that spreading Michael's ashes on his birthday felt like the right thing to do. I finally realized I was holding the entire family back from letting go.

Scott lays down his card to pay for dinner after much insistence, and Logan and Kyle chip in for the tip and dessert as allowed. When the check slip has been signed, we all walk the short distance together through the city down to the river. There's distant music from a sports bar a few blocks down, but there are no home sports games today, and the dinner crowd has cleared.

The sun is finishing its descent into the horizon when we get to the river. My skin raises with goosebumps under my dress feeling the temperature drop. Although some people pass us jogging, we're the only ones loitering near the cement's edge.

Scott holds the urn in his hands, and we all wait for his direction. No one knows what to do now that we're here.

"We should all spread a portion of the ashes," Scott says with authority blunted by sadness. He opens the box and removes the urn. Elaine takes a small step toward him, signaling she wants to go first. Her chin quivers as she accepts it with shaking hands.

We wait on the sidewalk as Elaine takes a few steps toward the water, stopping as it touches the shore. She whispers quietly, keeping her words private, but she keeps glancing up at the sky, so I know who she's talking to. My tears spill over seeing the mother of the man I love so heartbroken.

She looks up one more time then reaches her hand into the urn. As the breeze passes, she spreads her fingers wide. A puff of ashes is released, and we watch as they float away. The Ambassador Bridge gives enough overhead light to see them taken away, decorating the landscape view of Canada that lights up across from us.

Elaine walks back to the group. Her face looks swollen, and her posture is defeated making her look older than she did just minutes ago. She extends the urn to Amber, who is being comforted by Logan. When Amber has taken the weight from her, Elaine collapses into Scott's arms.

Amber holds the urn silently. Her shoulders tremble as she hangs her head. In one single handful, she let's go of what's left of her little brother. We watch again as they glisten in the bridge's light before being carried over the river.

Amber passes the urn to Logan, who hands it off to Miller, Harper, Scott, and finally Kyle.

Kyle stands at the river's shore, looking down at the small waves as they lightly lap the rocks beneath his shoes. He rubs his hand over his face as he shakes his head; his mannerisms so much like Michael's it hurts. His words are indecipherable as his voice cracks and breaks, pulled apart by heavy sobs. With a fistful of ashes, his lips release a loud cuss, and he opens his palm facing the ground, letting the colorless fragments of Michael fall.

He returns to me with puffy blue eyes and a clenched jaw. He shakes his head.

"I'm so sorry," he whispers in raspy devastation. My gaze starts to drop to his hands, but I snap my eyes closed, afraid of what I'll see inside the urn. When I open them again, Kyle stares back at me with quiet desperation.

We shake our heads, searching each other's eyes, pleading for answers to the question our hearts bleed. Where did our best friend go?

I'm gasping in breaths but I'm still suffocating. My head drums, reverberating through my chest. When my fingers touch the urn, an icy wave rushes throughout my body. Kyle's hand grips my elbow to support me, but my head only gets lighter, and a layer of cloudy static begins closing in my peripheral.

"Breathe," he exhales, pulling me closer to him. He speaks through tears, "I'm right here. We're all here for you, Anna."

"Do you mind if I do this alone?" I release a breath between us through blurry eyes, the tip of my nose reddened by sadness and the cool early summer wind.

"Of course," Elaine touches Scott's arm, which signals the rest of the group to step back. Kyle pushes the urn into my chest, but my feet refuse to move. The group disappears to sit at a picnic table up the trail.

I focus on each foot as it moves in front of the other.

One, two. One, two.

I count each time my heel meets the cement, each strike a drum of agony.

Finally, I get to the river, watching the water rise to flood the small bed of rocks in a hushed collapse before gently receding. I stand on the same rocks that the water soaks, unbalanced and heavy with fear, unsure what my next step is. How do I say goodbye?

"Hi," I whisper as I take a seat on a larger rock that lacks the stain of the tide. I wonder if Michael can hear me where he is. My mouth stays locked, refusing to release the words tangling in my mind. I sit in painful silence before taking another deep breath, begging the air filling me to bring peace in with it.

In the distance, my family sits at the picnic table as they hold each other, desperate to comfort their own broken hearts. Kyle holds Miller. Amber shares a pack of tissues with Harper. I see the family Michael and I created, the people we brought together.

"We couldn't have picked a better family." I wipe my eyes. Black mascara smudges coat my index finger. "You did good here."

The city lights cover the stars, but I still feel shadowed by the vast darkness.

"I hope you're up there. I hope your prayers worked, and you're in the heaven you always talked about."

An unrestrained sob bursts out, and I bury my head in my hand. I can't decipher the rush of emotions; anger, sorrow, pity, frustration, fear, and primitive sadness send my body folding into itself. I bend into my thighs searching for comfort.

"I can't believe you left me behind," I sob deeply, my cry carrying through the wind. "Why did you leave me here without you?"

Michael's lifeless body stains my mind, and I cry for the loss of him. I cry to release the anger I've held against him for making the choice to leave, the frustration of not being included in that decision before he made it. I let go of the resentment of myself for not being enough to make him want to stay. I'm released from the blanketing hatred for a sickness that doctors couldn't heal that I've covered myself with. I cry because it feels good. Acceptance of the life lost washes over me.

A hand touches my shoulder softly.

"Can I help you?" Miller asks, her eyes still glistening.

I nod.

Miller lifts me up with little help from my legs and embraces me fully. We lean against each other, crying with the urn between us. She tucks her thumb into the sleeve of her hoodie and wipes my cheeks gently.

"I love you," Miller says, letting me go. She takes a few steps backward to give me space but remains within reach.

I stare down into the half-empty jar in disbelief, confused how one moment has become my entire life. One day that has bent every succeeding second to be shaped around it. One minute in a bar changed my life forever. One sentence from a doctor ruined it. And now, in just one moment, it will all be gone. I don't know how to say goodbye.

I flinch as my fingers brush the dust. I take a small handful and let it go with the wind, then fill my hand again and repeat. I continue until I'm exhausted from the bounce between emptiness and anger. Small clouds of ash fly into the air one after the next; pinches of my life being carried away. When there aren't any ashes left, I let out a sob and feel Miller's arms around me within seconds.

Her embrace tightens as I cry into her shoulder. My fingers dig into the urn, then relax completely, causing me to drop it.

"No," I say, muffled, "I don't want it to be real."

We stand frozen in time and space until the rest of the family comes to us, and I become aware of the cluster of their arms and the warmth of their bodies.

When we break, Elaine picks up the urn and sets the top back into place. Miller grabs my hand, and we all walk up to the Detroit River parking lot, which seems much further away now that we're exhausted and longing to be home. We say our goodbyes quickly. Miller offers to drive Harper and Kyle back to my house, noting to stop at the store for snacks, giving me time alone.

The drive home slips from minute to minute as I replay the last couple hours, and soon I'm pulling into the driveway.

Butler greets me when I walk in, bumping his head into my hands to be pet as I mindlessly take off my shoes. Nothing has changed since this morning, but there's an eerie silence that's fallen throughout the house, like the world has responded with muteness to my pleas.

I slip out of the black dress I bought specifically for today and toss it into the garbage before going upstairs.

The cold water numbs my skin as I hang my head over the sink. Black water droplets contaminated with mascara fall as I run soapy hands over my cheeks. I'm drying my face, avoiding my reflection, when Butler's bark alerts me that the group has arrived. I rush to put on shorts and one of Michael's sweatshirts then jog downstairs.

Harper and Kyle are lugging in three suitcases, and Miller is carrying a box of wine as they all tumble through the door.

"The Irish get drunk instead of sad when they lose a loved one," Miller says grunting as she lifts the box onto the kitchen island.

"And I decided we're all Irish tonight," Kyle adds as he rubs Butler's head. It's astonishing how much his mannerisms mirror Michael's—a result of growing up together, I'm sure. I watch him move, desperate to absorb the fading echoes of Michael he unknowingly carries.

As he stands up, his eyes fall to the Patriots sweatshirt that swallows me. It's pilled and there's a handful of holes giving away decades of use. The once bright red and white logo has faded and cracked. His lips tighten with suppressed sadness.

"Let's put our stuff in the guest bedroom, we can work out where everyone is sleeping after a few glasses of wine," Harper rolls the suitcases about two feet from the door. She abandons them at the bottom of the stairs and walks over to the kitchen.

Kyle rolls his eyes and obliges to Harpers unspoken request to carry the bags up.

"What are you in the mood for?" Miller starts pulling bottles from the box. Red wine, white wine, vodka, tequila, more wine.

"Did you clean out the party store?" I chuckle halfheartedly.

Their bright energy lights up the dull house, but it feels incomplete without Michael gluing us all together. I can't seem to find anything more than sullen gratitude for their company.

"We couldn't agree," Harper shrugs.

I laugh, Harper cries, and Miller tells stories of Michael. Kyle sits with us and smiles but with uncharacteristic coldness. I continue the stories, and Miller joins Harper's tears.

The air conditioning blows powerfully around the room, so we cover ourselves with heaps of blankets, sprawling comfortably, taking up the entirety of the large couch. We're nothing more than sand hills with eyes holding glasses of wine.

Harper is the first to say she's getting tired, and Miller is quick to follow. Kyle's eyes redden as they speak, but he doesn't join in their exit. Miller and Harper agree to share the guest bed. I don't protest, needing some time alone to absorb the truth of the day.

"Want another?" I ask Kyle as I pour myself more wine.

"Sure."

The glug of the bottle spills into the emptiness around us. When I set it down, the whirl of the ceiling fan fills the hallow space.

There's movement upstairs between the bathroom and guest bedroom—giggles and tripping, the sound of rushing water, a toilet flushing, the clicking of a door. Then we're returned back to the silence.

Kyle exudes thick tension, unreleased words begging to be set free.

"Today was long," I prompt, refilling my glass again.

"Today sucked." Kyle inhales, downs the little wine left, and holds his glass out to me for more.

"So, you guys are moving to Newport?" I sigh. Everyone's life continues at some point, so I shouldn't be surprised that Kyle's is moving forward too.

"Well, I am. Anita's still trying to figure things out," Kyle pauses. "I didn't want to say anything in front of Mrs. Leathem, but I wouldn't make any plans to travel to Boston for the wedding if I was you."

"What do you mean?" I put what's left of my energy toward keeping a straight face and preventing jaw from falling in surprise.

"Life hasn't made it easy for me to be a good fiancé," he says simply, but I understand. He lost Michael, the closest thing to a brother that he's ever had, and his dad passed away less than a year before that.

"Grief makes us neglect the people we love," I say ashamed, thinking of Mason and how much I've ignored Amber's requests for me to see him. "If it's meant to be, Anita will understand. If she doesn't, it wasn't God's plan for you anyways."

"You sound like Michael," he chuckles, his lips thinned again as he suppresses his emotions.

"That's the best compliment anyone could give me." My eyes burn as I speak, but I'm smiling.

"I just need a fresh start. There isn't a place in Boston that I don't tie to Michael or my dad. I need to start over somewhere else. I need to escape their memories." Kyle lets out a breath, then sits back in his chair more relaxed. "I can't afford Boston anyway."

"And you think Newport is going to be cheaper?" My eyes widen in surprise. We both laugh.

"At least I'll be getting a house and not a studio apartment. If I'm going to spend a million, I'd at least like a yard of some sort." His smile fades and his head falls again.

We sink back into silence. I get up and start folding the blankets Harper and Miller were using, giving Kyle an opportunity to excuse himself from the conversation. He doesn't say he's tired or ready for bed. Instead, he leans forward, cupping his glass with both hands, letting the liquid warm between them.

"I have something for you," he says without looking up.

His single sentence is abrupt and heavy with emotion. I walk around the couch back to my spot warily.

"Michael," Kyle's voice catches on the syllables. The tears drip off his chin as he continues to hang his head.

I move closer to him and put my hand on his arm for comfort. He covers it with his in acceptance.

"Michael wanted me to give you something," he reaches in his pocket. I hold my breath.

He pulls out an envelope folded over itself a handful of times. Its creases are deep as he opens it up.

"I don't know what it says. I didn't open it. He told me one day he was going to send me something to give to you when it was all over. It came in the mail a week after he…" Kyle trails off, unable to finish his sentence.

I stare at the paper in his open hand, extended to me. It's addressed to Kyle. The ink is smudged, showing signs that he's been rubbing it, out of nervousness I'd guess, but I'd recognize the handwriting anywhere.

"Thank you." My hand shakes as I reach out for the envelope. I brush my fingers over the faded letters.

"I'm sorry I didn't give it to you sooner. I didn't want to mail it to you. I didn't know the right time." Kyle's crying openly now. I lean over and hug him, burying my face in his shoulder.

"Don't be sorry, you were his best friend. He trusted you with his last goodbye." I pull away and wipe my eyes with the sleeve of my sweatshirt.

I contemplate opening it now, but today doesn't feel like the right day. I'm not ready to say my final goodbye. I clutch it in my hand, sad sweat seeping into the softened paper.

"I'm going to head to bed," I rub his arm one last time. "Let me know if you need anything. Sorry all we have is the couch."

I can't bring myself to get the air mattress out, to unpack the memories tied to it.

Kyle nods a goodnight.

Upstairs, I pace between the walls of the bedroom, the minutes flying by with indecision. I have to tell Elaine; she had the same questions I did. Why didn't he write a letter? Why didn't he say goodbye?

But I don't want to open it now. I don't know when I'll be ready, but it isn't now. Do I call her when I open it? Will she be mad at me for hiding it? Will Kyle say something to her?

After at least an hour of contemplation, when my feet start to feel worn from the carpet, I stick the envelope in the drawer under Michael's sink. The same spot he kept the bottles of pills. The last place he went while he was still here, the final thing he touched. I decide to open it another day.

MONDAY
JUNE 25, 2018

I WAS OFFERED A promotion today. Michael was the first person I wanted to tell. In the frail pause between seconds, a single beat of suspended time, excitement overtook the truth, and I instinctively reached for my phone to call him.

I hold onto these rare faults of my mind, when I forget he isn't here. They're fleeting and fragile, but allow a flicker of relief, where I don't bear the enormity of his absence. For the briefest of moments, I get to experience life with Michael again.

Rhett could see the churning thoughts in my mind. He put his hand on my shoulder and teared up with me. I said thank you, just two words, but he heard all of the unspoken ones. He felt my gratitude for being so patient, for supporting me in my grief, for believing I'd come back and excel even when I couldn't see the future.

I cried when I got home. Uncontrollable, primal cries left my body as I grieved Michael's loss again.

Since then, I've been watching videos of Michael, desperate for his voice. I've scrolled through pictures of us aging back to when we first met and watched videos of him laughing and being silly. I relive each memory as it plays in front of me—laughing at the same times I laughed in the videos, missing his goofiness.

I pull up voicemails to absorb the sound of his voice, let it wash over me, memorize the inflections in his words. The times he giddily shared good news that he couldn't wait to tell me and frustrated venting that he promised to continue over dinner.

> *"Babe! I'm done! Only one more semester and then I'll be done for good. I'm so happy. I'm picking up pizza now and coming over to celebrate."* The voicemail clicks. I try and fail to remember the joyous look on his face that day. Why didn't I etch it into memory?

> *"Michael look at the camera!"*
> *Michael stands shirtless, showing off his slim figure, which had become more masculine by the time we moved to Michigan. He holds a garden hose in one hand in an attempt to water our small yard of grass while Butler zooms through the stream crazed by the warm September day. Butler stops with his butt playfully in the air, and Michael flicks the water in his direction, sending him running around in circles again.*
> *"No, I know it's a video!" He bellows, shaking his head with a smile as he flashes the hose at me, droplets of water clinging to the camera.*

> *A group picture outside TD Garden with Michael, two of his friends next to him, and me on his back. All of us in Bruins jerseys, and a sea of smiling people behind us.* I can still smell the alcohol covering the city street after a Celtics or Bruins win, and I know the aroma of PBRs or Rolling Rocks floated off us that day, too.

> *A picture of Michael, Harper, and her then-boyfriend at dinner raising drinks, each with a half-eaten plate of burgers and fries in front of them. Michael's watch*

looking glitched on the screen, its shine catching in the flash of the camera.

"Michael, wake up. Santa came," I whisper on the other side of the camera. His mouth is open, and a small, dried drool patch stains the corner of his mouth.
"Five more minutes," he mumbles, still mostly asleep.
"But it's Christmas morning."
"Hmmm, that's nice."
Michael's face is inflated as the camera zooms into the drool spot, flashes up to his closed eyes, then zooms out.

Michael sways from side to side in the kitchen of Harper and my apartment, humming along to country songs as he rolls out store-bought pizza dough.
"Can you grab the sauce and spoon some on here?" He looks up as he forms a crust by pinching the dough. He sees me recording and reaches with outspread sticky fingers, which results in a squeal from me and the end of the video.

"Are you recording this?" Michael's laughing, folded over, "you have to get a picture." He stands up straight and wiggles his eyebrows as I take a few shaky steps backward. His face is hidden behind the low beam of the ceiling.
"I don't think this is the one for us," he says behind the wall. After weeks of searching for an apartment, we came across this one, which had to be crossed off the list because the ceilings dropped down in various spots, and Michael was too tall to stand.

A dozen pictures of Michael raising a toast at a bar in a football jersey with me by his side, each one getting progressively more chaotic, starting with us smiling, then a blurry one of us laughing, and ending with me falling into him, his arm pulling my head in as he leans to plant a sloppy kiss on top.

I drift to sleep before the sun has fully set, tucked between couch cushions, covered in blankets, warmed by the fire, and calmed by a video of Michael attempting to make a sushi roll in our kitchen. When it ends, I instinctively reach over and loop it back to the start.

WEDNESDAY
OCTOBER 10, 2018

WHEN CAROL WALKS IN, I'm sitting in a small two-person booth toward the back corner of the eclectic café—they serve alcohol at night, so I don't think they qualify as a coffee shop after dark. She shakes off the rainy snow that's collected on her purple woven coat and unwraps the scarf from her neck before spotting me across the room, her lips curling into a smile.

The space between us is lined with mismatched, oddly colored frames filled with artsy images of black-and-white flowers and pencil sketches of famous historical figures. A half-wall topped with lively green plants divides the room. Their dark leaves drip down toward the tables below. Along the adjacent wall, shelves crowded with books stretch from corner to corner. The space is small but provides enough seating for about four dozen people. Elegant industrial hanging lamps cast a warm glow over the crowd gathered here tonight.

"I see we're still only *considering* sobriety." Carol smiles as she stuffs her winter gear into the corner of the booth opposite me.

"Wine was never part of our deal," I say smugly and raise my glass of red.

Carol provided much-needed comfort on the first night of the grief group. Amber and Harper may have pressured me into it, but I'm thankful I started the habit and even more grateful for Carol's unending support.

Since then, Carol and I have met regularly at a conveniently located coffee shop. She acts as a mentor, guiding me through the different steps of grief, but there is a motherly undertone in the advice she gives. She supplies an understanding that others lack and takes the place of a relationship I've missed for too long.

During our last two coffee dates, I had begun contemplating sobriety. With the anniversary lurking nearby, I'd started relying on alcohol to silence my brain's chaos.

Carol goes to the counter to place an order for her usual coffee—black decaf, no cream, no sugar—then walks back to me after they call her name. Her hands wrap around the glass mug, seeking its warmth.

"How's your week been?" I ask casually.

"How are you?" Carol asks gently, ignoring my question. She leans over her coffee, studying me as she waits for my response.

"This week has been rough," I admit with a nod followed by a sip of wine. I look down at my fingers' reflection in the glass, studying their contortion.

"I imagine a lot of grief is resurfacing."

I nod again silently, feeling a familiar sting building in my mind. I say nothing.

"Have you been taking any of the steps we discussed?"

I shake my head, remaining quiet. I haven't started searching for a therapist like she suggested, and I've stopped attending grief group. I've been feeling myself slipping backwards lately so I've been avoiding anything that draws attention to my lack of progress.

"We've all missed seeing you at group."

"Obviously my mental health has missed it too," I cynically joke, pointing to my reddening eyes.

"You're welcome anytime," she shrugs and sips her coffee. "It would be nice to have someone who's further along than most of the newbies. You could share some wisdom. I bet it would be healing for you, too."

"I don't think anyone cares to hear what I have to say. Look at me."

"I care." Her words hang between us, their sincerity evident.

"I can't believe it's almost a year." My words splatter into the air as a tear escapes. I quickly wipe it away in embarrassment. "I'm here today to listen to you, Carol."

"I know."

We sit, both muted, as I hold back words I can't find. No string of vowels and consonants could capture the shape of this pain. After a few minutes of comfortable silence, I ask Carol how her week was again. She answers this time, catching me up on the changes to the church space.

They recently received a donation to renovate the public housing to give the families staying there more privacy. They didn't hesitate to jump into construction, and Carol has new progress reports whenever I see her.

She talks about her parents, who are both getting too old to keep up with the demands of the farm they own. Carol speaks with poise and care. She doesn't complain or gossip as she talks; rather, she describes the situation and discusses her adjoining emotions.

In return, I tell Carol about the changes at my job, trying to match her posture and avoid complaining. I tell her about the modifications I've made to the house over the last few months; I bought a new lampshade for Michael's office in the loft, hung a new picture in the guest bedroom, rearranged my bookshelf, and bought a new coffee table for the living room.

"Why did you decide to make these changes?"

I sit on her question for a minute trying to find, and avoid, the honest reason. My mind bounces between possible answers, hiding from the truth. I contemplate the consequences of the thought becoming spoken words.

"It's almost been a year. I…" I pause, not wanting to say the reasoning out loud. "I can't live there still."

"Live where?" Carol inquires cathartically.

"In a constant state of pain. Stuck in the thought that if I change anything, Michael will be gone for good."

"Anna, do you know that he *is* gone for good?"

Her words float in front of me, almost tangible. I still have moments when I convince myself otherwise, even in the stillness of the house. So of course I *know* he's gone, but I have no answer for whether I've *accepted* it or not.

"Partially," I answer.

"Despite what you think, you're doing good, Anna. I'm impressed."

"I need another glass," I respond immediately, unable to acknowledge her words. Her compliment holds an unwanted truth, an honesty that feels like a betrayal to Michael.

When I get back, we change the subject to the upcoming holiday season. We share our travel plans. I tell her that I'll be going to Boston to visit Michael's parents for Thanksgiving. Amber asked me to come over for Christmas, but I haven't decided whether I'll be accepting the invitation, which I talk over with Carol.

After Carol finishes half of her second cup of coffee, and I've finished my third glass of wine, we start to pack up.

Out the window, I catch a glimpse of the thin layer of accumulated slippery wet snow. The streetlight reflects off the translucent white covering the ground, making it evident, even in the darkness, that winter has begun. The sleeting fall continues to illuminate the parking lot hazily.

Although the coffee shop is heated and the wine has made me warm, the chill seeps through into my bones, knowing I have no one at home waiting for me.

"I didn't realize it was supposed to sleet tonight. Such an early snowfall this year," Carol says, following my gaze out the window. "It'll melt by morning. I know it will get warm again before Thanksgiving. The weather always gets better before it gets worse."

I don't respond immediately, but I put my coat back down. Carol follows, pushing her coat back into the booth as well.

"Carol?" My voice cracks from the constrained sadness.

"Hmm?"

"How do you know which memories to save?" Sloppily, I wipe my tears with the back of my hand. I see a flicker of sorrow before she looks down into her almost-empty mug.

"You don't," she says boldly, her head still hanging. "You pray that you save the important ones and keep the others tucked away to be resurfaced at the right time."

"I don't want to forget," I sniff. A warmth covers my fingers wrapped around the empty wine glass. Carol reaches over and rests her hand on mine.

"You won't forget, Anna."

"But what if I do?"

"Michael is not someone who can be forgotten." Her hand squeezes mine, and she gives me a mournful yet kind smile.

"Will you tell me who you lost?" I ask, balancing courage with caution. In response, the color drains from her usually tight-knit expression, and her mind escapes somewhere else in silence.

I've never asked why Carol leads the groups she does. I've never pried to find out where her knowledge of grief comes from, if it's personal or if it's been acquired through university education. I've never felt compelled to. Sometimes, for a split second, her pain reflects back in the discussions at grief group.

Her words feel heavy with the weight of experience tonight.

After much contemplation, she removes her hand from mine and sets it back on the mug in front of her. She nods and collects herself, pulling her mind back to the present.

Carol tells me about her daughter, Rosie. A sweet six-year-old who dreamed of being a ballerina, always singing and dancing across the wood floors in preparation for her future debut. She had blonde, stringy hair, never brushed and always a mess, and bright pink, thin lips permanently curled with joy. Rosie would insist on reading the bedtime story to Carol, making up the words confidently. Carol said she filled their house with life. That she and her husband, Mark, kept their foundation rooted in their small, smiling girl.

I've never heard Mark's name, but I know there is no ring on her finger.

With swelling eyes, Carol explains that Rosie was outside dancing in the rain one Friday morning.

"It was only a second," Carol says, tucking in her lips. "She was only outside without us for a second."

Rosie wanted to dance outside in her new raincoat. Mark was

straightening his tie; Carol was brushing her teeth. They let her, knowing they'd be outside in only a minute. Mark was quick to follow her, but before Carol had even made it to the door to wave to Rosie in his backseat, the world spun into a fog of screaming. She didn't understand what happened, only that the motionless body of her lively baby was floating in the shallow cattail pond.

"It was an honest mistake. It was both of our faults," Carol says. "She wanted to dance in the rain. We were almost ready. But all it took was just one second."

Her eyes burn red, but the words continue to fall from her lips. "The doctors said she died almost instantly. Studies show it takes less than thirty seconds to drown. I know that should have helped me feel better. But it only made things worse. There was no chance to save her from our mistake. From what we let happen."

"I'm so sorry," I say, grieving with her, crying for her.

"Mark and I were never the same. I placed the blame on him. I couldn't forgive him for a mistake that was my fault too. He couldn't stop drinking. Neither of us could find God in the situation. We lost our faith, he lost his job, we lost the house. And then we lost our marriage."

I don't know what to say. My stomach clenches in pain for her, for Mark, for their daughter. And for Michael, for the child we'll never have. I gently thumb the falling tears from her cheek.

"Eventually, I forgave God," Carol says after a long silence.

"What do you mean?"

"I hated God for a long time. He could have stopped it—even in my hatred, I still knew He could have stopped it."

"Why didn't He?" I ask in search of answers for Rosie and, selfishly, for Michael. "Why didn't He stop it if He could have?"

"Because Rosie was an angel. She could accomplish God's purpose for her little life from heaven. So, she got to go home early."

Carol says this confidently, but the tears don't slow down. I respond silently, stunned by Carol's answer, confused by her acceptance, heartbroken for both of us.

"Michael believed in God." My voice is raspy. "Do you–"

My sentence stops, and I allow myself to cry softly in the dim light of the emptying coffee shop. Carol says nothing, though I sense she knows the anticipated question.

"Do you think he's with Rosie?"

"I do." She smiles warmly, "I think Rosie is dancing up there, and Michael is cheering her on. I think they found each other like we found each other."

I ask Carol to tell me more about Rosie. As the words are released from captivity, Carol becomes lighter with a hint of cheer. She smiles occasionally as she thinks back to a memory I assume she's kept imprisoned for a long time. I become less absorbed in my own grief as we hold the burden of Carol's together.

Time passes and they do a last call signaling closing. We complete the task of clearing our dishes off the table and walk out together; two women, four puffy red eyes. The air sends a chill through my coat instantly, but, rather than shivering, my body floods with an unfamiliar peace. I close my eyes, the cold soaking into my cheeks, staining them pink, and take in a breath of crisp air. The snow stopped after about a half an inch of slush accumulated. I wipe off Carol's car for her for good measure.

"Thank you for sharing with me," I lean in to hug her.

"Thank you for listening," Carol replies once we've pulled back. Her eyes still glisten in the streetlight's reflection, but I can see the gratitude shimmering through.

I take the long way home, enjoying the mostly untouched watery snowfall that coats the trees lightly in a glass-like shimmer. Michael loved the first snow of the year. He fills my mind the whole ride home. I make it home without crying. Maybe my eyes are too exhausted, but I remain optimistic in thinking it's because I, like Carol, can find joy in the memories.

I'm reminded, when I pull into the driveway dusted with snow, that I'll have to hire someone to clear it this winter. I doubt the neighbors want to continue their generosity for another year.

I turn off the car and sit, staring at the house. The tall, thin structure Michael and I called home. The building that mirrors Michael even in its architecture. Memories of him have soaked into the grass and embedded themselves in the walls.

It's amazing how easy the broken find each other without knowing it. I'd worked with Rhett for over a year before he told me about his late wife. I've spent hours with Carol spilling intimate details of my sadness, and she never brought up her own heartbreak. I imagine most people have a story of loss. I'm confident that if I talk about my grief, more stories will follow from the people around me. We all find each other in the dark.

SATURDAY
OCTOBER 13, 2018

Dear Anna,

Hello, beautiful.

I don't know when Kyle will give this to you, but thank him for standing in the space I couldn't. Take care of my mom and dad, Amber, and Mason. They all need you, even if you don't think they do.

I know I've made many promises that I can no longer keep, but I have one more—I promise you'll be okay. It may not feel like it now, but I promise you will be. Things will get easier, even if they don't get better. I hope all the dreams we had are coming true. I hope you laugh. I hope you feel lighter. I hope you still enjoy summer thunderstorms and putting up the Christmas tree. I hope you find a church for Sunday mornings and spend every holiday with

Mason. I hope you get to the live the life I promised you, in some capacity.

There's so much I'm sorry for. I'm sorry I left without warning you. I'm sorry I didn't allow you to help me make the decision. You would have told me to stay, and I would have listened. Leaving you is the hardest part about this. Knowing I can't hold you tight and say goodbye breaks me. I'm sorry I'm the reason you feel alone. I want to comfort you more than anything. Grief is a valley, I'm sorry I'm not there to be your strength and carry you to the other side.

The time we had together was shorter than either of us expected. But our life was full of good things. Since I met you, you have made everything better. Dinner, traffic, football season, long workdays, the silence. You became my home and my foundation. Thank you for taking such good care of me, I know it hasn't always been easy.

Please know this wasn't about you. I've been living with no purpose. I can't work or take care of us the way I promised. My body has failed me. I can't escape the pain even in my sleep. My bones feel like they are breaking when I stand up, and it takes all my energy to breathe. I can't go a day without double doses of pain meds. Eventually a handful of pills every four hours would turn into a continuous morphine drip and really, what's the difference between living like that and not living at all? You're not living either, I've watched my sickness dull you. We can't continue like this. I won't let you suffer because of me. I didn't think this was the way having cancer would turn out for me, but it feels like it's the only compassionate option. My body will be in the ground, but this frees my soul—and it frees you.

Anna, my Anna, I love you forever. More than anything that's ever lived.

See you when you get here,
-Michael

EPILOGUE

THURSDAY NOVEMBER 28, 2019

"WHY ARE WE EVEN watching this?" Amber says as she places a small boat of gravy onto its holder and lights the candle beneath it. She winks at me, knowing the playful banter she's initiated. I smile, always impressed by her stubborn loyalty to the New England Patriots. Logan has transferred his love from the Pats to the Lions.

"This is the year! They're due for a win!" Logan raises his empty beer, clinking his bottle to Miller's. But she has no interest in the football game on TV; her attention remains fixed on the baby cradled in Logan's arms.

"For the loss," Connor, Miller's fiancé, says, shaking his head at Logan's blind hope as he passes him a fresh beer. I'm not sure why any of us accepted him into the family, he's a Packers fan.

As he sits next to Miller, Mason zooms around the corner, clumsily holding three Spider-Man action figures to his chest.

"Miller, come see my superheroes!" He grabs Miller's hand with his free one, leaving her no choice but to follow him to his bedroom, although she would have gone willingly. Over the last couple of years, Miller has become another sibling in the bunch of us, even adopted in by Michael's parents as their fourth child—they took me in as their third. They have so much love to give, and, with the loss of a son, they want to keep family close regardless of their bloodline. If Michael loved them, Scott and Elaine will carry on the returned love in honor of him.

Although they've accepted Miller as a daughter, and Amber treats her like a sister, Mason only sees her as a consistent playmate and often claims her full attention during family gatherings.

A cute but piercing cry comes from the living room, and I rush there before Miller can.

"I'll take him. Amber needs you to cut the turkey anyway." I reach for the tiny, blanket-wrapped body. While Mason has quickly grown into a little person at the age of four, Micah is barely three months old, so new that he still has baby acne.

The announcement of Micah came shortly after Miller's engagement. The addition of the new family members lifted a lingering sadness draped over the family. Our joyfulness reminded me of the times we were all together before Michael's diagnosis.

When the one-year mark passed, I started spending more time at Amber's to prevent slipping back into depression—something my therapist recommended. Mason, only three, teetered around like a small drunk man walking into things or falling and hitting his head. I admit the waddling toddler sparked smiles and laughter that had been buried too deep for anything else to reach.

Mason had a habit of gaining too much momentum while he ran, which often sent him flying forward. Without regard to what he hit or how hard his chin bounced off the floor, he always got right back up. It amazed me how quickly he would use his little arms to lift himself off the floor and go back to moving, recovering without hesitation.

He taught me how to pick myself up; I taught him about rock music. We had weekend sleepovers with superhero movies and board games. Amber and I would bring out the wine when he went to bed. When the sleepovers became less frequent, Amber created a Sunday dinner tradition. Scott and Elaine would join us, but they returned to Boston in the spring. They've talked about moving to Michigan permanently now that there's another baby around and a promise of more with Miller's engagement.

So when Amber invited me over for dinner, I didn't think it was anything special. I didn't think she'd be announcing a pregnancy.

It was over cherry pie and ice cream that she sprung the news and proposed the name for the baby boy growing inside her: Micah, after Michael. I cried instantly, nodding through the tears falling onto my plate. I wanted nothing more than to have his legacy live on, and this new life, with an unlimitedly bright and joyous future, was the perfect way.

"I am thankful for…." Logan starts the inevitable round of praise. He looks over to Amber lovingly, "I'm thankful that we are here today, for my beautiful wife, and now *two* strong sons."

A series of melancholy thanks follows: Miller for finishing grad school and her new fiancé, Connor for being welcomed in so warmly, Amber for a second healthy baby boy, Mason for Spider-Man and Ghost-Spider, and Scott for my recent open-minded exploration of a local church.

"I'm thankful for the beautiful daughters we've added to the family." Elaine reaches over from next to me, squeezes my hand like Michael used to, and smiles at Miller across the table.

It's my turn.

I have too much to be thankful for.

The table is set like a buffet. There are plates of steaming mashed potatoes, greasy cheesy potatoes, homemade pies, and green bean casserole. The freshly sliced turkey sends rosemary traveling through the air.

Every chair is filled by someone I love; parents that I've adopted in the absence of mine, Miller who's considering moving to Michigan as she starts to think about a family of her own, and sweet Mason who has his eyes closed and hands folded as if we're saying grace.

I had an amazing marriage full of memories I can cherish forever, which is more than a lot of people can say. A husband who taught me God's grace without trying.

I'm learning to accept that I'll never be the same. I can't be the version of myself that existed with Michael, but I work every day to be somebody that he would be proud of.

"I'm thankful–" The first tear falls, and I pause, close my eyes, take a deep breath in. Another familiar squeeze, I imagine it's Michael with my eyes closed. I squeeze back and smile at Elaine through blurry eyes. "I'm thankful for Michael, for teaching me how to love, and for bringing me my family."

This causes a moment of silence that we all allow to happen. When I no longer feel like I'm going to cry—when the feelings of love and joy exuding from the people around me overcome the sadness as it eventually always does—I reach for the green bean casserole.

"Now can we dig in?" And with that, the passing of dishes begins.

The End

Acknowledgements

First, I have to thank Jesus Christ for giving me breath in my lungs. For the gift to write and a matching zeal. Writing this took a lot out of me and He created the perfect storm for me to use my passion to heal. Thank you for being present and bringing peace and comfort in some of the worst days of my life. For using my heartbreak to inspire me endlessly. I owe my life to You.

Thank you to anyone who made it to this section! Thank you for reading my book – the words I wrote when I *had* to write, when I had nothing except writing. I've sprinkled remnants of my life throughout these pages and every chapter is deeply personal. This is not a perfect novel, but it was the truth of my emotions during my healing and I can't express my gratitude that there was someone – **you** – who wanted to read it. I struggled with things to add to make it more: more thrilling, more exciting, more erotic. But I decided not to. I wanted it to be the truth of loss, a never-ending battle between joy and grief. So thank you for fighting the battle with me.

I am incredibly thankful for my friends and family who supported me through the writing process and held me during my darkest days. I hope to emit a fraction of the love to you that you've shown me. Thank you Kristen, Lexie, and my mom, who read the earliest drafts of this novel. Thank you for being honest in your editing.

The acknowledgments wouldn't be complete without thanking Dr. Christopher Lao at the University of Michigan (the Spartan in me hurts writing that). Thank you for being someone I could trust, for befriending my dad, and for being there until the last days. To Juan, the neuro ICU nurse, for being gentle in your care, keeping my mom company when I couldn't, and for crying with us at the very end.

Most of this was written from Caliber Coffee (thanks Bri for feeding me) and Red Bicycle in The Nations (the neighborhood is not complete without you). Thank you for allowing me to take up space for hours on end. My apartment was too small for the enormity of my emotions.

Thank you to everyone who made this book happen logistically: my editor and friend Hayley Angle, my sister Chloe for choosing one of the character names, my mom for searching through hundreds of MRI and CT scans.

Lastly, thank you to Anna and Michael. I healed a little more with every addition to their story.

Connect with the Author

Gianna Giacoletti is the debut author of *The Vastness of the Valley*. Although she currently resides in Nashville, she is proud to be from Michigan. When she's not writing, she enjoys traveling, going out with friends, and cheering on her favorite sports teams.

While it's rare for tragic love stories to end ideally, they possess the unique ability to resonate deeply with all, and their honesty lingers long after the book is closed. Gianna encourages readers to share their own experiences of resilience, struggle, and grief. You can connect with her via email or social media to learn about future projects, undoubtedly inspired by life's mix of joy and loss.

Email: giannagiacoletti@gmail.com
Instagram: @gianna_giacoletti

www.ingramcontent.com/pod-product-compliance
Lightning Source LLC
Chambersburg PA
CBHW020933310726
48980CB00007B/752/J

* 9 7 9 8 9 9 3 4 1 4 0 1 0 *